PALM DESERT KILLING

and

The Val & Kit Mystery Series

FIVE STARS! "Have fallen in love with Val and Kit and was so excited to see there was a new book in the series. It did not disappoint. Val and Kit are true to form and it was fun to get to know Kit's sister."

FIVE STARS! "Each book in this series is like hanging out with your gal-pals! The characters, Val and Kit, are very well developed."

FIVE STARS! "Everyone needs a pal like these two!! Love Val and Kit! Can't wait for their next adventure!!"

FIVE STARS! "Val and Kit are such fun. Time spent with them is always a joy. I love the intrigue of these books, but nothing entertains me more than the wit and humor. It's so wonderful to see these great friends interact. They make you want to join them for a cup of coffee or a glass of wine! Looking forward to the next adventure."

FIVE STARS! "I love all of the Val & Kit mysteries! Great reading! Lots of laughs and suspense with Val and Kit."

FIVE STARS! " ... This series is a fun read. There's friendship, suspense, mystery, humor and a bit of romance for good measure. I can't wait to read what happens next."

FIVE STARS! "Love the authors, love the characters. This series gets better and better!"

FIVE STARS! "When meeting an old friend for coffee and a chat, do you think to yourself 'Wow, I really miss them. Why do we wait so long to catch up?' That is exactly how I feel every time I read a Val & Kit Mystery. Like I just sat down for a hilarious chat over coffee and cake followed by wine and chocolate. These girls are a hilarious mix of Laurel and Hardy with a dash of Evanovich sprinkled with Cagney & Lacey. Comedy, love and mystery: a brilliant combination."

FIVE STARS! "Val and Kit are hilarious! I love a good girlfriend silly caper. I cannot wait until the next book comes out. I see a big fan base growing here."

FIVE STARS! "Easy reads, page-turners and full of fun can describe this series. Though these books aren't deep and overwrought, the characters are wonderfully developed. I can see each of them so clearly in my mind's eye. For me that's the mark of a good read. Delightful and entertaining. I can't wait for the next installment. Thanks, Roz and Patty!"

FIVE STARS! "I love these stories and hope there will be more to come. I was reading in the car and laughing out loud. My husband looked over and just shook his head. Thanks again for another good one."

FIVE STARS! "I love these books. . . . The authors always give us a big cast of suspects, and each is described so incredibly. . . . It's like playing a game of Clue, but way more fun. . . . The authors make the characters so memorable that you don't waste time trying to 'think back' to whom they are referring. In fact, it's hard to believe that there are only two authors writing such vivid casts for these books. So come on, ladies, confess . . . no, wait, don't. I don't want to know how you do it, just please keep it up."

Palm Desert Killing
A Val & Kit Mystery

Rosalind Burgess
and
Patricia Obermeier Neuman

Cover by

Laura Eshelman Neuman

Copyright © 2015
Rosalind Burgess
and
Patricia Obermeier Neuman
All rights reserved.
ISBN-13: 978-0692499702
ISBN-10: 0692499709
www.roz-patty.com

Blake Oliver Publishing
BlakeOliverPublishing@gmail.com
This is a work of fiction.

Also by
Rosalind Burgess
and
Patricia Obermeier Neuman

*The Disappearance of
Mavis Woodstock*
A Val & Kit Mystery

The Murder of Susan Reed
A Val & Kit Mystery

Death in Door County
A Val & Kit Mystery

Lethal Property
A Val & Kit Mystery

Foreign Relations
A Val & Kit Mystery

Dressing Myself

Acknowledgments

We once again (but never enough) thank our partners in crime—our cover girl extraordinaire, Laura Eshelman Neuman, and our brutally and beautifully honest beta readers: Michael Gerbino, Kerri Neuman Hunt, Jack Neuman, John Neuman, Betty Phelps Obermeier, Bruce Obermeier, Clayton "Pete" Obermeier, Sarah Paschall, Emma Tracy, and Melissa Neuman Tracy.

We dedicate this book with love
and gratitude to Sarah Paschall.

Hours spent proofreading – $0
Making us laugh – $0
Inspiring us – $0
Her friendship – Priceless

Palm Desert Killing
A Val & Kit Mystery

The Val & Kit Mystery Series

CHAPTER ONE

When I heard the loud rat-a-tat-tat on my front door, I bolted up in bed at lightning speed. The bright red numerals on my digital clock read 1:05. I grabbed my reading glasses, as if they would offer some protection, and prepared to wait. For what? To get a closer look at any intruder? After a few seconds of silence, I sucked in a big gulp of air, the kind doctors instruct you to take just before they shove one end of a cold stethoscope against your skin.

Okay, whoever was knocking had bypassed the super security system in the entrance of my building. But the dead bolt on my front door would keep me safe. If only I had remembered to lock the darn thing. If only I had remembered to plug in my cell phone for recharging or, even better, had brought it into the bedroom with me.

Rat-a-tat-tat started up again, and my breathing was becoming dangerously shallow. I'd surely pass out before any would-be housebreaker, no matter how courteous, assumed there was no one home and kicked the door in.

When the knocking started a third time, I had a sudden burst of bravery, no doubt brought on by a lack of oxygen to my brain. I jumped out of bed and grabbed the aluminum baseball bat I kept in my closet, the one I'd found discarded next to the Dumpster outside my building.

With the bat gripped tightly in both hands and held high over my right shoulder, I crept out of my bedroom and across the short distance to the front door. I did at least have a peephole in working condition, and stretching up the inch or so necessary to peer through it, I got a good look at my interloper.

Kit. Kit James. My best friend for more than forty years.

She was staring straight at the peephole, one hand on her hip, the other waving an envelope in my direction. She looked pissed.

"Will you open this door, for crying out loud? I know you're standing there, Val."

"How d'you know that?" I yelled back, twisting the unlocked dead bolt several times before opening the door. I felt my breathing return to normal, glad my blood pressure hadn't caused an explosion over the beige carpet. "And why didn't you use the key I gave you?"

I watched her shove the envelope into a tiny black Chanel evening purse (which probably didn't have room to hold my key) and bend down to retrieve a cardboard drink holder containing two paper coffee cups. She brushed in past me as I was wondering just how far she'd had to go to find an open Starbucks.

I remained at the door, hoping I looked outraged. "Is everything okay?"

She placed the coffee holder on the counter in my galley kitchen. "Yes, but I need to talk to you."

I shut the front door, secured the dead bolt noisily, and stepped toward her.

She had removed a lightweight evening coat, revealing a black silk dress with half of the back missing. It was the kind our mothers used to call a cocktail dress, although I don't think they do anymore. "What were you planning to do with *that*?" She looked down at the bat that I was now using as a short but sporty walking stick.

"I thought you might be a burglar or something—"

"Were you planning to bunt me to death? Really, Val, you must get—"

"Not a gun. No, I don't want a gun. You know my feeling on guns."

"Okay, okay, calm down. But I'm getting you a gun."

"Thank you, Sarah Palin. And why in the world are you here in the middle of the night, and why wouldn't you call me first, before barging in?"

"Honey, I'd hardly call that barging in, although if I'd wanted to, I could have. You didn't lock the dead bolt, did you?"

"And you even stop to buy coffee? It's after one, Kitty Kat. Who buys coffee at one in the morning? Where do they *sell* it at one in the morning?"

She didn't answer, but instead took one of the Starbucks cups and moved the few feet from the kitchen to the living room to reach my couch.

"Well, at least you look very glam," I said, joining her. "Have you guys been out somewhere nice?" As I spoke, I ran the fingers of my right hand through my chin-length blond hair, conscious of the spikes that had formed at the back of my head (and also aware that I was overdue for a cut and highlight).

I watched as she took a sip of coffee and shook her head a little, her glossy auburn locks perfectly framing her delicate face and brown eyes. For fiftysomething, Kit looks terrific. "Dinner with the CPAOI," she said.

"I think I just saw a commercial for that disease. Or have you and Larry joined the teamsters?"

"Oh, you're close, and yet surprisingly wrong. Certified Public Accountants of Illinois. Big dinner downtown. And I did try to call you—"

"Sorry, my battery's dead, and I meant to charge—"

"Don't you have a landline anymore?"

"Got rid of it."

"Oh, that was a shrewd idea." She all but rolled her eyes.

"I rarely used it, and I save thirty-three bucks a month."

"Gets better all the time." She crossed her slim legs, and I noticed her shoes had tiny rhinestone bows on the backs of the heels. So elegant.

"Personally, I think it's far more dangerous to be in a coffee shop after midnight—look, forget that. What's going on? I have to get up early for work tomorrow. I don't have time to discuss potential home invasions."

"This is what you sleep in?" She eyed my oversize gray T-shirt, which fell below my knees and was emblazoned with letters announcing that *New Orleans got style, baby!* I'm pretty sure it was Louisiana's claim to any kind of fashion know-how that she questioned, not the shirt itself. She took another sip of her coffee and then dramatically removed the envelope from her purse and placed it on the coffee table in front of us. "This arrived."

"Who sends letters anymore?" I asked, thinking *only my mother and the government.* I prayed this one was from the government.

"It's from Nora," she said quietly.

"Nora?"

"Yes. Nora. My sister—"

"I know she's your sister, for Pete's sake. But what's the problem?"

"You'll see. Read it." She handed me Nora's letter, which was written so perfectly and with such a flourish, it could have been the handiwork of Emily Brontë.

The date and location in the top right-hand corner of the heavy parchment read *Tuesday, September 1. New York, New York.* The salutation read *Dearest Katherine.*

"Yeah, I know," Kit said, reading my thoughts perfectly. "Apparently, she wrote it in the 1800s."

"So she's coming to visit?"

"Seems like it."

Nora's calligraphy advised that she was attending a conference in Palm Desert, California, and would be breaking her journey in Chicago. "Breaking her journey?" I questioned Kit.

"I guess that's when she plans to water the horses."

"*If convenient, I'd enjoy spending two nights with you and Larry,*" I continued reading. "Oh, so what she means is, she's coming here for a visit."

"Right."

"By herself."

"She doesn't mention a *traveling companion.* She's arriving Friday. You're not working, are you? I need you to be around."

"Me? Why?"

"You have to ask? You know Nora."

I did indeed know Nora. It would have been impossible to go to high school in Downers Grove and not know her. Up until the time she graduated as the valedictorian and then mercifully left for college in Michigan, Kit and her big sister had often been referred to as, well, Nora and her *little* sister.

But Kit is no *little* anything. Once the brilliant Nora Juckett removed her first mortarboard and was safely out of the state, the sisters assumed opposite lives. Kit graduated from high school two years later, and four years after that she received her undergraduate degree from the University of Illinois. Meanwhile, Nora had graduated from the University of Michigan with a major in economics and a minor in history and then took some time off to learn Mandarin, in Hong Kong.

Things progressed smoothly. Kit married Larry James. Nora entered Harvard Law School. Kit had a baby son. Nora landed a much-sought-after associate's position with a prominent New York law firm. Kit joined the Junior League and had her sofa reupholstered in the very latest fabric, according to *Architectural Digest*. Nora moved to an apartment in Manhattan that had a doorman.

***

I arrived at the office on Wednesday looking like someone who hadn't gone to sleep before three in the morning.

I work as a Realtor at Haskins Realty for the owner, Tom. We are assisted in our quest by Perry Haskins, Tom's thirty-year-old nephew, and Billie Ludlow, our twentysomething office manager, girl Friday, personal assistant, and the best damn coffee maker outside of Starbucks.

I turned on my computer and began checking e-mails. I'd have to wait until Billie arrived for coffee, but truthfully, the venti latte I'd enjoyed with Kit earlier was still with me.

"You look like hell." Tom Haskins was suddenly standing in the doorway.

"Ah, Tom, just what every woman wants to hear from her boss first thing in the morning, so thanks for that." I reached into my purse for lipstick, blush, a paint roller, anything that would cover my lack of makeup and general looking like hell. "I didn't hear you drive in."

"That's what German engineering gets you, Pankowski." He turned to look through the glass front of the office and admire his automobile.

"The ability to arrive silently and scare the crap out of people?"

"Yeah, the Germans are cool that way."

"Then it's a wonder they didn't win World War II, or even the first one, come to think of it." I continued digging and came up with some powder blush that was cracked and dry and had probably been in my purse for the last decade.

"Why are you in such a foul mood?"

"Well, I had a late-night caller—"

"How late?"

"Late. After midnight—"

"Man or woman?"

"Well, I don't see that it's any of your business, but since you ask—"

"Woman, definitely."

"How'd you figure that?"

"You're not wearing makeup, and if you'd left a guy in your bed—"

"Back off." The only thing I'd left in my bed was the TV remote.

"Geez, don't get so touchy. You could have had a man over to your rabbit hutch. It's not impossible. You're still young—youngish. Middle-aged—"

"And I'm not getting any younger listening to your drivel—"

"Hey, I'm just saying that when you fix yourself up, you're not bad-looking. But if it wasn't a man, it had to be your drama-queen girlfriend."

I was too tired to argue, and seeing Billie's car pull in, I realized I was suddenly ready for more coffee. "Okay, it was Kit."

"She hasn't got you involved in smuggling illegals into the country, has she? Or are you two planning to kidnap a senator?" He took a seat at Perry's empty desk, his long legs stretched out before him.

"So funny. But no. She wanted to discuss her sister coming for a visit this weekend."

"Hmm." Tom leaned back in the chair. "She can't do that during normal daytime hours?"

"She could, but she chose not to. You remember her sister, Nora?" When I looked up, Tom was taking advantage of the swivel chair, his back facing me as he studied the wall next to Perry's desk. A lone calendar hung there, displaying Corvettes in several colors.

"Nora," he repeated slowly, before changing the subject. "Why is Perry's calendar completely blank? Is he planning to do any work at all in September?"

"I'm sure he has all his appointments on his phone," I said, although I wasn't sure at all. "And back to Kit's sister. You must remember her. I think she was a year behind you in high school."

"Everyone was behind me in high school."

"But unlike you, she was really smart. And pretty. Like Kit, only not so much. You must remember her."

"Kit? Pretty?"

"Kit's gorgeous, and don't even go there."

"So her sister is coming to pay us a visit."

"Kit and Larry. Not me; not you."

"But Kit does need you to hold her hand, right?"

I stopped and thought about Tom's comment. He was right, of course. On the rare occasions Nora visits the Midwest, Kit generally has me in tow. Her doing, not mine.

"So how long will the biggest brain from Illinois be in town?"

"Two nights. So you do remember Nora?"

When he didn't respond, I stopped running a brush across my cheeks and looked over to Perry's desk. Tom was leaning forward, elbows on the desk, palms flat on the surface. The starched white cuffs of his shirt poked out from under the sleeves of his gray suit coat. He is a large man, but elegantly so, like an ex–football player who has kept in shape.

"Well, do you remember her or not?"

He was slowly nodding. "Yes, I remember Nora, all right." Then, in a sudden burst of energy, he asked, "How long does it take Billie to get out of her car and start brewing cappuccino? It's been like an hour."

"Less than two minutes. And you think *Kit* is the dramatic one?"

***

After Nora left Downers Grove to begin her academic superstardom, most of what I've learned of her life has come, not surprisingly, from my mother. Kit speaks of her sister's achievements only when pressed and is generally low-key about all things Nora. It isn't jealousy; they're just different and somehow have never found a comfortable fit into each other's lives.

Nora reads only books made of paper; Kit loves her Kindle. Nora devours *The New York Times*; Kit gets all she needs from *People* magazine. Nora finds Facebook obtrusive (for a genius, she is rather lame at anything techy); Kit has over seven hundred friends. For vacations, Nora has joined an archaeological dig in Northern Egypt and volunteered legal aid to Doctors Without Borders in Africa; Kit exchanges Christmas cards with the concierge of The Venetian in Vegas.

So it was my mother who advised me that Nora walks to work every day and takes a cab only if it's raining. Her description of life in Manhattan makes Nora sound like a superbrainy Holly Golightly with a few dozen degrees stuffed into her evening bag. I learned that on Sunday afternoons Nora likes to visit The Frick, her favorite art museum, on the Upper East Side. And my source has kept me abreast of Nora's love life: first a top-notch lawyer, then a top-notch doctor, then the CEO of a Fortune 500 company (who apparently wasn't required to be a top-notch anything; he was a CEO, for heaven's sake).

And who's next, Mother? The President of the United States?

Don't be ridiculous, Valerie. Nora has no time for politics.

Oh, right. So that's *why she isn't the First Lady. No time.*

Despite the two-year age gap between Nora and me, my mother never really got over her disappointment at my ending up with Kit as a best friend instead of the much more desirable Nora.

When we were growing up, Kit and I spent little time with Nora. But that was mainly her doing, not ours. I always thought she was nice, but she lacked Kit's charm and wit and her younger sister's zany sense of drama. And let's face it; Nora may be brilliant, but so is Kit. Just in a different way.

And, as it turned out, maybe in a much more useful way.

CHAPTER TWO

Like a bear returning to his cave after a successful forage, Tom retreated to his office as soon as Billie served up his cappuccino. He closed his door (the only one in the place), leaving us plebeians to do what he pays us to do: make him some money. Mind you, Tom the grizzly bear can—and does—turn into Tom the teddy bear as fast as we can say *I sold a house* or *I need help.* I've known about his soft side since my brother, Buddy, first brought him home. They were in high school, and I was still three years away from entering the hallowed halls of the Downers Grove Trojans.

I took a sip of my own cappuccino and thanked Billie again. "This is probably the best thing that's going to happen to me today, Bill."

"Why do you say that?" She sat down at her desk, sipping from her own cup.

"I didn't get much sleep last night, for starters. And I have a stressful weekend coming up."

"Oh no. Sorry to hear that. The usual sleeping problems?"

"No, this time I can't blame it on age. At least not *mine*. Maybe Kit's. I think she might be getting a little . . . neurotic, as Tom might say. She came over in the middle of the night, upset because her sister's coming this weekend."

"Nora?"

"How do you know Nora?" I didn't wait for an answer. Not because I was being rude—I'd never be rude to Billie, of all people—but because Billie knows *everything*.

Early in our relationship I quit trying to figure out how she does it and just accepted the gift for what it is. She's better than the local newspaper and faster than the Internet. She's no *bigger* than a fifth-grader, but she's a lot smarter than a college professor, therapist, and gossip columnist combined.

"Kit has to entertain her," I said, "which means I have to—hey, got any ideas for what we could do, where we could take her? Something different, and someplace we wouldn't have to talk much?" I gave a sympathetic chuckle, knowing that would make it easier on Kit.

"Let me check a few things. I'm sure I can come up with tickets to something appropriately highbrow." She winked. "She's some kind of genius, right?"

"Thanks, Bill," I said, two words I utter a dozen times every day. "And yes, she's pretty smart, although not more so than Kit." As always, I felt an urge to defend Kit against her sister. It came from years of hearing my mother refer to Nora as the Downers Grove Einstein, and Kit as simply the "other" one.

Just then Perry arrived, dressed immaculately—and flamboyantly—in a cream-colored suit, black shirt, and polka-dot bow tie. "I see Uncle Tom's here. Is he mad?"

"At you?" I asked. "Never."

"I thought I was late. We have a meeting at . . ." He flipped his wrist to look at his watch. "Oooh, fifteen minutes ago. Traffic was bad, Val."

"You have a ten-minute drive at most through the residential streets of Downers Grove," I reminded him.

Billie giggled, and Perry's handsome face formed a grimace.

And then we heard the grizzly himself call from his cave. "Perry? That you? And our meeting was *thirty* minutes ago. In here. Now."

That's an obvious disadvantage of our small office: no one is ever out of earshot.

The *do I have a choice* look Perry threw at Billie and me made it clear he'd rather have a meeting with Kim Jong-un, but he followed his uncle's voice nonetheless.

Ten minutes later I was in the middle of a phone call with Kit when they emerged from Tom's office. She's one of the rare people who can ever beat Billie at anything, and indeed, Kit had procured tickets to Blue Man Group for Saturday night.

"Okay, this is going to be perfect," she'd said in answer to my hello. "Nora doesn't get in until seven Friday night, so by the time we finish dinner—you are coming over for that, right?—she'll be ready for bed. Her Eastern-time body clock, ya know. We'll take her shopping Saturday, you and I, and then I got five tickets to Blue Man Group for Saturday night. And she leaves for Palm Desert early Sunday morning." Kit sighed in relief, as if her sister had already come and gone.

Not for the first time since my daughter, Emily, had pointed it out on our last trip to Door County, I was reminded how like my mother Kit is (which is more than a little unsettling since my mom is no big Kitty Kat fan). I could just picture Kit sitting at her kitchen counter, reading from her list of planned activities. No need for a discussion with any of the participants.

"Five tickets? Why five?" I asked, instead of posing the real question, which was *why Blue Man Group?* Not the conservative Nora's entertainment of choice, surely. "Who else is going?"

"I'm not sure yet."

I was aware of Perry slinking back to his desk, avoiding all eye contact with Billie or me and beginning to type furiously, stopping for just a second to run his finger over the screen as if it were a printed sheet of paper. I averted my eyes, not only because Perry had yet to turn his computer on, but because it was obvious he'd just been given a verbal kick in the rear end.

He was followed by the designated kicker himself, his Uncle Tom, who moved over to my desk and stood looking at me as if I were talking to him instead of Kit.

I put my hand over the phone's mouthpiece and whispered, "What?"

"Going where?"

"I'm talking to Kit," I said, my irritation increasing my volume above a whisper. Then I resumed my normal voice and said to her, "Why would you get five tickets if you don't have a fifth person? They're not cheap—"

"I'll be the fifth person," Tom said, loud enough for Kit to hear.

"You don't even know where we're going," I said.

"So tell me."

"Blue Man Group."

"What the hell is that? It sounds dumb."

I knew that having Tom accompany us was a bad idea on so many levels. First, Tom was an even less likely fan than Nora of the experimental music and comedy that Kit and I so adore. But he would undoubtedly enjoy Blue Man Group—or even the Bolshoi Ballet—more than he would an evening with Kit. They are oil and water. Cat and mouse. Predator and, well, predator. I don't remember them ever liking each other, from the first time we hung out together in high school.

That was at my house. Kit was spending the night with me, and Tom and Buddy stopped by to grab swim trunks. They were going to an impromptu pool party at some girl's house.

14

"You're wearing those? In public?" Kit asked Tom, pointing her finger at his too-short trunks in a paisley-like design of various shades of blue.

"Yeah, I'm wearing these," Tom said. "Who's this?" he asked my brother, pointing a finger back at Kit.

"Friend of my sister's," Buddy said. "Might as well *be* a sister, she's over here so much."

"Humph. Isn't having Val as a sister enough?" asked Tom, who has only one brother.

"Thanks, Tom." I assumed that was some kind of compliment and flashed him a goofy smile because I had a secret crush on him. I just wished I hadn't let my mother trim my bangs the night before; they were way too short. (I had been aiming for a Dorothy Hamill but ended up with a Mamie Eisenhower.)

"Yeah, you're all right, Val. You're the best kinda sister. But you . . ." He pointed at Kit again. "You're too mouthy for your own good."

Nevertheless, the boys had stayed for a while, deigning to chat with little sis and her friend, regaling us with a story that involved their day on dirt bikes. I laughed way too hard at Tom's probably exaggerated account (feeling my bangs recede even farther), but Kit wasn't easily impressed.

Finally, off the guys went, Buddy carrying a pair of trunks in colors just as bold as Tom's. And Kit and Tom's relationship—which amounts to their paths crossing through me and through the friendship Tom has with Larry—was all downhill from there. In many ways, as with Kit and my mother, they are just too much alike.

I love them both, but hate to be with them at the same time. So I said to Tom, "No, you can't go."

"Why not?"

"Just a second, Kit," I said into the phone, trying to silence her until I could pay proper attention again. I looked up at Tom, and in a tone I hoped would convey I meant it, I said, "Because you'd hate the show even more than you hate Kit."

"I do not hate Kit. And besides, I'd like to see Nora."

Obviously, Kit heard Tom's bellow, which had penetrated the shield my hand was supposed to form. "Yeah, Tom! Why not? He can be the fifth." She cackled, and I assumed she was thinking *that'll teach Nora to come visit.* "That'll teach Nora to come visit," my pal said aloud. It didn't surprise me. We read each other's minds like that all the time.

"Why did you even buy five tickets?" I asked again, not so much because I wanted to know—it was too late to make a difference—but because I was frustrated that I'd have to put up with an evening of Kit and Tom together.

"I was given the tickets. You know the Whittackers; they were supposed to go as a family, but her mom got sick . . ."

I was no longer listening, instead making a mental note to be sure that Tom and Kit were seated as far from each other as possible.

***

Kit and I awaited the arrival of Nora as if the Duchess of Cambridge were about to step through the front door. It was almost eight o'clock, and Kit had insisted I arrive at six. "Just in case she gets on an earlier flight. She loves to do that to me. Catch me off guard, not quite up to speed," Kit had said.

As if Kit is ever off guard, ever not up to speed. At the moment, her elegantly set dining room table and the aroma of beef stroganoff served as proof.

Nora had insisted she would get a limousine out to Downers Grove from O'Hare. Her firm, after all, would pay for it, so no need for Larry and Kit to put the miles on their vehicle.

"That was considerate of her," I said to Kit, as we waited on one of her living room couches, both of us slightly tipsy from too much pinot grigio. One of the perils of being ready for company way earlier than necessary. Especially company that Kit dreaded.

"What? Making us feel our vehicle isn't good enough for Her Royal Highness's heinie?"

"C'mon, Kit," a deep voice said from the living room entrance. Larry, my good friend since he and Kit started dating in high school. "Give her the benefit. She was probably sincerely trying to be considerate."

Kit shook her head at her husband but didn't speak, as if what he'd said was too ridiculous for her to comment. Then she returned her attention to me. "Want Larry to get you more wine?"

"No. Not unless you want me to pass out before Nora arrives."

"*I* want to pass out before Nora arrives. Here, Lar, fill me up, will you, pleashe, please?"

Oh dear. I wondered what lay ahead. Larry looked at me and widened his eyes until his eyebrows rose about an inch. Obviously, he was wondering the same thing.

"Kidding! You guys, I'm kidding," Kit said, all signs of slurring gone. "Sheesh."

And then we heard the slam of a car door. None of us moved until the doorbell rang, and then we all rose and Larry made a beeline across their spacious living room to the front door.

Nora had arrived.

CHAPTER THREE

Nora looked good. Somehow taller and a little slimmer than I remembered her. She was wearing a light-gray cropped jacket and deeper-gray straight skirt that landed at her knees. On her feet were simple black leather pumps, not too high and not too low, with a semirounded toe that said *I'm classic, yes, but oh-so-stylish*. Her hair was a lighter shade of ash blond than I'd last seen her sporting, falling a couple of inches past her chin, precisely cut and delivering the same message as her shoes.

Instinctively, I looked down at my own feet, encased in sandals. I knew it was against the law to wear white after Labor Day, but did that also apply to sandals? They did have two-inch heels plus an intricate pattern of woven leather straps, and it was warm out, but still . . . sandals?

"Nora!" Larry said from the front door, giving his sister-in-law a hug and taking her leather Tumi suitcase. "Only one bag? This is all you've got?" He waved it around as if it were full of feathers. "Boy, your sister should take packing lessons from you."

"Ah, dear Larry," she said. "Actually, I do have another one in storage at the airport. There was no reason to transport it out here, so I'll pick it up when I fly on to California."

"Good thinking." Larry nodded. Then, turning back to where his wife and I stood in the living room doorway, he said, "Kit, isn't that good thinking?"

"Ah geez," I heard Kit mutter as she left my side and held out her arms for a hug. "Nora, you look wonderful; come in, come in. Look, Val is here."

On cue, I stretched out my own arms for an embrace, and since Nora remained at the front door, I felt rather like a sleepwalking zombie heading in her direction. "Good to see you again," I said. "How was your flight?"

"Actually, it was uneventful. There was a low-flying nimbostratus cloud formation most of the way, but of course we were above it—"

"Yes, yes." Kit took her sister's arm and led her into the living room. "Those damn nemo clouds can ruin a good flight—"

"No, not really. Actually they are quite harmless—"

"Val, come help me in the kitchen," Kit said. "Nora, take a seat and get comfy. I bet you're exhausted."

"No, not at all. Actually, I slept for one hour and fifteen minutes on the flight—"

"Good for you. Larry, fix Nora a drink. A big one. Val, this way."

I followed Kit into the kitchen, noticing that my sandals sounded like steel-toed boots on her tile floor. "She looks good," I said, as soon as we were as far away from the living room as possible without leaving the kitchen.

As if that weren't far enough away, Kit opened the French doors to the patio and stepped outside. "Geez," she said, looking over my shoulder to be sure we hadn't been followed.

"What? What's wrong?"

"She's driving me nuts already; that's what's wrong. I think we need reinforcements. What's Tom Haskins doing tonight?"

"Playing poker. But I don't see why—"

"Good. Nothing important. Can you call him and tell him to come over—"

"Er . . . no. Poker *is* important to Tom, and why do you need reinforcements, as you call them, anyway? I think it's going well."

"Oh, you do, do you? Clearly, you can't hear anything over those tap shoes you've got on."

"Will you just relax? Everything is fine. We'll have a nice dinner and then call it—"

"Are you sure you can't phone Tom? Maybe if Larry calls him."

"Forget it. Tom is not driving from downtown at this time of night. Just start serving dinner, and try to enjoy the evening."

"If you say so." She sighed and stepped back into the kitchen, throwing a towel over her shoulder. "But all I'm saying is this: when you ask a person how her flight was, the normal response is *just fine*. I don't care if the plane took a dive and you were flying upside down. What you *don't* do is describe the freakin' cloud formation."

"Okay." I took the salad bowl she handed me. "So she's a little intense."

"Or a little nuts. And by the way, why are you wearing flamenco shoes?"

***

For dinner Nora changed into an ankle-length pink silk caftan. On her feet she wore gold slippers encrusted with tiny teardrop pearls. In contrast, my noisy sandals looked like they belonged on a construction site.

"Tell me about you, Valerie," she said, when we were seated at the dining room table.

"Oh, Val is just setting the real estate world on its ear," Kit answered for me, as she entered the room carrying a large covered serving dish. "It's just one multimillion-dollar home after another with this one."

"And are you actually still working for Tom Haskins?"

"For? Who said anything about *for*?" It was Kit again, embellishing where I didn't believe it was needed. "She's running that corporation, hands down—"

"Yes, Nora," I said, before Kit had me overtrumping Donald Trump. "I do still work for Tom, and business has picked up a lot in the last year. You'll see Tom tomorrow at Blue Man Group. I know he's looking forward to seeing you again."

"How is he?"

Kit couldn't wait to answer. "The same unbearable oaf he's always been—"

"He's great," I said.

"And this Blue Man Group thing . . . you'll have to tell me what that is about. Actually, I'm not up on the latest music."

"Music?" Larry piped up from his end of the table, where he was scooping salad into a bowl. "I didn't know it was music. Is it music, Kit?"

"It's wonderful," she said.

"So you don't even know."

"Of course I *know*, Larry."

"So what is it?"

"Oh, for crying out loud, just pass the salad." Kit placed her large dish in the center of the table and made a show of removing the lid. A delicious aroma filled the room. "Beef stroganoff," she announced, picking up a ladle from the sideboard.

"Smells delicious," I said.

"Actually, stroganoff originated in Russia, not Hungary as some people think," Nora added.

"Oh, do tell," Kit said sweetly, her lips drawn in a thin line, "and here I was thinking it came from St. Louis."

"Actually, the Russians use smetana; it's a form of sour cream."

"Yeah, well, I add a dollop of Daisy. It does the trick." She was standing behind Nora's chair, the ladle perilously close to the back of her sister's head.

Larry rose from his seat. He removed the utensil from his wife's hand and placed it in the stroganoff. "I don't care if it came from a soup kitchen on the South Side. It looks and smells delicious. Let's eat."

***

I was home in bed by ten thirty, and at ten thirty-five the phone rang.

"Hi, Tom."

"Hey, Kiddo. Just checking in."

"Checking in, or checking up?"

"I don't know what the hell that means. How was Nora?" That's the thing about Tom. No guile or deviousness. If he wants to know something, he just asks.

"She was good. Nice. Asked about you."

"She's still got the smarts, then."

"Yeah. But it's an odd sort of smarts. She's a little disconcerting."

"What are you talking about, Pankowski?"

"Well, she's pleasant enough. But she's childlike in the way she blurts things out. Usually it's brilliant, but—"

"Glad to hear it. Now, about this Blue thing tomorrow—am I gonna hate it?"

"Definitely."

"That's what I thought. Thanks for getting me roped in."

"Hey, you invited yourself. If you don't want to go, make an excuse."

He paused for a few seconds. Then, "Nah. I'd like to see Nora."

***

I arrived at the James house at six on Saturday evening, and Larry greeted me at the door.

"No Tom?" he said, kissing me on the cheek.

"He says he'll meet us there."

"I thought for sure he'd bail after he checked out this group on the Internet."

"Well, Tom doesn't do the Internet. I've already assured him he'll hate it, but he insists on coming. Where's Kit?"

"Upstairs in the bedroom. You better go see her."

I waved to Nora in the living room, where she was seated on one of the couches, engrossed in Kit's *Elle* magazine. She was wearing skinny jeans, a fringed red leather jacket, and some adorable cowboy boots with silver buckles. In my conservative black jacket I felt like I'd be chaperoning a Nashville singing sensation. "Hi, Nora, how ya doing?" I said in passing.

"Hi, Val. Actually, I'm just catching up on some of Kit's fashion magazines."

"Go for it," I said, before taking the stairs up to Kit's bedroom, where I found her sitting at the dressing table sipping a glass of wine.

"Hey," I said, flopping on her bed. "How'd the shopping go?"

"Good. I dropped her at Neiman's and picked her up three hours later."

"Sorry I had to bail," I said. "But really, that was my biggest client who called—"

"No worries. You were there for the hard part. I don't think I could have sat through the entire lunch with just Nora."

"She looks cute," I said.

"Yes, for a rodeo. But does she have a clue as to what to wear to this type of thing?"

"Do you?"

"Hell no." She rose and studied my khaki pants and jacket. "That's what you're wearing?"

"Well . . . er . . . yes. And before you start—"

"No, no, Valley Girl. You look good."

I watched as she pulled a similar pair of pants and a checkered shirt from her large closet. Before putting them on, she bent down to check her makeup in the dressing-table mirror. "Did you notice anything odd about Nora?" She poked at her eyelashes with a pinkie finger, as if to separate them. Then she finished the last gulp of wine.

"Odd? I thought she was—"

"Wait. I don't mean regular Nora-odd. I mean odd, even for her."

"Not really. She seems as nice as she ever was. What are you getting at?"

"For starters, she's really vague about this thing she's going to in California."

"Palm Desert, right?"

"Right. And when I pressed her for details, I learned the elevation of the place, the demographics, and the friggin' climate for all twelve months. Oh, and Bill Gates has a home there. But I never found out what she's going there *for*."

"I thought she mentioned a seminar."

"Yes. But what's it about, and where exactly is it being held?"

"So you didn't ask the right questions."

"Me? You know better than that. How difficult is it to just say what hotel you'll be in?"

"I'll ask her. Don't worry."

"Did I say I was worried? Come on. Let's go see if Annie Oakley has saddled up her horse yet."

***

24

On the drive to see Blue Man Group at the Briar Street Theatre, Nora informed us that, actually, the venue was once owned by Marshall Field and was originally used as a stable.

Larry pulled his SUV up to the main entrance and let us out. The sidewalk was crowded, and we three moved closer to the building amid the throng of people to wait for Larry's return.

I scanned the crowd, looking for my boss. Normally, Tom Haskins makes some kind of magical entrance wherever he appears. Suddenly, above the din of the crowd, we heard the sound of a car horn, and then Tom's Mercedes pulled slowly to the curb, defying anyone to get in his way.

"Oh, how gauche," Kit said, bending a little to get a look at Tom in the driver's seat.

He gave an unenthusiastic wave and then pulled farther down the road, stopping at the valet-parking podium, which I hadn't even noticed before. Had they set it up just for him? Slowly, he emerged from his vehicle, looking handsome in his custom-made navy-blue suit and matching blue tie. At least he had picked the right color.

I pushed through the crowd toward him. "You made it," I said, unnecessarily.

"I live five minutes away, Pankowski. It wasn't a stretch. I could have walked."

"Then why didn't you?"

"Nah, this is better." He handed the valet guy a twenty and then took my elbow. The crowd parted as he steered me forward to where Kit and Nora stood waiting.

Then, in a completely un-Tom-like gesture, he kissed Kit on the cheek. Next, he reached for both of Nora's hands. He held them for a few seconds, staring at her, transfixed, and then he placed a gentle kiss on the back of each hand. It was so out of character, I almost asked for some identification. "Nora Juckett," he said, a sweet smile covering his face.

"Actually, it's Nora Bainbridge. I don't think I mentioned that I got married."

Kit made a croaking sound and then asked, "What the *fuck*?"

CHAPTER FOUR

Bainbridge." Kit shook her head as she helped herself to a waffle from the stack Larry had left on the granite counter for us. He'd also prepared a plate of bacon and sausage. Just his typical brunch that my friend and I always enjoy with our Sunday morning paper. "Leave it to her to marry someone named Bainbridge. I'm surprised she doesn't insist he change it to *Brain*bridge, to suit that pride and joy of hers inside her skull."

Stopping her rant just long enough to take a sip of coffee, she continued. "But why the hell wouldn't she tell me she was getting married? Or at least that she *was* married, once it was a done deal?"

I had barely arrived, but Kit knew I'd soon have to leave for my open house. So she hadn't wasted any time getting straight to the topic she was obsessing about. "It's not like you guys are all that close," I said. I've always secretly—sickly?—been glad that Kit and her sister are not close. Even though I adore my brother, Buddy, he is, well, a *brother*. I've thought of Kit as my sister ever since we were ten years old, and she's always seemed to like me more than Nora. "Besides," I added, regretting my comment, "maybe she wanted to wait and tell you in person."

"Yeah, right. So blurting it out to Tom Haskins while we're standing on the sidewalk was her big plan?"

I could see that Kit was upset by her sister's announcement, so I stepped carefully. "I don't think it's easy for her to confide in you, Kit. I think maybe she's a little intimidated." As I spoke, I loaded my plate with two waffles and generous helpings of bacon and sausage, but in keeping with my newly started diet (okay, *re*started), I self-righteously ignored the butter Kit pushed toward me. I did, however, take advantage of the warm syrup.

"*Nora* intimidated by *me*?" Kit used her fork to cut a waffle in half and put it on her plate, where she added a small pat of butter and a drizzle of syrup. "Ms. Brain intimidated by Ms. Average?"

It's true. As smart as Kit is, she isn't what any teacher ever deemed book smart. But *I* know—and I was surprised Kit didn't seem to—that she has a keener intelligence in all the important life matters than Nora ever could. "What did she say when you got home?" I asked.

There'd been no opportunity out on the sidewalk or during the show for any of us to question Nora. And she seemed content to discuss anything *but*, whenever we did have a moment to talk.

As we'd waited for our cars after the show and overheard others commenting on the enchantment that was Blue Man Group, our walking Wikipedia gave us a minilecture on how the group was formed in 1987, how two of the three founders had been friends since junior high, yada yada yada. For someone who claimed no knowledge of the group, she certainly knew a lot about it. I'd never experienced something so surreal turn into something almost mundane so quickly.

"What she said when we got home was *good night*," Kit answered me.

"Did you *ask* her about her marriage?"

"Of course I did. But she rambled on about it being a long story and said she really needed to be fresh for her early flight this morning. So I got up at four just to have a chance to ask her again, but she was already gone. I planned to drive her to the airport, ya know, but she'd arranged a limo service. So, why did she go to all the trouble of scheduling a layover here and then not talk about her big news?"

"I'm guessing she planned to and then changed her mind."

"Ya think?"

"Hey, Val." Larry joined us in the kitchen, wearing the same navy cotton sweater and khaki pants he'd worn the previous Sunday, confirming he was heading to the golf course. Kit loves golf almost as much as Larry does, not that she plays it but because it gets him out of the house. More specifically, it gets him out of his den and away from his TV and computer screens, two things she considers an utter waste of time unless *she* is the one facing them.

"Hey, Larry," I greeted him. "Thanks for this grub. How are you today?"

"Glad Nora's gone."

"Larry!" Kit and I said in unison, not because we couldn't figure out why he'd said it but because it was uncharacteristic of him to do so. Larry has the fair and balanced mind of the accountant that he is. It was unlike him to voluntarily weigh in so heavily against anyone.

"I'm just saying what my better half is thinking." He grinned as he grabbed a napkin full of bacon and his to-go cup of coffee from Kit. Then he winked and told us to have a good day, as he headed out the door to the garage.

"I could just strangle her." Kit placed another waffle and more bacon on my plate. "Eat, for crying out loud."

"I'm eating, I'm eating," I said, my mouth already full.

"I mean, really. She gets married, and then she mentions it so casually—and of all people, to that idiot Tom Haskins."

"Yeah, that was a bit off. I don't know what's up with those two, but . . . well, at least she told someone. Larry outdid himself on these waffles, by the way."

In my attempt to get Kit off the subject of Tom, I grabbed the unopened newspaper that lay on the counter and leafed through it until I found our favorite parts. I began to silently read the housing section—something I do only on Sundays and only at her house—and listened as she read aloud from the advice column, which she loves to make fun of. It's one of our greatest pleasures. And then I had to get to work.

***

Tom stopped by my open house—not unusual for him, but his manner from the moment he walked in the door shouted unusual. Instead of his characteristic I-own-the-place stride, he practically tiptoed, and I knew it wasn't because of the white carpeting.

"You okay?" I asked.

"Yeah, I'm okay. Why wouldn't I be okay?" Good. The real Tom was poking through.

"You just look like . . . like something's wrong."

"Wrong?" His belligerence was beginning to remove the almost-timid look he'd worn when he first arrived.

"Well, *off*," I clarified.

"Did you see Nora this morning?" he asked, changing the subject to what I realized must be the reason for his visit and also for his weird behavior.

"No, I did not. But what is it with you and Nora?"

"What the hell do you mean by that?"

"I mean, you act all weird about her."

"I do not."

"Tom, it's weird you even agreed to go out with us last night. And you were all gaga around her, and now you're showing up here just to ask about her. That's weird."

"Forgive me for showing an interest in our high school friend. I would have thought you'd praise me for that, not condemn me."

"Condemn? You're being so dramatic, which is also weird."

"Oh, forget I asked. Forget I came by." He turned to leave.

"Tom." I hurried over to him and grabbed his hand, leading him into the living room and pushing him gently onto the couch. Then I sat down beside him. "Tell me about you and Nora."

***

I couldn't get to Kit's fast enough after the open house to tell her what Tom had said, but I didn't get the chance.

She was on the phone to Nora when I knocked twice and then entered her house. I followed her voice to the kitchen, and as soon as she saw me, she pushed the speaker button on her phone and then laid it on the counter. It was obviously the beginning of the conversation because Kit said, "I just wanted to make sure you got there okay. How was your flight?"

I thought Nora sounded stranger than usual when she answered, "It got me here."

"Dammit, Nora, tell me about this husband of yours."

I wasn't surprised at Nora's silence, given Kit's outburst, which *also* hadn't surprised me.

Just as I saw Kit open her mouth, no doubt to repeat her demand, judging by the stern look on her face, Nora spoke. She said it quietly, but her words rocked both Kit and me as if an earthquake had come all the way from California through the phone.

"He's dead," Nora said, as calmly as if she were telling us he had blond hair or size-ten feet.

"He's *what?*" Kit asked. Then she added, "Val is here." She looked at me as if I had an explanation.

But all we heard in response was what sounded like Nora quietly crying. It was alarming to listen to. In all the years I'd known her, I'd never seen her shed a tear.

"Nora," Kit spoke again, her tone softening. "Just tell us what happened."

"I did. He's dead." It sounded as though Nora was softly blowing her nose, and I imagined her using a linen handkerchief instead of a tissue. It sounded more like she was suffering from a late-summer cold than a late spouse.

"Dead?" Kit repeated, as if she expected her sister to come up with a better answer.

"Yes. Actually, I think he was murdered."

"Okay." Kit took a seat on her side of the counter and reached for a pen and notepad, as if she were about to make a grocery list. "Start by telling me where the hell—where you are staying."

"I'm at The Palms Hotel. It's a resort and spa. Actually very nice—"

"And this husband of yours—"

"He's dead, I told you—"

"Okay, okay, forget him for now. This conference . . . is there really one or—"

"Yes. I was supposed to meet Arthur here—"

"Arthur?" Kit picked up the phone and briefly covered the mouthpiece. "*Arthur Bainbridge*, that's her husband," she whispered, looking across at me.

"I'm three feet away," I whispered back. "I can hear her."

Kit set the phone back down. "Okay. Val and I are coming out there." She stopped, expecting, as I did, a torrent of reasons why that was not a good idea.

But instead, Nora said, rather weakly, "I'll arrange a room for you. I'll see if there's one vacant on the concierge level with us. You'll like the spa, actually; it's very lovely—"

"Forget the damn spa; I just need to see you and find out what's going on. Val, go home and pack a bag. We're going to California."

CHAPTER FIVE

Leaving town for who-knew-how-many days was a little harder for me to arrange than for Kit. First, I had to tell Tom.

As soon as I got back to my apartment, I sent him a text message (since I know he rarely responds to texts). I typed quickly, advising him I was going to California for a couple of days to see Emily, my only child, who lives with her husband in Los Angeles.

Then I called Billie, but since I got no response, I left her a more detailed voice mail telling her I wasn't sure when I'd be back but that I'd keep in touch. I reminded her to remind Tom that I was owed a million vacation days at the very least, and he better not have a heart attack. I also gave Billie the name of the hotel.

Next, I called my mother, who lives in Door County, Wisconsin, with her new husband, William. "Mom, I'm going to California for a few days to see some people; I just wanted to let you know."

"You're driving all the way to California? From Illinois to California?"

"Of course not; we're flying."

"We?"

"Kit and I."

"Oh, I see." She sounded like she didn't see at all, and I heard her yell to her husband, "*William Stuckey!* Valerie and that Katherine are going to California."

"Who do they think they are, Lewis and Clark?" I heard him yell back and then laugh heartily before adding, "Good for them." I have grown to really love William and thank God that he seems to love my mother.

"So I just wanted to let you know," I hurried on. "I'll be gone only a couple of days, but I'll call once we get settled."

"Who are these people, Valerie?"

"Well, Emily, for one. And you know Kit's sister, Nora; well, she's out there for a few days, and she invited us to come visit." Since my mother's so in love with Nora, I knew that would soften the blow.

"Why didn't you say so in the first place? Why do you always have to beat around the bush, Valerie? Just be sure to tell Emily her grandmother loves her, and Luke too; and you tell Nora congratulations."

"I will, and—wait, *congratulations*? What do you mean, *congratulations*? For what?"

"Well, her marriage, of course. Although I believe it's more correct to offer the bride best wishes, and congratulations only to the groom—"

"Wait a minute. How do you know this?"

"It's common knowledge, Valerie; everyone knows that congratulations should—"

"Not that. How do you know Nora got married?"

"She mentioned it in her last letter."

"Letter? She writes you letters?"

"Yes, from time to time. The last one said she and Arthur Bainbridge were getting married. Don't sound so shocked, Valerie; some people do still put pen to paper."

"Did she mention anything about this Arthur Bainbridge?"

"Well, he sounds just marvelous. You know Nora could have her pick of any man. And I do believe he's a few years older than her—"

"What's a few years?"

"Well, let me think. Maybe twenty-five."

I didn't need a calculator to figure out that made him close to eighty. But I waited for my mother to continue, since she would spill everything she knew if I just gave her time.

"He was the owner of the law firm where Nora works. He's retired now, but he does lecture occasionally and sometimes teaches. He sounds like quite the catch."

"He does indeed," I said. And of course he did. He was older than the hills, probably filthy rich, and more important, he could possibly be dead already. Who wouldn't want a guy like that for a husband? I wondered if he had a brother.

I said good-bye and hung up and then called a few clients to tell them they could reach me by cell anytime. There was really nothing pending that needed my immediate attention, so I felt comfortable leaving on such short notice. I felt excited too.

So I began to pack, first pulling out my only suitcase from the back of the closet. When I was married to David and lived in the Big House, we owned a perfectly lovely set of luggage. When I left and moved to my little apartment, David had oh-so-generously said I could take it. That was magnanimous of him, especially since he'd won it in a raffle at his golf club. But I'd let him keep practically everything we'd ever owned together. My apartment was too small, anyway, and I wanted to start over with new things. He could keep it all. And especially the damn luggage. It was still packed with memories of happier times, particularly when the now-twentysomething Emily was younger and still living at home and we occasionally took family trips.

In some bizarre act of defiance, a suitcase had been one of the first purchases I'd made for my new life. I wheeled it across my bedroom floor now, noticing how one of the wheels still wobbled precariously, as it had the last time I'd used it. The zipper wasn't much sturdier. I was hoping I had time to run out and buy a new one, when my cell rang from within my purse.

"Val?"

"Kit, I'm glad you called. Do I have time to go buy a new suitcase? I mean, we're not leaving tonight, are we?"

"I made reservations on a flight leaving O'Hare tomorrow morning at six forty. We fly to Palm Springs and then pick up a rental car."

"Okay, just let me know how much I owe—"

"Nothing. I'm using Larry's mileage points to get us upgraded and—"

"No, seriously, Kit, I can't let you pay my fare—"

"Too late. Already done, and I don't want to hear another word about it. I'm just calling to tell you we'll pick you up at five. Larry is going to drive us to the airport."

"Okay. But the ticket discussion is not over. And by the way, there are a couple of things I need to tell you."

"Go on," she said impatiently. Then, more softly, "Valley Girl, I'm so glad you're coming with me. You're the best friend anyone could have."

"I'm happy to go, silly." It was unlike her to sound so sentimental, and I almost didn't want to continue. But I had to share what I knew. "Um, I spoke to my mom, Kit. Apparently, she and Nora are pen pals—"

"That doesn't surprise me," she said, although it had really surprised *me*.

"Well, this might." I told her about my mother's knowledge of Nora's marriage and her description of Arthur Bainbridge. When I finished relating our conversation, Kit remained silent, and I let the news sink in.

After a few seconds, she spoke. "He sounds loaded."

"Isn't he supposedly dead, which would kind of make Nora loaded?"

"If he really is dead. And if she really married the schmuck. You know how dramatic Nora is."

"Are you saying you don't believe her?"

"I don't know what to believe. That's why we have to go there and find out. Dammit, I should never have let her leave."

"That was hardly your fault—"

"Did I say it was my fault? If it was anyone's fault, it was Larry's."

I didn't respond, although I knew that was definitely, most certainly not true.

"So," she said after a few more seconds, sounding suddenly tired, "I'll see you tomorrow. And really, Val, thanks so much for doing this. I couldn't do it alone."

That made me a little nervous, since I wasn't exactly sure what it was we were going to do. But I also knew there was one other thing I had to tell her. "Before you go, there's something else you should know about Nora."

"Oh *hell*," she said. "What now? Let me guess. One of your police confidants told you Nora murdered this Arthur person and—"

"I don't have police confidants, as you put it, and what I have to tell you came from Tom."

"Ha! Even worse. Did she have him put a hit on poor Arthur?"

"So now he's *poor* Arthur?"

"Look, I don't know shit about the guy. But if Tom Haskins is involved, you can bet—"

"Tom has never even met Arthur, as far as I know. But apparently your sister called Tom a week ago and asked him for some advice—"

"She asked Tom Haskins for advice? What the hell kind of advice could he give her, or anyone, for that matter? The man is a complete—"

"If you'll let me finish, I'll tell you. It seems Nora is in the process of buying a house in upstate New York. Somewhere very expensive. And even though she couldn't, of course, use Tom's realty services up there—"

"Or anywhere else, for that matter—"

"She wanted his opinion on the price. She sent him the specs and asked him to check around and see if it was a good deal."

"Naturally. That's what *I'd* do, since Tom is such a real estate magnate—"

"He is very knowledgeable, Kit. I know I'd like his advice before spending a lot of money on a house."

"Yeah, but you'd seek Tom's opinion on bunion cushions—"

"Shall I continue?"

"Yes, continue." She sounded weary. "Tell me what brilliant bullshit Tom was handing out that day. And by the way, why didn't she just ask her new husband?"

"Well, that's the thing. She didn't mention a husband, so Tom didn't know she was married; he assumed she was just asking him, an old school friend, for his opinion on a matter he was familiar with, before she plunked down a lot of money."

"How much money are we talking?"

"Fifteen mil."

***

The flight to Palm Springs was smooth. Kit was quiet throughout most of the journey, and I read my Kindle peacefully. I had just reached 34% of my Janet Evanovich novel, which Kit had already read, when she suddenly sat up straight in the seat beside me. "I'll tell you what happened," she said.

"Don't you dare tell me the ending—or the middle. I'm only a third—"

"Not the damn book. It's Tom Haskins. Now I see why he was slobbering all over Nora at the Briar."

The only disadvantage to the Kindle, as far as I could see, was my inability to slam it shut in any great statement. So instead, I turned it facedown on my lap. "First, Tom was hardly slobbering all over Nora. He kissed the back of her hands—"

"Yeah. What normal man, let alone Tom Haskins, does that? Unless of course he's come across a woman with fifteen million smackeroos—"

"Tom would not care a fig about Nora's money. Believe me, he has plenty of his own." I don't know that for a fact, but judging from the expensive condo he owns, the luxury car he drives, and his custom-made suits, it's a reasonable assumption.

"But he's a gambler," Kit said, "and trust me, money comes and goes with those guys. You said yourself he didn't know there was a Mr. Nora in the picture—"

"If he'd wanted to, he could have found that out easily enough. And why are we even having this conversation? Tom did nothing more than offer Nora some advice."

"So what did your precious Tom say when you told him we were going to California?"

"He said have a good trip." That was, of course, a lie. Although I never expected Tom to return my text, I had expected him to call me the night before—not only because it's a pattern of his, but because I hadn't yet given him the details of that day's open house. I was a little concerned that I hadn't heard from him.

"I still say there's something up with that guy and Nora." Kit leaned back again in her first-class seat.

"Why must you always make him the villain?"

"That's not true. Anyway, the villain shows up at around 64%." She looked down at my Kindle.

"Kit, that's mean."

"No; I'm kidding. You'll figure it out much sooner."

***

We didn't speak again for the remainder of the flight. When we reached our destination and deplaned, we waited in silence for our luggage to appear.

My brand-new neon-pink nylon suitcase with four sturdy wheels rolled down the carousel upside down with a big black mark that looked suspiciously like a man's footprint stamped on one side. It was followed by Kit's two perfect Gucci bags in a classic gray-and-black tweed edged in leather. Somehow they stood upright and looked as if they were still on a showroom floor.

Perhaps it was the miserable journey my sexy suitcase had suffered, while hers had arrived unscathed, that prompted Kit to take my arm. "I'm sorry, Val. Please forget what I said about Tom. You know how grateful I am to you for coming with me."

"Yes, I know; please don't start all that again."

"Right. And I'm sure Tom has nothing whatsoever to do with this."

I nodded. But I wasn't as sure as she suddenly claimed to be.

I found a luggage cart, and we made our way to the car-rental desk, where Kit had reserved a Cadillac. Her only comment, once we had loaded our bags and she was finally behind the wheel, was that they certainly didn't make Cadillacs the way they used to. Since I'd never owned one, I had no opinion.

Using Kit's GPS, we found The Palms Hotel easily. It did look, as Nora had indicated, very swank. When we got to the front desk, Kit addressed a young man standing behind the counter. He was wearing a maroon blazer with a tag attached to the top pocket displaying the name Mauricio. He gave us a minismile. Not quite *happy to see you*, more like *why are you bothering me?*

"I'm Katherine James," Kit said. "My sister, Nora Juckett, is a guest here, and she made a reservation for us."

"Bainbridge," I added.

"Huh?" Mauricio responded. He was handsome in the California way, meaning although he was a desk clerk one day, he could be starring in his own action-thriller movie the next.

"Bainbridge," I repeated. "Her name is Bainbridge."

"So, am I looking for a reservation for Bainbridge or what was it, Junket?"

"You are looking for James. Katherine James. That's me." Kit had removed her American Express Gold Card and was tapping it impatiently on the desk. "My sister made the reservation."

The guy was unimpressed with her Amex card and looked as though he didn't care if Jerry Brown himself had called in the reservation. Instead, he started typing rapidly on a keyboard, looking at his screen every few seconds. Suddenly he gave us a full smile. "Sorry, no reservation for James."

"I just told you, my sister—"

"Ma'am, there is no reservation for James. Katherine, right?"

"Okay, then, do you have a Nora Juckett— Bainbridge—listed in that little computer of yours?"

"Are you Ms. Juckett or Ms. Bainbridge?"

"Are you deaf? I've told you, I'm her sister. Katherine James."

"Sorry, I can't give out information on other guests."

"But do you have a reservation for James?"

"I certainly am not deaf, so I heard you the first time you asked. And the answer is still the same. No reservation for Katherine James."

"Maybe Kit James?"

"Still no."

I cut in quickly. "What about Arthur Bainbridge? Do you have a reservation for him?"

"Sorry, still can't give out information on guests here."

"Okay," I said, "how about this? Is there a conference or seminar taking place here? Something to do with the law?"

"Are you attending the conference?" Mauricio asked.

"Yes," Kit said. "I'm an attorney." Then, as an afterthought, she looked at me. "This is a member of my staff."

Mauricio was starting to look bored. "I still don't have a reservation for you. Or your *staff member*. But I can make one now if you like, as long as you can share. I do have a room available. Double, two kings, on the concierge level. Would you like me to confirm it?"

"I'd like to confirm my foot in your ass," Kit muttered, handing him her card.

"Sorry, ma'am, I didn't quite catch that?"

"I said I'd like to confirm—"

"She said would you please have our luggage taken to our room," I cut in again.

He glanced over the desk and gave our luggage a quick peek. My pink suitcase was lying on its side, footprint on display. "Hmm," he said, sliding a printed sheet of paper toward Kit.

She signed it and then grabbed the two key cards he produced, handing one of them to me. We left the ungracious Mauricio and entered the expansive lobby.

"How come you get to be an attorney and I'm just a member of your staff?" I asked, as we headed in the direction of the bar.

"Val, attorneys do not buy their luggage at The Dollar Store."

"It's not from—oh, forget it."

A little sparkle had returned to her demeanor, or maybe it was just her new position in the legal world. Either way, I was glad to see it. "I'll meet you in the bar," she said. "Oh, and order me a pinot."

"Wait—where are you going?"

"I'm going to find out if Nora is staying in this fleabag. Won't be long."

"And how're you going to do that?"

"I'm an attorney now, remember? It will be simple." And then she turned and left.

CHAPTER SIX

I had no desire to go to the bar by myself, so instead, I made my way to our room. I debated whether to tell the bartender my plan, because I knew Kit would ask him if he'd seen me. But I decided she'd figure it out—now that she was an attorney—if indeed I didn't bump into her when I got to the concierge level.

I no more wanted to ask Mauricio for directions than I wanted to sit at the bar alone, so I went in search of the elevators, making only a couple of wrong turns before I found them tucked discreetly just around the corner from the bar. In the process, I noticed The Palms Hotel was anything *but* a fleabag. Actually, as Nora would say, it was the very definition of posh.

And our room was as luxurious as the rest of the building. But the massive beds covered with floral duvets and matching pillows of all shapes and sizes couldn't compete with the view I uncovered when I opened the floor-to-ceiling white wooden shutters.

The San Jacinto and Santa Rosa mountains soared high above the Coachella Valley toward a sky that was pure blue, unmarred by even a wisp of a cloud. The Valley itself was studded with palm trees swaying in a gentle breeze and bursts of color from hot-pink bougainvillea, orange and yellow poppy and hibiscus blooms, and purple, red, and pink petunias that I knew smelled as sweet as they looked. I also knew that outside my window stood more shops, restaurants, and entertainment than Kit and I could ever begin to explore.

Even if we didn't have a mystery to solve.

The thought of that mystery brought me back to reality. So did the thought that my daughter was only two hours away, and I had no idea what I should tell her about my sudden visit to paradise. Nor could I decide what to do about either predicament just yet because my thoughts were interrupted by my cell phone's ringtone: the theme song to *Law & Order*. I smiled, remembering when Emily told me my new phone wasn't really *my* phone until she uploaded— downloaded?—that tune on it, as she had with my old phone. I was hoping this call was from her.

But it was Tom.

"What the *hell* are you doing in Palm Desert? Why are you—and I assume your dingbat friend—following Nora out there? Can't you give her a minute of—"

"Tom, methinks your concern for Nora involves more than just helping her assess some real estate."

"What the hell do you mean by that?" I could tell he was chomping on a cigar. Whether it was lit depended on where he was and if he was in the mood to flout any rules that might forbid it. He seemed to enjoy both experiences— lit and unlit—equally, like a baby who's happy to have a pacifier replace his bottle. For a while, anyway.

"I mean I still don't think you've told me the whole truth about you and Nora. Your concern for her is . . . well, just not like you."

"You sayin' I'm not nice?"

"No, I'm saying you seem overly concerned about Nora. The only times I've seen you like this are when you have a special lady in your life. Oh, Tom, you and Nora haven't—"

"No, we haven't. Haven't what?"

"Never mind. I've got to unpack and go find Kit. Or Nora. Or Arthur. Or someone." As soon as I'd finished thinking out loud, I regretted it.

"What do you mean? You don't know where Kit and Nora are? And who's Arthur?" I could tell he was as upset as a baby demanding the real deal. I was sure if his cigar wasn't already lit, it would be within the usual five minutes it took him.

"I just mean I have to go join Kit and Nora . . . in the hot tub. Arthur is Nora's husband. What do you know about him?"

"I don't know anything about him." I heard Tom sigh, and I could picture him setting his lit cigar in an ashtray, if one was within reach.

"Tom. What are you not telling me?"

"I'm not telling you nothing."

I wasn't sure if his double negative was his usual butchering of the language for effect or if he was trying to convince me of an untruth. Pretty sure it was the latter, I was equally certain he wasn't going to fully disclose the truth just yet. I knew I'd get it out of him eventually, but I had no time at the moment to waste on a futile attempt. "Tom, I have to call Emily, let her know I'm here, and make some plans. This conversation is going nowhere."

"Yeah, and neither are you going nowhere again without *asking* me if you can take some time off." There he was, once more confusing the issue with his double negative. "What kind of operation do you think I'm running?" he asked.

"The very best kind, Tom. The very best." I knew flattery wouldn't get me across the street, let alone across the country, with his blessing, and so I said a quick good-bye. I hoped next time I talked to him, I'd know enough about Nora to be able to coax still more information out of him.

As soon as I disconnected from Tom, I pushed my speed dial for Emily. While I listened to her phone ring, I lay down on the bed closest to the bathroom, staking my claim. I knew that once Kit took a sleeping pill, put on her eye mask, and inserted her earplugs, she'd be comatose until morning. I, on the other hand, would be good for at least two nocturnal trips to the bathroom.

"Mom. I was just going to call you," my daughter greeted me.

"Yeah? Well, you have to be faster than that to beat your ol' mother."

"Oh, Mom, fifty's not old."

"Fifty*some*."

She giggled. "You'll never seem old to me, Mom."

"And you'll always be my baby, Em."

"Really? Luke says I'm *his* baby." She giggled again, but there was something different about her giggle. An intensity? A nervousness?

I sat up, ready to pay full attention to the center of my universe. I suddenly craved a hug, and knowing she was so close made it almost unbearable.

"Speaking of . . . I—I mean we—have something to tell you, Mom. I'm so glad you called, although I really wish we could do it in person—"

"Well, you're in luck then. You'll never guess where I am."

That was a mistake. When I proceeded to tell her I was in Palm Desert, she did indeed insist her big revelation should wait until we were together. And so we hung up after promising that we'd see each other, somehow, within the next twenty-four hours. I assumed my not-yet-famous actress-daughter had news of her latest movie or TV role, so I let it go in order to focus on the Juckett girls, as I will always think of them. I decided my unpacking could wait, and headed out to find Kit and her sister.

After taking an unintentional tour of the grounds—the indoor and outdoor pools, hot tub, gym, movie theater, restaurant, and a few of the shops—I found myself back by the bar where Kit had ditched me an hour earlier.

And there she was. I saw her cozied up at a table in the far corner with a man who looked old enough to be her father—at least in the dim light, which made her look closer to thirty than fifty. Okay, fifty*some*.

Disgruntled that she apparently hadn't worried when she didn't find me in the bar, I marched over to her table, not considering the fact that I was interrupting what might be a revealing talk she was having with . . . could it be Arthur? *Could* he still be alive? *Oh, please God, let that be*, I offered a silent prayer. *Let this just be a glorious vacation and chance to see Emily.*

"Kit," I said, "I see you were worried when you didn't find me here."

"Why would I worry? You sitting in a bar alone is the last thing I'd expect to find."

"I've sat in a bar—"

"Val, this is Arthur Bainbridge. Arthur, my best friend—and a good friend of Nora's—Valerie Pankowski. Arthur says Nora went for a hike—"

"Arthur?" I said, sounding as if I'd never heard of him. But before I could ponder the strangeness of meeting a presumably dead man, the situation grew still stranger.

"Yep. Found Arthur," Kit said. "But now it seems Nora is missing."

CHAPTER SEVEN

S teady on, old girl. I didn't say Nora is missing, exactly. She trotted off for a stroll or hike or some damn thing. She said something about the Art Smith Trail, I think. She'll be back shortly. No need to fuss." Arthur Bainbridge stopped talking long enough to briefly glance at me. Then he continued, addressing the vacant chair at the table. "Val, is it? Sit down and I'll get you a drink. Wine? Yes? If you can't get a decent glass of white wine in California, where can you, eh? Only don't let the French hear you say that. Or the Italians, for that matter. Start another bloody war." He rose, and even though there was a waiter standing close by holding an empty silver tray, Arthur said, "One can never find a waiter in this place. I'll just pop over to the bar. Won't be a tick."

He was a tall, thin man, impeccably dressed, with a clipped white moustache covering his top lip. Although it was hardly the latest fashion in male facial hair, on him it looked elegant.

The second he was gone, I sat down next to Kit. She had her elbows on the table and held her head in her hands. I grabbed her forearm. "He's *alive*!" I whispered, as if we'd just opened an ancient tomb and found the occupant still breathing.

"Apparently."

"So why would Nora say he was . . ."

"Dead?"

"She *said* murdered. What the hell—"

"Who knows? Why does Nora say, or do, anything? Because she didn't get enough love as a child? Because it's Monday?" She sat up straight and took a sip of her wine. "Nora loves the drama; you know that."

But I *didn't* know that. Her life, as I had observed it from afar (and via my mother), was more Mary Poppins than Macbeth. She appeared to seamlessly hopscotch from accolade to triumph, sidestepping anything nasty.

But that, it seemed, had changed.

"Well, at least her husband is alive," I stated the obvious once again, hoping to lead Kit toward the half-full glass.

"But he's so old." She groaned.

"And British. That's a British accent, right?"

"He's ancient."

"But British; don't you think he sounds—"

"He's older than Methuselah—"

"*Okay.* He's getting on a bit. But quick, before he comes back, tell me how you found him."

She glanced toward the bar, where Arthur was talking to a young woman wearing the same type of maroon jacket as Mauricio. "He found me. I was just about to bribe one of the morons who work here to give me the Bainbridges' room number when Professor Higgins tapped me on the shoulder and introduced himself. Said he recognized me from my picture." She paused to take a sip of her wine.

"Your picture? Well, I guess Nora could have shown him—"

"*Or* he heard us talking to Mauricio, who, by the way, I am going to speak to the manager about—"

"Never mind that now; tell me what else Arthur said."

"They got married one week ago. She is his official ball and chain—his words, not mine." She stopped speaking and began gazing thoughtfully at the light fixture above our table.

"Go on. What else did he say?"

"Not much. He had a late breakfast with the enchanting Mrs. Bainbridge this morning, and as he put it, the old thing took it into her head to trot off for a stroll through the wilds of Palm Desert. Hasn't been seen since."

"How long ago was this?"

"I don't know. Didn't you notice, he's older than dirt?"

"So what happened to our hotel reservations?"

"He said there must have been some ghastly mix-up—"

"Now you're sounding British. Don't say *ghastly*. Did he know we were coming or not?"

"It seems that Rain Man, aka Nora Bainbridge, forgot to mention that little detail. But not to worry; he's pleased to meet us. Everything is tickety-boo."

"He really said tickety-boo?"

"Something equally dopey. I might have heard that on *Downton Abbey* or somewhere."

"But I'm guessing that means good, right?"

"Apparently. But he's a million years old—oh, shush; here he comes. Arthur!" She sounded thrilled to see him, as if he'd just returned from discovering the Indian subcontinent.

He laughed in return and placed a glass of wine before me. "For you, Val. And I'm not quite that old. I'm only eighty."

Kit looked at her watch. "Look, Arthur, I'm getting worried about Nora. Shouldn't she have returned by now, or at least called? I've tried her cell several times."

Arthur waved her off; I mean he literally waved a wrinkled hand with professionally manicured nails in her direction. "Oh, I wouldn't worry. She's got Irene with her . . ." As he spoke, he gazed intently toward the bar entrance.

"Irene?" Kit said. "Who the fu—who in the world is Irene?"

"Didn't I mention?" His focus returned briefly to Kit, then moved on to a painting of mountains on the wall above her head. "Irene is my niece. She's an extraordinary girl. Third year at Oxford, reading law. She's over here on holiday. Those two have a lot of catching up to do, blabbing for hours, I have no doubt. Look, why don't I get us a table in the dining room—"

"No." Kit rose. "I'm not comfortable with this; I'm going to look around myself."

"I'll come with you." I rose too.

"Really, ladies, I assure you there is nothing to be alarmed about. I expect Nora left her mobile in the hotel room, but if it will make you feel better, let me give old Irene a ring and see what's what."

Then he stood as well, and waving that hand of his—this time in a *stop, sit, and stay* motion—he stepped away from our table and took a cell phone from his pocket.

"Should we contact the police?" Kit asked, as soon as Arthur had moved out of earshot.

"Well, that might be a little premature," I said, patting her arm as we both sat back down.

"We're not delivering a baby here, Val. We've got a missing Nora."

"And seems like a missing Irene—"

"If she even exists—"

"You don't think—"

"That Arthur is full of shit? Yes, I think I do. Why didn't he mention this Irene before? And when have you ever known anyone to tolerate Nora's blabbing, as he so charmingly put it, for hours? *Ever?* The whole thing seems off."

I took the last sip of my wine. "Hmm, I agree. And why does he always look as though he's addressing a jury when he's speaking? Why can't he make eye contact?"

"Probably a courtroom tactic he picked up from his pal Abraham Lincoln."

While we were talking, Arthur had disappeared from the bar, and we were just about to leave when he came rushing back, returning his phone to his pocket.

"Crisis averted, ladies. Spoke to old Irene. I was right; Nora did leave her phone here. They hiked a bit farther than they'd planned, but they are safe and sound and on their way back. No need to call out the dogs. Should be about half an hour or so. Nora sends her love, apologies, and all that. Said we should meet them in the dining room, as I suggested. So, why don't you two go and freshen up, not that you need to, of course, and we'll meet back down here in ... let's see . . . an hour? That suit?"

All of this was addressed to the large clock hanging over the bar. But it was clear Arthur Bainbridge was used to rapidly barking out orders and expecting them to be followed.

Kit, however, remained seated, and I did the same. "Is the food any good here?" she asked, elbows on the table, looking up at Arthur.

"For California, it's exemplary." He smiled, then looked at us directly as he held out his arm in a *leading the way* gesture. Like an usher showing us to the door. "So, ladies, I'll see you in an hour or so, but you'll have to excuse me for the present. I just ran into an old chum in the foyer, a chap I used to know in Cape Town. So if you don't mind, I'm going to have a long-overdue chin-wag."

Kit and I watched Arthur hurry out of the bar. "*Chin-wag?*" I repeated.

"It means chitchat. Everyone knows that. And I think we need to go and have a little chin-wag of our own with Mauricio. I have a question for him." She stood up and

54

grabbed her purse; I followed her out toward the reception desk.

"Well, I don't think *everyone* knows that," I mumbled, catching up with her.

The bad news was that Mauricio was still in the same spot, clacking away on his keyboard. The good news was that he looked up, saw us approach, and then rapidly disappeared through a concealed door behind the desk. A few seconds later a similar-looking young man appeared in his place. His badge announced to the world that his name was Tarique. I braced myself for whatever hell it was Kit was planning to put him through.

"Yes, ma'am," he said, with the same minismile as his colleague. "How can I help?"

"I need to know what time the turndown service is this evening."

"Are you registered here?"

"I ain't got no double-wide parked outside, if that's what's worryin' yer, Tareeeek. Of course I'm registered here; why else would I even care what time you throw a Junior Mint on my—"

"May I have your name, ma'am?"

"Katherine James."

"Ah, here it is." Sounding unimpressed, he did at least look at his watch. "It'll be done about eight o'clock. Anything else I can help you with?"

"I'll let ya know, buddy boy." She turned, grabbed my elbow, and steered me toward the elevators.

"Kit, what are you planning?"

"For starters, Nora said they were also on the concierge level, so it shouldn't be too difficult to figure out which room they're in."

"Oh, Kit, the rooms are lovely. Wait till you see the view—"

"We don't have time for any damn view. I need to be certain my big sister is okay. Not to mention, *why* didn't they have a reservation for us when we arrived? I don't believe the mix-up bullshit; Nora always does what she says she's going to do. And why didn't Captain Crunch know we were coming? It's totally unlike her not to have told him, or for her to not be here to greet us." She nodded her head for emphasis. "I'm wondering if *she's* even checked into this dump."

I was about to remind her that it was the furthest thing from a dump she'd ever seen, but I had to agree that it was unlikely Nora would forget to make our reservation. As I watched my pal lean against the wall of the elevator, her chin raised, her eyes never leaving the illuminated buttons as we passed each floor, I was filled with compassion for her. You gotta love a little sister like Kit.

On the concierge level the elevators opened into a large, round room with a wall of windows revealing the glorious California landscape. There were several coffee tables, each surrounded by sleek, armless chairs. A long bar had been set up, covered with an assortment of fruits, nuts, and items that looked so healthful as to be almost unappetizing. A wide variety of drinks ranging from greenish fruit-and-vegetable concoctions to a pitcher of margaritas completed the offerings.

From one end of the area a wide corridor extended with doors on either side, and I spotted our room. Two doors down from it, a cart storing extra linens and toiletries was parked. Kit hurried toward it.

"Hello?" She peered into the open room closest to the cart.

A middle-aged Latina appeared, coming out from what looked like the bathroom. "*Sí, señora?*" she said.

Kit glanced at me, slightly nodding her head to indicate I should move back a few steps. Like I might not want to hear this. Next, I saw her open her purse and produce our key card, waving it for some kind of identification. Then she opened her wallet and removed some folded money.

An exchange followed between them. Apparently, Kit said something funny, because the maid laughed. Then she put her hand to her heart and nodded her head in a gesture of gratitude. She took the money and slipped it into her apron pocket. Kit looked at me triumphantly, so I assumed it was safe to follow. We three walked to the end of the corridor, where the maid used a key card that hung from a chain around her waist to unlock the door.

"We'll be quick as bunnies," Kit said.

"Bunnies. *Sí.*" The maid laughed. Then she put a finger to her lips to shush us.

"Yes," Kit whispered back, "quiet as mice. This is Mrs. Bainbridge's room—*Nora* Bainbridge, right?"

The maid nodded in confirmation. "*Sí, sí,* Bainbridge." Then, after looking at her watch, she held up one hand to Kit's face, palm outward, her fingers splayed to indicate we had five minutes.

Kit nodded, then turned to me. "Val, go get the stuff."

"Stuff?" I asked, alarmed. *What stuff was she talking about?*

"For the bride and groom. The wedding stuff. It's in that ratty old pink suitcase in our room. Go, quickly. We have only five minutes to decorate for the wedding couple."

Not really sure what I was doing, I ran to our room and dragged out my once-beautiful pink suitcase that had already lost most of its neon luster. When I returned, the maid said, "First I go check no one is home."

As Kit and I stood outside the room waiting for her to give us the all clear, I whispered, "So what exactly is it we're looking for?"

Kit sighed deeply, looking frustrated that she had to explain something that was so obvious to her. "Okay," she said slowly and quietly. "We do at least know that Nora, or someone called Bainbridge, is staying in this hotel. In this very room—"

"Yes, your plan worked, and you're very clever—and by the way, would it kill you to let me know what the plan is before we're halfway into it?"

"I make it up as I go along; you know that."

"Understood. But here's the thing; now that we know this is Nora's room, what are we looking for?"

"Proof."

"Of what? You know she's here; the maid confirmed it. You spoke to Nora when she called from here yesterday— was that only yesterday? Seems like we've been here a month—"

"She called me from *somewhere*. I'd just like a little proof that it was from here. Hell, I just want her to be okay. Just find me something of Nora's in this friggin' room. That too much to ask? Or do you have something else you need to be doing—"

"No, nothing else. Oh, and while we're at it, should we maybe poke around and see if we can dig up something on your new brother-in-law?"

She flung her arms around me in a quick movement. "Since we're already here, it can't hurt, right?"

But before I could tell her I was only joking, sort of, we heard a piercing scream, and the maid rushed out of the room, pushing past us. She stopped in the center of the hall, still screaming and grasping a gold cross around her neck. "Go, go, go see . . ." She raised an arm and pointed a shaking finger toward the open room.

Kit was the first one into the bedroom, one of three rooms off the main living area.

Lying on one of the king-size beds was a woman. She was facedown, as if she had fallen there, her head surrounded by a dark-red pool of blood on the designer bedspread. Her arms were outstretched, and from her neck a pair of scissors protruded.

"Oh no!" Kit stepped closer to the dead body.

"It's not . . . she's not . . ." I remained standing at the door to the room, unable to move.

"Nora?" Kit bent down to peer at the profile of the woman. "No." She put a hand to her chest, taking a deep breath. "No. Not Nora."

I joined Kit and also took a deep breath, at the same time feeling the sting of tears form. "Irene, perhaps?" I asked Kit.

"Could be. Welcome to the Golden State, old thing."

CHAPTER EIGHT

I prefer this *part of the Golden State*, I thought, as Kit and I hiked in the mountain range I'd been admiring out my window that morning. Not exactly vacation-type hiking or even exercise-type hiking. And certainly not graceful hiking.

On the off chance I'd have an opportunity to use them, I'd packed the hiking boots Emily had given me for Christmas, as a gentle hint to get back out to Southern California and explore more trails with her and Luke. I'd tossed them into my suitcase at the last minute, smiling at the contrast between the neon-pink lining of my rolling bag and the dark-brown leather of the boots. I proudly thought that pretty much summed up my daughter: a delightful mix of girlie girl and tomboy.

Kit, of course, was lucky she'd packed something as sporty as her pool flip-flops. But then Kit has a bit of an obsession with flip-flops. She owns them in all colors and every imaginable material, and she even has a collection of flip-flop magnets that threatens to overtake her Sub-Zero fridge.

I watched as the desert sun shone on the rhinestones of her flimsy footwear. In fact, I rarely took my eyes off her feet, since I was so sure they were about to slip off the narrow hiking path that took us up, up, up in search of Nora. And maybe Irene.

The police had arrived within minutes of Kit's 911 call, followed of course by seemingly half the staff of The Palms Hotel. They weren't accustomed to murders in their piece of paradise. Murder was just something they read about in *The Desert Sun* (paper version for those over fifty, online for the younger set), something that took place in neighboring towns, and usually gang-related killings. Dead bodies in buildings as ritzy as the one we'd checked into that morning were unheard of.

Until now.

While the technical people did their thing with vials and cameras and evidence bags, a couple of detectives who looked like surfers with their deep tans and bleached-blond hair grilled Kit and me. They never seemed to quite believe our total ignorance about the woman in the bed as well as the whereabouts of the room's registered occupants.

At last Kit did tell a little white lie that allowed us to leave. She promised we'd go right to the station and give them a detailed statement as best we could.

But Kit had something else in mind for us to do before we showed up at the station. We stopped by our room so she could change out of her wedge sandals into her sparkly blue flip-flops that complemented her pedicured toes. When she saw my boots as I reached down to the closet floor for my own flip-flops—plain black rubber, thank you very much—she gave the first inkling of what she had in mind. "Bring the boots, Valley Girl. We're going for a hike."

"Wha—?"

But she was already headed down the hall, so I scooted after her, boots in hand.

She seemed desperate as she got behind the wheel of the rental car, started it, and drove out of the parking lot as if the building were about to explode behind us. I remained silent, as the situation seemed to call for. She clearly had a plan, and whereas the logical assumption was that it involved hiking, she almost immediately pulled into the Starbucks on the corner of El Paseo and Monterey. Surely she wasn't stopping for a jolt of caffeine or to partake of the shopping El Paseo is famous for.

"Arthur said Nora was hiking on the Art Smith Trail." She'd whipped out her phone the minute she threw the car into park and was obviously consulting her BFF Google.

"How on earth could you remember that?" I asked. Kit is no better at remembering names than I am—names of *people*, let alone hiking trails. It's part of our basic nature, not to mention our age.

"Art Smith Trail? Arthur? Kinda easy, ya know."

"Yeah, I guess. But what do you plan—"

"I plan to see if Nora's there."

"Why didn't you tell the police that she was on the Arthur Trail?"

"Art Smith Trail. Sheesh."

"Whatever. Why didn't you tell them?"

"I need to make sure she's okay." Kit looked worried.

"Well, all the more reason to tell the police where she is."

"I need to find her first. Find out what she knows. And coach her about what to say."

"She's a smart girl. She'll—"

"Val. C'mon. We both know she's a genius. But she doesn't have a clue when it comes to staying out of the sun, let alone saying the right thing to the authorities."

I couldn't argue with that, and so I waited the couple of minutes it took before she whipped her car into reverse and backed out of her parking spot. Soon we were headed up Monterey—more picturesquely known in some parts as the

Pines to Palms Highway and more mundanely in others as Highway 74.

We didn't have far to go before we saw the sign announcing the Art Smith Trail, and Kit pulled over and parked by the only other vehicle there, an Escalade with Oregon plates.

September is still hot in the desert, especially that day, so it takes a special kind of hardy to hike. The word *hardy* didn't seem to fit Nora, much less Kit and me. In fact, the word *fit* doesn't belong in the same sentence with Val and Kit, although for my part, that is something I am eternally vowing to change.

Apparently, starting immediately. "Get your boots on," Kit said. "What are you waiting for?"

"Well, I thought we'd have to drive farther. I didn't know ol' Art was this close."

"Now you know. So hurry." She grabbed two water bottles that she'd undoubtedly taken from the hospitality table and handed me one as soon as I climbed out of the car.

As we walked along the flat valley that led to the mountain trail, feeling like the only two people left in the world, I remembered the Oregonians whose vehicle we had seen parked and was comforted by the fact that they were surely somewhere nearby.

Although we spied no other fellow human beings, I saw at least a dozen lizards of various sizes, from a few inches to almost-as-big-as-a-breadbox. Luckily, they either froze on the rock they blended in with or scurried by so fast I didn't have a chance to scream or even feel more than a second of fright.

Kit, who otherwise might have been more dramatic about such sightings—although she's the bravest woman I know—was on a mission. I doubt she noticed a single reptile.

When we reached the base of the trail, we looked up in silence, awed by both the splendor of the mountain in front of us and the fact that we were about to ascend it.

Typically, I had gone just a few feet when I tripped on a rock and fell. "Oh crap, Kit. Just crap."

"That the best you can do? Seems if ever the eff word was warranted—"

"This isn't funny."

"Ya know, it kinda is."

"Do you want to find your sister or not?"

"You're right." She helped dust me off, and we carried on, as Arthur might say.

I had to force myself to quit worrying about Kit's footwear and my own fear of heights and look down the steep—and growing ever steeper with each step—embankment every minute or so to look for Nora. And maybe Irene. We still couldn't be sure that was her body on the bed.

Somehow, Kit managed to walk and peer over the side at the same time with all the agility of an acrobat, which only made me even more nervous for her and her flimsy footwear.

I'm not sure what we expected to see when we looked down and around us. Nora lying hurt? Or dead? Or Nora hiking down a switchback across from us? But we never saw a soul—hurt, dead, or otherwise. Granted, we didn't go very far before we were uncomfortably hot and breathless.

"Do you see anything?" Kit asked, looking back at me briefly about ten minutes into our trek up.

But I was already too out of breath to talk. "Uh uh," I grunted.

She paused and looked down into the rock formations between two mountain peaks. "What did you say? Ya know, this would be pretty if it weren't so rocky and dusty. Ugh. Look at my flip-flops. They're ruined."

I thought the view was spectacular, not only looking down below us, but also looking over the valley to the mountains on the other side of the highway. Magnificence as far as the eye could see. But seriously, I couldn't even grunt again. My chest burned, and I felt parched. I took a drink of water.

"It makes you really appreciate the settlers who headed West." Kit had stopped, standing ahead of me, one hand on her hip, the other forming a shield over her eyes to keep out the blinding sun. "What do you suppose they'd think of our cell phones and Google Maps, not to mention visors and sunscreen? Val? Why aren't you talking?"

"Can't." I think the huffing and puffing that followed my answer finally enlightened her. I sat down on a big rock next to a jumping cholla cactus that held a tiny nest filled with hummingbird eggs the size of Jelly Bellies. I pointed to the natural wonder with my own kind of wonder.

"Cute," Kit said. "Although I could go for a real Jelly Belly about now."

I rolled my eyes and waved for her to go on without me. I felt certain she wouldn't go far enough away for me to have time to get scared. And frankly, even a rattlesnake under the rock I was sitting on couldn't get me to budge another step.

I watched, impressed, as Kit climbed higher and went around a bend. But within minutes, I saw her coming back down. At a faster pace. Good. I'd been counting on the descent being easier.

"Let's go," she said when she reached me. She held out a hand to help me up. "No way Nora would have made it even this far, not unless she was flown here by helicopter. She's a city girl."

Apparently, our residence in a Chicago suburb made us the outdoorsy type.

I remained silent for a while, still breathless and needing to concentrate on not going so fast that I'd miss a turn in the path. Doing so would plunge me over the edge and no doubt impale me on one of the cacti.

But then I broke the silence with a laugh. I felt mean, but it was involuntary. Kit had picked up too much momentum and was beginning to slide, arms flailing and voice screeching obscenities. We were close enough to the base by then that I figured the worst she could do was fall and sit on a cactus. She finally managed to gain control, but not before one of her flip-flops fell into a deep bed of rocks and cacti. I could only imagine the creatures that might be lurking there.

Kit no doubt had the same vision because she just kept walking, hobbling along with one tattered flip-flop and one filthy bare foot.

By the time we arrived at our car, we were drenched in sweat and had drunk every drop of our water. Kit immediately blasted us with maximum air-conditioning.

And then she announced that she was driving us to the police station.

But I told her I wouldn't be going in until I made a call to the only law enforcement officer I knew. A Downers Grove, Illinois, police detective named Dennis Culotta. I hadn't seen or heard from him for way too long, but I really wanted his advice.

I really wanted to hear his voice.

CHAPTER NINE

Why in the hell would you call *him*?" Kit was tapping her phone's keyboard for directions to the police station. It was located on Gerald Ford Drive.

Her question was a good one. Although I'd chosen to believe Detective Dennis Culotta and I had some kind of connection, he had abruptly disappeared from my life, leaving just a voice mail letting me know he'd be out of town for a while. I had no idea where *out of town* was, and the *while* had turned into forever.

But I called him anyway and listened to his voice repeat the same message I'd heard too many times to count. Then I hung up. Kit was right. There really was no need to talk to him. He'd advise us to do exactly what we were doing—go to the police and give a formal statement.

"Okay, let's do this." I shoved my phone back into my purse.

Kit set her cell on the seat beside her and took a few seconds to apply lipstick. Then she pulled her Ray-Bans down from her forehead and shoved them over her eyes.

I could feel that the ends of my hair against my neck were wet with perspiration. I noticed Kit, however, showed no signs of our sweaty hike—if you didn't look down at her feet, both of which were now bare. I leaned down and picked up my flats from the car floor. "Here," I said. "Wear these."

We rode in silence—except for the GPS directions, which we followed carefully. My occasional glances at Kit and her lack of conversation confirmed that she was worried. I reached over to pat her arm before finally speaking. "I'm sure Nora is fine. You're right, though: she would never have hiked that far up the trail. It nearly killed me—" I stopped speaking, appalled at my choice of words, but they elicited no response from Kit.

When we reached our destination, she put the car in park, turned off the ignition, and leaned forward, her chin resting on the steering wheel.

"C'mon, old thing," I said, but my attempt at levity resulted in Kit removing her shades and throwing me a frozen stare.

"Why would she marry a guy like that?" she asked, her voice barely above a whisper.

"Ah, honey, we spent only an hour with him. He could be really nice."

She didn't reply, which in itself was scary, but instead leaned back and opened the car door. She sighed. "Let's go."

"Okay. Let's get it over with."

***

"And neither of you ladies had ever seen the deceased before?" The detective's name was Tag Mason. It sounded like something a Hollywood movie studio had dreamed up. He was in his midthirties, tall, with sun-bleached hair and a prominent square jaw that accentuated his handsome features.

"Correct." Kit pointed to the part in her statement that reported just that.

"Hmm." Detective Mason glanced over the statement again.

"Hasn't Arthur Bainbridge identified her?" Kit asked, eyes wide open, eyebrows raised.

"Why? Do you think this Mr. Bainbridge would know her?" Tag Mason responded in the infuriating way police officers have of answering a question with another one.

"Know her? A shot in the dark here, Detective—she *was* found in his room. So surely—"

"Tell me about him."

Before Kit could point out that we'd already done so, and it was in our statements, I put a hand on her arm to silence her. "As we said, Detective Mason, we'd never met Mr. Bainbridge before today. All we know is that he and Nora were married recently."

"So you have at least brought him in?" Kit asked again.

"Another detective will question Mr. Bainbridge."

"So you are talking to him?" Kit's frustration level rose higher.

By way of response, Tag Mason reached into a drawer in his desk and took out a plastic bag, the kind I use to house my tuna sandwich when I plan to eat lunch in the office. Only difference was, this one had the word EVIDENCE stamped across it and a pair of bloody scissors inside. We all three stared in silence.

Tag was the first to speak. "Do you recognize the contents of this bag?"

"Recognize?" Kit replied. "Is it some kind of newfangled gardening tool—"

"Is it the murder weapon?" I asked, hoping to move this exercise along so we could go.

Tag nodded, giving me a nonverbal A+. "You ever seen it before?"

"No, Officer, not unless they were the ones sticking out—"

"Detective," he corrected me, shoving the bag back in the drawer. "We'll need fingerprints from you ladies. Just for elimination purposes. And until we find Mrs. Bainbridge, any of her DNA you could provide would be helpful."

"Are there fingerprints on the—"

"Gardening tool? No. Wiped clean. Or the killer used gloves."

"Can we leave now?" I asked. "We'll come back with some Nora DNA."

"Yes, you can return to your hotel. I'll be sending a team over to collect DNA specimens. By the way, where did you ladies go, after you left the hotel and before you got here?"

While I was thinking of a response, Kit decided to tell the truth. "We took a short hike on the Art Smith Trail. Looking for my sister."

"Anyone see you?"

"No one human. And before you ask why . . . someone's got to be looking for Nora."

And for her husband, Arthur, I silently added.

After we had been questioned by the police in the hotel room and were on our way out for our impromptu hike, we'd taken a cursory look in the lobby and bar area of the hotel. But Arthur Bainbridge was nowhere to be seen. By then the place was full of uniformed police officers, mingling with concerned guests. As we passed the check-in desk, I noticed a female officer talking to Tarique and making notes.

Now Tag Mason closed the file that contained our statements and stood. Obviously, our session with him was over. "You ladies should plan to stick around. We'll probably have some follow-up questions. And of course if you remember anything you didn't mention in your statements . . ."

Kit looked astounded. "Stick around? Where the hell do you think we're going—"

"Of course," I said, managing a smile. "C'mon, Kit. Let's get out of here." I took her arm to help her up, but she wasn't ready to budge.

"About my sister," Kit said, a little more calmly.

"Yeah, we'll need to speak to her, once she surfaces."

"Once she *surfaces*? She's not a damn floating device. You better get your people off their asses and—"

"She's very upset, Detective," I said. "We're both upset." The last thing I wanted was for Kit to alienate the Palm Desert police.

"Are you even looking for her?" Kit asked.

"We have dispatched a team around the perimeter of the hotel property. Don't worry; we'll locate her."

"Please contact us if you learn anything," I said. "You have our phone numbers. We'll be waiting for an update."

Tag nodded, looking as though he couldn't wait to get rid of us.

Before Kit could say another word, I yanked her arm again, and this time she rose.

"I'll be expecting to hear from you," she told Tag. "And it better be soon."

"Keys," I said, holding my hand out as soon as we were out of the station. "I'll drive." I knew Kit had put me on the rental agreement as an approved driver.

She placed the keys in my hand, and I opened the passenger door of the Caddy for her. "Where to?" she asked. "Where should we go?"

I prefer it when she has a plan mapped out, and even though I was literally in the driver's seat for the moment, I wasn't sure what I should do next. "How about we go back to the hotel and get something to eat," I said.

"I can't eat a thing until I know where Nora is."

"But you should." I felt guilty that I was suddenly ravenous. "Let's go back to the hotel and grab some room service. How about that?"

She gave a *who cares* shrug, and I started the car.

***

Back at The Palms Hotel we headed across the lobby toward the elevator. I noticed Tarique was still at the check-in desk, and he averted his eyes when he saw us. I steered Kit's arm in the right direction, and she gave me a weak smile.

"I'm not an invalid," she whispered into my ear.

"I know, Kitty Kat," I whispered back, as the elevator doors opened and we got in. "I know."

When the doors opened again on our floor, we stepped out to the previously empty lobby, and I saw an older couple sitting in two of the chairs. A quick glance down the hallway on my left showed a uniformed policeman standing outside Nora and Arthur's room.

"Howdy," said the man in a distinctive Southern drawl. He stood up and extended his hand. A giant of a man, he looked to be way over six feet tall and somewhere on the wrong side of seventy. "Dale and Louetta Powell from Tulsa, Oklahoma. Pleased to meet you."

We both shook his hand and smiled at Louetta, who remained seated. She may have smiled back, but her features were taut from what looked like an expensive face-lift. Not a good one, but an expensive one. Her too-long silvery-blond hair moved with her when she nodded her head at us, but her face wasn't moving for nothin'.

"Val and Kit," I returned his introduction.

"Pleased to know ya, Val and Kit," Louetta said from her chair. "Y'all heard what happened here?" She indicated the door and the policeman at the end of the corridor.

I could almost feel Kit come to life from her frozen state. "Yes, we heard. It's terrible." She took the chair next to Louetta, leaning close in a conspiratorial manner. "How long have you two been staying here?"

"Three days is all," Dale replied for his wife. "Can I get you gals a drink? Might as well; it's on the house."

"I'd love some white wine," I said, taking a seat.

"Me too," Kit said.

"Comin' up." Dale left our group, taking the few steps over to a couple of silver wine coolers on one of the tables.

"How long y'all been here?" Louetta asked. Again, I couldn't tell if she was smiling or not, but her manner was friendly.

"We just checked in this morning, but it's been one hell of a day, Louetta." Kit smiled for her. "Did you see the couple staying in . . . in the room . . ."

"Oh, honey, he was here when we checked in. A very dignified gentleman. He told Dale he was waiting for his wife to arrive, didn't he, honey?"

Dale had returned, holding two wineglasses, which he placed on the coffee table before us. "Sure did. Nice fella. But I understand that the gal they found in the room wasn't his wife. Someone else entirely. Seems like that fella had a regular ol' harem going."

"Do you know who she was?" Kit took a sip of wine.

"Nope." Dale moved over to his wife and crouched down in front of her, patting her knee in a touching gesture. "Ya need anything, honey?" He gave Louetta an adoring smile.

"I'm good." She reached out to touch his shoulder. "Go on and sit down now." She nodded in the direction of his vacant chair.

Reluctantly, but with easy agility for a man his size and age, he stood and returned to his seat and took a swig from a beer bottle. "Ain't got a clue what's happenin'," he finally finished answering Kit's question. "Police don't tell us nothin'. We were locked out of our room for a couple of hours while they did things in the hall like you see on TV, fingerprintin' an' all. Sure don't expect to be sitting out in the hallway when you're paying—"

"Oh, *Dale*," Louetta shut him up. "Y'all have to excuse my husband." She waved a hand in his direction. "He's tighter than Dick's hatband." Despite her frozen expression, it was easy to see she had once been beautiful, and she still

73

had a trim figure. She reached down to the coffee table to retrieve her drink, and I noticed a huge diamond on her engagement ring, plus a whole row of smaller ones on the accompanying band. Ol' Dale might have been tighter than the proverbial hatband on this Dick fellow, but he'd sure spent a pretty penny on his wife's rings. "Honey," she said, addressing her husband again, "why don't you go down to the lobby and fetch me a newspaper. I think I saw an *Atlanta Journal* in that shop down there—"

"They won't be selling an Atlanta newspa—"

"Then get me a Yankee one, honey. Just go."

Dale finished his beer in one gulp. "I'm going, I'm going." He smiled and rose, tipping his fingers in a little salute in our direction. As soon as we saw the elevator doors close behind him, Louetta leaned over and patted Kit's knee.

"My husband is way out of his element here. He rarely leaves Oklahoma. I about had to hog-tie him to get him this far."

"Are you vacationing?" I asked.

"Oh no, honey." Again, I had the feeling she would have smiled if she'd been able. "I had a little doctor visit. A follow-up, you might say. Sometimes you gotta leave your home state to get things done. So, what about you gals? Are you from California?"

"No, we're from Illinois," I said. "Chicago area."

"Oh my. So you're a long way from home too. What are you doing here, if you don't mind me asking?"

"Visiting family," Kit said, before I could respond. "Louetta, about the man in the room . . ."

"Hmm?" She took a sip of her wine, and her sharp blue eyes studied us over the rim of her glass.

I felt a twinge of sadness for Louetta. Had she disfigured her own face in an attempt to regain her lost youth? Well, hell, why else does a woman do that? But I hoped she had at least done it for herself, and not for Dale. "You never saw his wife?" I asked.

"I did catch sight of a gal leaving the room on Sunday. She was done up in that spandex stuff, like she was going running or something. Not sure if that was the wife or not. The older fella coulda been her daddy. I didn't speak to either of them myself, understand, but I heard Dale talking to the fella when we first checked in. He never did meet a stranger. But I told Dale I was sure that man was a big ol' fake."

"How do you mean?" Kit asked, trying to sound nonchalant, but not fooling me.

"Oh, pretending like he was British. Worst English accent I ever heard. He told Dale he was from Manchester originally. Claimed it's south of London. But I know it's northwest of the capital. I figure he took ol' Dale for a country hick, and he's probably right. Dale wouldn't know Manchester from Macon, Georgia. But see, I've been there. A few years ago, before . . . before I . . . just before things needed to be done . . . I traveled through England with a group of gals from Tulsa. On a tour of sorts. Very lovely country, I might add."

"And you don't think this man was really English?"

"Hell no, I don't. He wasn't fooling anyone, 'cept of course Dale. And he doesn't count."

We finished our drinks and then left Louetta. There was something worldly about her, and I thought briefly I'd enjoy getting to know her better.

But Kit was already rushing down the hallway to our room.

As soon as I closed the door, she threw one of her suitcases on the bed and ran the zipper around the edge. "We need Wi-Fi," she said, locating her iPad.

I opened the menu of amenities The Palms Hotel offered, all neatly bound in a leather folder. "It says it's free. I'll call down and get the password."

"Good. Let's see if Arthur Bainbridge has a wiki site." She sat on one of the beds and inched backward so that she was leaning against the headboard, her iPad on her lap.

Meanwhile, I wrote down the password that the woman who answered my call gave me. "Here." I handed the piece of paper to Kit. "By the way, what did you think of Louetta?"

"I think she should sue her plastic surgeon."

"Yeah. Definitely. But I liked her."

"Me too."

"And what was all that about Arthur not being British?"

"Ha!" Kit replied. "I knew he was fake."

"You knew?"

"Of course."

"Well, if you knew, why didn't you call him on it?"

"Okay, I didn't know. But I would have figured it out eventually."

"I'm sure you would have."

"Did you notice how he could never look you in the eyes?"

"Er, yeah. I think I pointed that out to you—"

"And all that British claptrap. Why would he pretend to be something he's not? Let's find out just who Nora really married." Kit began tapping furiously on her virtual keyboard and after a few seconds, stopped and looked up at me. "Son of a bitch." She said it calmly and without expression, not unlike our new pal, Louetta.

I joined her on the bed and began to read the page on the screen.

Arthur Bainbridge, founder of Bainbridge, Littlefield and Stein. Attorneys at Law. New York, New York. Arthur Bainbridge is currently in semiretirement. Kit closed the site and then clicked open the one below it. This showed several photographs, all taken at events that Bainbridge had attended. In most of the pictures the attendees were in evening dress of some kind. Arthur appeared distinguished and elegant in various tuxedos.

"Holy shit." Kit moved the cursor through each shot.

"And thank you, Louetta," I said.

The Arthur Bainbridge presented to us via the iPad looked to be in his early eighties. He was clean-shaven and wearing thick-lensed glasses. His posture was okay for a short guy with a definite paunch.

But no way in hell was he the same man staying at The Palms Hotel and claiming to be Arthur Bainbridge, the one we'd had drinks with just hours before.

CHAPTER TEN

It was dark, and I could tell the thought of Nora being who knew where was unbearable for Kit. "What if she *is* up in those mountains, Val? And why don't they have a search party up there?"

"How do you know they don't?" I asked, but I didn't remind her that Tag the Boy Detective said she wasn't considered missing for twenty-four hours. And I didn't tell her my bigger fear was that they *were* looking for Nora—as a murder suspect. Instead, I said, "We have to call the police, tell them about this guy posing as Arthur."

"Val, I don't want to talk to them again until I speak to Nora," she said. "I want to . . . warn her . . . prepare her."

"But Kit—"

"Val, she's *my* sister. I can handle this."

I considered dropping the subject, but it was too important. "Calling Detective Mason is the right thing to do," I said firmly, steeling myself for an argument, but surprisingly, none came.

"You do it," she said suddenly and quietly.

"Me?"

"Yeah, you. He liked you better than me."

"Okay, if you're sure. I don't mean about him liking me more. I mean about—"

"I know what you mean, for crying out loud; just do it, Val."

I dug my phone out of my purse, along with Detective Mason's card, and stepped out onto the balcony. As I punched in his number, Kit followed me and stood at the open door, watching closely.

I gave Tag Mason a brief description of our Internet search, explaining that the man we had drinks with was an impostor. For good measure, I followed up with Louetta Powell's assertion that Arthur Bainbridge probably wasn't even British.

"So?" Kit asked, as I turned my phone off and headed back inside. "What'd he say?"

"He said thank you for this vital piece of intel and he would act on it immediately."

"Really? He said that?"

"No. Not really. He was chewing gum, so it was hard to understand, but he definitely said hmm."

"*I knew it.*" Kit sounded triumphant, as if I'd just confirmed her suspicion that the police were basically doing nothing.

"Look, Kitty Kat, at least we've said our piece. And remember, at the station he said they were searching for Nora."

"Around the hotel grounds. Big whoop."

"Well, I'm sure they don't tell us everything they know." I'd also been disappointed at Tag Mason's lack of enthusiasm, but I wanted Kit to believe they were on top of things.

"Ya know, I almost wish they did think Nora is the murderer," she said, flopping down onto her bed. "Then they'd *really* look for her."

"I thought she probably *was* a suspect. Or that we suspected she would be a suspect."

Kit looked at me and shook her head. "Wanna say *suspect* one more time?" Her edgy tone, directed at me, was something I'd seldom if ever heard in the forty years we'd been friends. But then she'd never had a missing sister before, one I knew she feared might be dead or, yes, a *suspect*.

As I joined her on the bed, my phone rang. Emily. I answered it and immediately regretted it. Kit needed me too badly right now. "Em, this isn't a good time. Can I call you back?"

"Oh, Mom. I just can't wait to tell you our news. When can I see you? I'm just going to tell you now. We're—"

"Emily. I can't talk now." I felt certain I'd figured out what she wanted to tell me, and I didn't want to spend the rest of my life associating the glorious news of becoming a grandma with what might turn out to be the demise of Nora. Besides, Kit really did need me. "I'll call you back the minute I'm free, okay, honey?"

"Okay." I could sense her disappointment and almost changed my mind. But before I could, she said good-bye and my phone went dead.

"She's dead," Kit said, and I looked at my phone, thinking for a minute that's what she was talking about. "I just know it. Whoever killed that woman in the bed killed my sister too. I just know it." And then she rose and began to pace. I watched her circle the room and me, all the while removing her makeup with some fancy little pads. In contrast, I ran my fingers over my eyelashes, pulling at any stray mascara lumps. When her face was squeaky clean, she crumpled back down on the bed. "What will I tell my mother? How can I tell her I let Nora—"

"Wait a minute. You didn't have anything to do with whatever's going on with Nora."

"No, but I was never nice to her. I never—"

"Let's not get sidetracked, Kit. Let's think what we can do to find Nora." I had to get her focus back to the present.

When her phone rang, we didn't hear it at first. It didn't help that it was partially covered by the throw pillow she'd tossed aside when she first got on the bed with her iPad. Because the volume increased with each ring, we knew by the time we did hear it, it was nearing the last one.

She grabbed it, and as she slid her finger across to answer, she said, "It's Nora!" Then she said into the phone, "Nora?" Next she hit the speaker button and held the phone out so I could hear too.

All I could think was how the Arthur impostor had told us Nora left her cell phone in the hotel room. But of course he was lying.

I decided we needed to start making notes to help us study what few facts we knew. Then again, if Nora was all right, maybe we could put this whole thing behind us and I could go see Emily.

I couldn't be sure Nora was okay, though, since I could barely hear her whispering.

"Nora, why haven't you called us?" Kit asked.

"I just did."

"Can you talk louder? We can't hear you. Why are you whispering?" Kit yelled, as if her volume could make up for what Nora's lacked.

Nora whispered a bit louder. "I'm okay, Katherine. I'm hiding at The Living Desert. I don't dare try to leave until they open in the morning. I'm sure I would set off all sorts of alarms. They probably have the system whereby—"

"This is no time for a science lesson—"

Nora gave a slight nervous chuckle. "That wouldn't be science, Katherine; more accurately, it would come under the discipline of—"

"Nora! I need an explanation of your whereabouts— and why—not a lecture on science versus physics or whatever."

"Actually . . . oh, never mind." Nora sighed, as if her little sister were hopeless. "I had to get away from there. Someone was following me at the hotel. So I came here, and now they've closed. I've been hiding behind a bush near the giraffes. They're so elegant—"

"Nora." Kit's severe tone sounded just like their mother's, and apparently it grabbed Nora's attention—for the moment, anyway.

"Sorry. I have too much to explain, and my battery's going dead. I'll leave here when they open in the morning and meet you in the mall in front of See's Candies at ten."

"Wait! What do you mean? Who's following you, and why, and how long—"

But by then Nora was gone. I watched Kit shake her cell phone, as if she'd been disconnected by her service provider and a good rattle would reconnect her. Finally, in frustration, she threw her phone onto the bed. "Where is this Lost Desert place? We have to go there immediately." She grabbed clothes from her closet and began digging in her purse for car keys. "Oh, this is just so ridiculous. Dammit!"

"Calm down," I said, even though I felt far from calm myself. And then I patiently explained that The Living Desert, which was far from lost, was a zoo and gardens on Portola Avenue, not far from our hotel. I also reminded her about the alarm system Nora mentioned, and that we could *not* climb over any fences or walls in the dark and go searching for her sister by the giraffes. And finally, after checking my phone, I told her Nora no doubt meant the Westfield Palm Desert mall, as it was the closest.

"Okay," she said, sinking into an armchair, her purse clutched to her chest, her head nodding in agreement at the wisdom I had somehow pulled out of nowhere. "She's alive. That's all I care about. For now." She rose and gave me a quick hug, and her newfound relief was palpable.

I wasn't counting on getting any sleep, but I got ready for bed nonetheless. And then I called Emily, only to get her voice mail.

As I lay in the darkness, I wasn't sure if Kit was asleep. I looked across to the other bed and could just make her out; she wasn't wearing her sleep mask, but lying on her back with her forearm covering her eyes.

"Ya know," she said suddenly, "this happened so many times when we were kids. We'd go to the mall, and somehow Nora would disappear, and my mother and I would have to look for her. Then we'd find her in the pet store staring at a fish tank, or in the bookstore crouched down behind a shelf reading. One time we were at the movies, and she suddenly was no longer in her seat and Daddy and I searched everywhere for her. Eventually, we found her in the projection room. I don't even know how she got there, but she was talking to this guy who ran it. I was so pissed at her because we missed the show."

"Yeah," I said. "I seem to remember—"

"The worst part is . . . this isn't nice . . . but sometimes when she disappeared, I hoped we'd never find her. Is that awful to say?"

"You were a kid. It's not awful at all. Siblings can be a pain."

"You never thought your brother was."

"Oh, sure I did, sometimes. And I know you did." I giggled at the memory of Buddy and Kit bickering.

I heard a rustle as she propped herself up on one elbow. "Yeah, sometimes he was a pain." I could almost hear the smile in her voice. "But with Nora, it was different. It was like she didn't belong in our family, Val. And she was always trying to get away. Know what I mean?"

"Yeah, maybe. But you always went looking for her."

I heard her lie back down, and for a few minutes we were both silent. But neither of us was sleeping.

"Kit," I spoke first.

"Yes?"

"Do you think we should call—"

"Mason Jar? Definitely not."

This time I agreed with her.

***

We found a place to sit with Nora, under a palm tree inside the mall. For someone who had supposedly spent the night with a bunch of elegant giraffes, she looked pretty elegant herself. She was wearing a stylish black-and-gray jogging jacket that hugged her upper body, with cropped leggings showing off her shapely legs. She'd pulled her hair into a ponytail, and I wondered how it all stayed in place. Mine never did, without a can of hair spray. As soon as she sat down, she grabbed the unopened bottle of water Kit handed her.

I had to tear my attention from Nora when Emily chose that exact moment to return my calls, the one I'd made before bed last night and the two I'd made before we left the hotel this morning.

"Sorry, Mom," she said in greeting. "It's been crazy busy here, for both Luke and me."

"No, Em, I'm the one who's so sorry. Now I can't talk again."

"Mom, is everything okay?"

"No. Yes. I think it is now. I'll call you in a bit, okay?" I barely said good-bye, so eager was I to hear what *Nora* had to say.

"Okay," Kit said, when Nora finally stopped gulping water and was ripping off the packaging from the bagel her sister had supplied. "Nora, I don't even know where to begin. Why don't you start by telling us why you think Arthur is dead."

"Actually," Nora began, taking tiny mouse-size bites out of the bagel.

What adult eats that way? I wondered.

And that led me to memories of my mother and her rules for dining. *Valerie, you are not a wolf. Slow down. Valerie, you are not in prison; no one is going to steal your plate.* And my favorite: *Valerie, there are starving children in Europe who eat slower than you.* (Really, Mom? Because I thought the starving children were all in Africa.)

"Wait." Kit held up a hand. "Before you begin, let me tell you the hell we've been through." I could hardly believe Kit's choice of words, but then she proceeded to give her sister an account of everything that had transpired since our arrival.

It surprised me how patiently Nora listened to what I was sure was a boring story compared to whatever the hell it was *she* had to tell *us*. She nodded her head with each tiny nibble. Not once did she interrupt to explain or teach. Until Kit got to the part about Dale and Louetta Powell from Tulsa, Oklahoma.

"Huh," Nora interrupted then, as soon as Kit said their names. "You met them?"

"Nora! You know them? How? Who *are* they?"

"I think I saw their names on a—" Nora stopped speaking as her face took on an expression of absolute terror. Then she stood and bolted. I mean, she *ran*. She knocked over a toddler as she sprinted away, looking back briefly, as if to make sure the little girl was okay. And she barely missed an elderly man with a cane, but paused to give him a pat on the arm. All the middle-aged folk were on their own. She bounced against them like a running back heading through the defense for a touchdown, as she clumsily but quickly made her way out of our sight, stopping for just one second at a trash can to dispose of the paper napkin she had scrunched in her hand. That was impressive.

Kit and I were both panting to get our breath as we halted our chase. Nora was long gone, and we were left feeling powerless to figure out what had triggered her bizarre behavior.

And then we saw.

Standing across from where we'd been sitting, but making a quick exit himself when he knew we'd spotted him, was the Arthur Bainbridge impostor.

Whoever the hell he really was.

***

We stood in See's, Kit nibbling on a piece of their famous Dark California Brittle and me devouring my second dark-chocolate turtle. This family trait, this nibbling of food that I'd never noticed before, was just too annoying.

"I'm really annoyed," I said suddenly, surprising us both. I should have added *at you.*

Kit turned the piece of candy she held in her fingers. "I think it's quite good. I was just comparing it to Godiva or Ghirardelli, and it's—"

"We didn't learn one single thing from Nora."

"That's hardly *my* fault, ya know. In case you didn't notice, let me bring you up to speed. Nora took off—"

"You didn't let her speak."

"I would have. I just wanted her to know what we'd been going through—"

"Kit, is that important?"

"I didn't know the Count of Monte Cristo was going to turn up."

"I think we should go to the police, tell them what just took place." I stooped over and picked up a piece of chocolate that had dropped to the floor. I hated to do it, but I threw it away. What a waste.

"We don't *know* what took place. So what would we tell them?"

"We know Arthur—or rather the guy we had drinks with—was here, and that when Nora saw him, she ran for her life."

"And they're going to believe us *why*? And what reason will we give them for not letting them know Nora was at The Painted Desert?"

"The Living Desert."

"I hope they don't have to rename it The Dead Desert by the time we figure things out."

"You're not making any sense, Kit. And if we call the police, they can try to locate Nora through her cell phone, can't they?"

"Ya know, you'd think they would have already done that."

"Well, maybe they will, now that she's gonna look more suspicious to them."

"Are you still annoyed with me?" she asked, after we'd been silent for a few seconds. She had an *I don't give a damn either way* look plastered on her face.

"Yes."

"Hmm." She linked her arm through mine. "But you'll get over it, right?"

"Eventually."

"Val, thank you so much for coming here with me. And you are so right; I should have shut my trap and let Nora talk. I just didn't know there was a time limit—"

"Okay. Enough already. I'm over it."

She smiled her infectious smile. "Good. Let's go back to that damn hotel."

And so within a half hour, we were back in our room, all but twiddling our thumbs. It was obvious we were both deep in thought, my own flitting from Emily—and whether I should try to call her right now—to the bigger problem of Nora. It was equally obvious our thoughts were unproductive, as neither of us spoke.

And then we heard a light tapping at the door. I looked through the peephole and saw only the back of a woman's head, but Kit soon shoved me aside and opened the door.

And there was Nora.

CHAPTER ELEVEN

I put down the phone and looked across the room at the sisters sitting on the edge of one of the beds. Kit had her arm loosely around Nora's shoulders.

"Food will be here in fifteen minutes," I said. "I ordered fries with our sandwiches. Hope that was all right."

"That was thoughtful, Val." Nora looked up at me. "Normally, I avoid foods with high levels of saturated fat, but just this once—"

"Will you forget the damn food and tell us what's going on?" Kit had lost all pretense of being patient.

"Where should I begin?" Nora looked helplessly at me, and I sat down next to her.

"Start from the beginning." I patted her knee.

"When I was born—"

"Not the beginning of your *life*," Kit said. "The beginning of this whole friggin' nightmare you seem to be in the middle of. Nora, do you realize there was a dead girl in your room—"

"No, no." Nora scrunched up her eyes and put her fist in her mouth.

"You have no idea who she was?" Kit asked.

"None."

"Was she Irene, perhaps? Arthur's niece?" Kit's brown eyes had never looked so intense.

"How would I know, and why would you think that? Actually, as I recall, Irene is in Bangkok; she's guest lecturing at the international university there. They have an excellent curriculum—"

"Enough!" Kit stood and then leaned over Nora, grabbing her shoulders. "I'm tired of your rambling, Nora. Tired of your games. And we certainly don't need a lecture on education in flipping Bangkok. So I'm going to ask you questions, and you better have some answers. No bullshit."

Nora's eyes widened at her sister's outburst, but she nodded in compliance. "Okay. Ask me anything."

"Good." Kit softened a bit. "Let's start with Arthur Bainbridge. He's your husband; you are married, right?"

"Well, technically—"

"*No, no, no.*" Kit released her grip on Nora's shoulders and took a step back. "I don't want to hear *technically* or any other BS; is he or is he not your husband? Simple yes or no answer. You're a lawyer, for crying out loud; imagine you are in court and you are the witness."

"Would I be a witness for the prosecution or the defense?"

"Just answer the question."

"Okay. Yes. Sort of. Actually, he *was* my husband. But now he's dead. I'm sure of it. So tech—I mean, essentially, since he no longer is alive, he's not currently—"

"Okay. Now shut up." Kit took a deep breath. "All right, we have established that at some point in the recent past you married Arthur Bainbridge."

Nora nodded vigorously.

I looked at my watch. Where the hell was the food? And why wasn't either of these two women concerned about it?

"So." Kit paced the room, doing a wonderful impression of a prosecutor. "You married Arthur Bainbridge, and the two of you planned to attend a conference in this hotel?"

Nora nodded again.

"Good. And you left Chicago and flew here on your own, expecting to meet your husband, Arthur?"

"Correct," Nora said.

"When did Arthur arrive in California?"

"He was scheduled to arrive on Friday morning."

"But when you got here, Arthur was not around?"

"Also correct."

"And you suspect that he's dead. Why?"

"Because he wasn't here. He'd checked in, but I couldn't find him. And then someone called telling me that Arthur was dead and I'd be next." She stopped talking after this startling announcement and looked as placid as if reporting a call from someone selling aluminum siding.

We waited a few seconds for her to continue. Kit took a deep breath, and I expected to hear her tell Nora that the man who introduced himself to *us* as Arthur was an impostor. But for some reason she didn't. "Then what?" she asked.

"Then I got a call from you."

"And speaking of that, why didn't they have a reservation for us when we arrived? What was that all about? You said—oh, never mind. Okay, let's back up. This person who called you: what exactly did they say?"

"They said Arthur was dead and I'd be next. I just told you that."

"Did you recognize the voice?"

Before replying, Nora turned her face away from her sister and toward the balcony. "The view is magnificent, isn't it?" Her voice was dreamy. "I can see the palms—"

"Nora," Kit urged.

"No." Nora turned her face back toward her sister, but she kept her eyes downcast, focused on her feet. "I didn't recognize the voice."

Kit sighed in disgust. "Okay. So did you consider calling the police?"

"Of course. That was my first thought." She hesitated slightly before continuing, turning her gaze back toward the balcony door. "I realized Arthur's things had been gone through, and some important papers were missing."

"What kind of papers?"

"He was working on a big case. I don't know the details. But Arthur was actually hired in a consulting capacity by the district attorney. He's not used to being on the opposite side." She laughed at the prospect, although the humor was lost on Kit and me.

"And these papers?" Kit asked. My neck was starting to get a kink from swiveling it from sister to sister.

"Actually a file, to be exact. Arthur had interviewed several witnesses in the case. Normally, he would have someone on his legal team do the research, but he took this one on personally. It's top secret."

"Why?"

"It has something to do with his first wife—"

"Oh! There's a first wife?" Kit asked, but I waved my hand in the air to shut her up.

"Yes. He was married before."

"Which century was this?"

"Kit," I said, "will you *please* be quiet and let Nora finish? Geez."

"Okay, okay, go on." Kit put four fingers over her lips, I assumed as a reminder to keep her mouth shut.

Looking a little grateful, Nora continued. "I know the file was important. Arthur had already agreed to come here and speak at this seminar more than six months ago, so he brought his work with him."

"That still doesn't explain why you didn't go to the police."

"I intended to. I really did. But my first thought was that the phone call was some kind of hideous prank and maybe Arthur was somewhere in the hotel, maybe in the restaurant or out by the pool. He's an avid swimmer, you know. The cardiovascular benefits from that type of exercise—"

"Focus," Kit said.

"Okay; I left the room and began searching. When I didn't find him in the hotel, I walked around the area. I was gone for an hour and a half, maybe two. When I got back to the hotel . . ."

"Go on," I urged.

"I spotted a man in the lobby that I thought I'd seen before in New York. I was shocked to see him here in California. I believed he had followed us out here. I think he might have taken the papers. He was the same man I saw in the mall when I ran."

"And you still didn't call the police?" Kit sounded irritated, although she hadn't been eager to call in law enforcement herself.

"No. I wasn't sure what Arthur was mixed up in. I didn't want to expose him. I also think this man was under the impression I was privy to Arthur's notes on the case. But actually, I know very little."

"Is Arthur doing something illegal?"

"No. Not Arthur. He's a very straight arrow. He's been a consultant to the New York judicial commission many times—"

"Yet you see some dude you're afraid of, you think your husband is missing or dead, you get a threatening phone call, and you still don't go to the police?" Kit was clearly astounded.

We waited for Nora to respond. "Actually, no."

***

Tag Mason looked annoyed. Not so much at the story Nora Bainbridge was spilling—which even to my untrained ear had more holes in it than a shooting-range target—but because he appeared to have somewhere else to be.

Getting Nora to agree to go to the police had been difficult. It was even more challenging to convince Kit that it was the best thing we could do.

But here we were.

"So, tell me again why you didn't contact us?" the detective asked, when Nora had finished telling her story.

"She panicked. She was afraid. She'd been threatened," Kit answered for her sister.

"You realize leaving the scene of a crime without reporting it *is* a crime?"

"Yes. Of course she realizes it; she's an attorney, for crying out loud."

"And actually, I didn't know a crime had been committed at that point," Nora said. "I speculated my husband was dead, but I had no real proof that I was correct."

Detective Mason took a stick of chewing gum from his pocket and popped it into his mouth. "And this man . . . this man you claim was following you . . . you think he's the same man that called and threatened you?"

"Yes. Quite possibly."

Kit turned her attention to Detective Mason. "And we've told you about this man posing as Arthur Bainbridge in the bar. When you questioned him, what did he say?" Kit sounded exasperated, like a harried mother explaining to a school principal that *her* child couldn't possibly be guilty of anything.

Detective Mason chewed lazily on his gum for a few seconds before answering. "That's the problem, ma'am. We were never able to locate him in the hotel."

"But you said that another detective would interview him—"

"And he will. Soon as we find him." His tone of voice suggested he did not believe this man ever existed.

***

Eventually, the Palm Desert police seemed satisfied enough to let Nora leave the station with us, although they stipulated that she stay in town until they finished their inquiries.

Once we returned to the hotel, Nora took up residence in our room since there was a policeman standing guard outside hers.

She immediately claimed one of the king-size beds, and we watched her fall asleep quickly. With Kit furiously tapping away on her iPad, I excused myself and went down to the lobby to call my daughter.

It was early in the evening, but the hotel was quiet, so I took an armchair by the waterfall in the lobby. I wanted to be calm, the way any prospective grandmother should be, and I figured the soothing sound of flowing water would help.

I tried to forget the turbulent events of the day and took a deep breath before tapping Emily's name on my phone's contact list.

She answered on the first ring. "Mom? Finally."

"I'm sorry, honey. It's been a little crazy here, and I wanted to wait for a quiet time to hear your news. So, go ahead. I'm by myself and all ears." As I waited a few seconds for her to speak, an image of a baby danced in my head. A miniature Emily or Luke.

"When am I going to see you? Oh, I just can't wait to tell you. We're moving to England—"

"Huh?" I held my breath. There could still be a baby, although it would probably be an English one. A baby that preferred cricket over baseball, and devoured crumpets (whatever they are) with gallons of tea. A child that shunned Big Macs in favor of fish and chips . . .

"Luke's company is transferring him to their office in England for a year."

"A year? England? What are you talking about?" I've never really been sure what it is my son-in-law does for a living. Something in computers, something very brainy, something that apparently required his presence across the pond for a year.

"Isn't that exciting? I couldn't wait to tell you."

"So no baby?"

"Baby? Mom—oh, is that what you thought the news was?"

"No, of course not. I . . . I'm happy for you and Luke. It sounds like a wonderful opportunity."

"Right. And England is not that far away. Well, a few hours longer to fly to England than to LA. But you and Kit can come visit, and it's going to be great."

Her enthusiasm killed my grandma persona, and I mentally put aside the baby booties I might have been knitting. I could hear the excitement and joy in her voice. "Honey, I think it will be great. I'm thrilled for you both."

"Really?"

"Yes. Really. Listen, I have to get back to the room, but I'll call you tomorrow and we'll arrange a time to meet in the next couple of days."

"Why the delay? Well, I've got a lot going on, anyway. But I can't wait!"

"I have to, um, help Kit—"

"No worries. Bye, Mom. Love you."

I made my way slowly back through the lobby, passing the front desk. I could see a new person was on duty, a young woman with a long flaxen braid straight out of a Disney movie. She was talking to a customer, and as I got closer, I saw her use the end of a pen to point out something on a printed sheet she'd placed on the counter between them. I stopped behind the man being served as a thought hit me.

"Is there anything else I can help you with, Mr. Tippon?" I heard her ask, as she flashed a smile, moving her heavy braid from her left to her right shoulder.

"Nope, that'll do it. Thanks." The man watched as she deftly slipped the key card into a paper folder and handed it to him.

"Enjoy your stay, sir," she said, as he lifted the suitcase at his feet.

He turned to look at me and smiled before moving a few steps away from the counter and checking the folder he'd just been handed.

"Now, how may I help you, ma'am?" Rapunzel turned her attention to me.

I took a step forward. "I'm staying in Katherine James's room. We're attending the conference. I wonder if you could call the Powells for me, please. Dale and Louetta. They're on the concierge level, but I'm not sure which room."

"Certainly. One moment." She clicked on her keyboard a few times, appearing to refresh the screen, and then clicked again. "I'm sorry," she said. "There's no one by that name staying in the hotel. Could I look up someone else for you?"

"No. No one else. Thank you."

In the elevator, I leaned against the wall as it sped to the top floor. When I got back to the room, both women were in bed. I could see Kit was wearing white silk tailored pajamas and a black satin sleep mask embroidered with the words *Fly Me to the Moon*. I changed into my Chicago Cubs T-shirt I use as a nightgown and crawled into bed beside her. "You asleep?" I whispered.

"Asleep? Who can sleep with loony tunes in the next bed?" she whispered back. "Did you reach Emily?"

I told her about the conversation with my daughter and followed up with what the lady at check-in had told me about the Powells.

I listened to her heavy sigh. "Why'd you check on the Powells?" she asked.

"I don't know. Just a hunch. The Powells are the only ones, so far, who have actually seen Arthur Bainbridge in this hotel. I thought it might be interesting to check out which Arthur it was that Dale spoke to."

"Yeah, good point, Valley Girl. And we gotta find out who the aging Lord Fauntleroy is," she said after a few seconds.

"Fake Arthur. Right," I murmured.

We were both silent for the next five minutes. Then Kit spoke again quietly. "Do you believe Nora?"

"Well, her story does sound slightly wacky."

"Where *is* the real Arthur?"

"Beats me."

***

The next morning I suggested we eat in the hotel restaurant, which was advertising a California Brunch from ten until two. I assumed this meant oodles of fruit, never my favorite thing for brunch—or any other meal—but I was hungry and didn't want to drive anywhere. So we three made our way down to the lobby and headed toward the entrance to the restaurant, passing some police officers standing in a group by the front desk.

"Have you noticed how handsome the police are out here?" I whispered to Kit, maneuvering around them. They could have been extras in an episode of *Baywatch*, and I almost expected Pamela Anderson to run by us in a red bathing suit.

"No donuts, I expect. They probably all jump out of bed every morning and eat a dozen mangos for breakfast."

The five or six officers in blue had formed a semicircle around one man in the center who seemed to be giving them instructions. He was not in uniform, but wearing Dockers and a blue shirt, his tie loosened at the collar, shirtsleeves rolled up to his elbows. As we got closer, I saw the man's white hair, his suntanned face, and his crooked smile as he shared what seemed to be a joke.

I stopped walking, grabbing Kit's arm and pointing across the lobby. "Kit, look who's over there."

"What the—" she said, peering into the group of guys. "Why is *he* here? Lock up your donuts, California."

But despite her disdain, I was finally able to take a deep breath for the first time since we'd landed. I just hoped I wouldn't throw up.

The cavalry had arrived, and Detective Dennis Culotta was leading the charge.

CHAPTER TWELVE

It was a crazy idea for us to go down to breakfast."
I barely waited for Nora to follow Kit and me back
into the room before I shut our door and locked it
with both the dead bolt and chain. "Like we want Nora to
be seen here?"

"It was your idea, ya know." Kit pulled her phone out
of her skirt pocket and plopped down on our bed. "You
were *starving.*" She'd set her phone down long enough to
surround my exact word with her trademark air quotes.

But suddenly I wasn't hungry.

It had taken a mere body in a bed for Kit and Nora to
lose their appetites, and I'd had to talk them into
accompanying me to brunch. It took Detective Dennis
Culotta for me to lose mine.

I should have had him arrested for theft of one hearty
and robust appetite. Except that I was too relieved to have
him nearby. I felt safe—or at least safer—for the first time
since we'd left Chicago.

I didn't, however, want him to see me the way I looked right now. No makeup, hair only finger brushed, and dusty shorts and T-shirt that I'd worn on our hike. I'd planned to clean up *after* eating. My priorities hadn't changed just because I was in California.

Nora, who was looking a little frayed around the edges herself, took a seat in one of the leather armchairs by the balcony door. "Who is this Mr. Culotta?" she asked.

"He's no one," Kit said.

"He's a friend of ours—" I started to explain.

"A friend of yours, not mine," Kit corrected me.

I sat down in the chair across from Nora, prepared to finish answering her question. She deserved an explanation. I casually picked up a copy of *C Magazine* lying on the table, trying to appear as nonchalant as possible. "He's a detective with the Downers Grove Police Department," I told her. "We've had some dealings with him in the past."

"And Val goes all gooey when he's around," Kit added.

"Ugh. That is not true at all. He's just very good at his job and—"

"He's a pain in the ass."

"He's far from that." I fanned the pages of the publication. "But what in the world is he doing in Palm Desert?" I asked no one in particular and didn't expect an answer.

Kit looked up from swiping away at her phone long enough to respond. "I was going to ask you that very question. I assumed you called him." She eyed me suspiciously, as if expecting a lie.

"Kit! You know I wouldn't do that without telling you. Did *you* call him?" I studied her face and eyes for telltale signs of a fabrication.

Just then both of our phones rang. If I'd noted my caller ID, I might not have answered mine.

But too late, I heard my mother's voice. "Have you seen our Emily? How is she? And I do hope you're wearing sunscreen when you go out, Valerie. Even at this time of the year the sun in California can be lethal."

Lethal? That surely was the least of California's problems, not to mention my own.

I moved over to the desk chair and sighed. "Yes, Mom, I'm wearing sunscreen, and no, I haven't seen Emily yet, but I talked to her last night, and we're going to meet—"

"What's taking you so long? I was thinking, Valerie, that you should meet her at the Getty Villa. I read in a gardening book that it's the most beautiful garden in Los Angeles. If you hadn't taken off without any warning, I might have accompanied you. I could have seen my granddaughter *and* the most beautiful garden—"

"Mom." I had to stop her. I didn't have time to get distracted. I felt guilty, knowing that my mom had *too much* time. If only she'd yield to William's pleas to take up golf, she could spend all the hours on the golf course that he did. I assured myself that wishing my mom fresh air and exercise wasn't selfish. "It's not that kind of trip, Mom. Sorry. You and I can come another time. You don't really want to travel with Kit, anyway—"

Did I say that out loud? I looked across the room at my pal, but she had her own phone pressed against her ear and didn't appear to have heard me.

"Yes," my mom said, "I suppose you are right. Having her in Door County was quite . . . the experience. Still, I would—"

"Well, another time. Look, I'll call you after I see Emily. I'll fill you in." I didn't want to go into the England story until I had plenty of time to do the *it's not the end of the world* reassurance I knew would be called for. My mother would point out everything from an increased threat of terrorism to the horror of Emily not having her own doctor or the food she was used to. Like she was going to a third-world country. "Bye, Mom. Love you."

"Give Nora a hug from me," I heard her say as I hung up.

I realized I'd sounded a bit like Emily had, signing off with me the night before. She'd been awfully quick to assure me it was no problem if we didn't get together immediately. I sighed. We daughters do have our own lives. But that's a lot easier for me to accept as a daughter than it is as a mother.

I turned my attention to Kit, who was on the bed resting her back up against the headboard and nodding into the phone. When she saw my call was done, she put her phone on speaker and laid it in the middle of the bed so we could all hear.

Her mother's voice floated through the air-conditioned room. Cool and cultivated, with just a hint of *gotcha!* As always when I heard Beverly Rudolph's voice, I felt like I needed to put on a sweater or turn down the air-conditioning. Growing up with Kit as my best friend, I'd avoided her mother as much as possible, which hadn't been that difficult since she didn't seem to be around much.

Beverly was taller and slimmer than both her daughters and beautiful in an aging–Angelina Jolie sort of way. Ethereal and lovely to look at from across the room, but you couldn't imagine her getting down on her knees and playing a good old-fashioned game of Twister.

Kit's mother was the antithesis of my own, who was always the first to show up at bake sales, having cooked all night. My mom often carried a few dozen handwritten recipe cards stashed in her purse for those who might want to know her "secret" for perfect oatmeal-and-raspberry-jam bars.

Beverly, on the other hand, arrived five minutes after the crowd, if she arrived at all, looking elegant in some divine outfit she'd thrown on, carrying a tray of two dozen chocolate éclairs, which she made no pretense of having baked herself.

She doesn't have a map to our kitchen, Kit loved to joke, but it makes sense to me that Kit has turned into a gourmet cook, insisting that almost every meal be made from scratch.

It also helps explain why Nora and my mom became pen pals (apart from being the only two people left on the planet who write letters).

"So, you two are in Los Angeles," Beverly said.

Nora and I had jumped on the bed beside Kit, forming a circle around the phone, like kids at camp waiting for marshmallows to turn brown.

"Actually, we're in Palm Desert, which is located—"

"Don't interrupt me, Nora. You know I hate that." Beverly's voice was icy, and I imagined she was wearing a silk caftan and matching turban, just the kind of outfit she could get away with and not appear ridiculous. "Why exactly are you there?"

"Nora is attending a conference, and Kit and I flew out for a little break," I said, when no one else spoke up. "This is Valerie Pankowski, by the way."

"Hmm," was Beverly's only comment. I looked across our little loop to see Kit's fifteen-year-old face asking her mother for permission to go to a Three Dog Night concert. Her mother had said she didn't care as long as she wasn't expected to drive us there.

That was in contrast to *my* mother, who had first argued with the fifteen-year-old me for over an hour that she didn't understand what a Three Dog Night was. Then she insisted she would drive, but pick us up thirty minutes before the concert ended to avoid possible crushing by the crowd or any riots that might break out. (Kit, incidentally, easily solved that problem by just giving my mom the wrong concert time, so we stayed till the end and still managed to avoid any trampling by overly excited teenagers.)

"So how did you know we were here, Mother?" Kit asked.

"I needed the name of a good tax attorney out here; our last one had a heart attack. So I thought Larry might be of some use."

The divorced Beverly Rudolph had remarried when the girls were in their twenties. The good news was that she and her second husband had moved to Phoenix. Even better news was that she rarely contacted her daughters, unless she absolutely needed something.

"Sorry," Kit said. "We should have let you know."

"No need for that. You have your own lives."

For the millionth time, I was grateful for my own mother, who would have had to be under the influence of some hallucinogenic drug to utter such a statement.

"Right," Kit agreed. "So was Larry able to help you?"

"In his usual fashion," was her reply, whatever the hell that meant.

"Alrighty then. So good to talk to you; you take care—"

"Not so fast, Katherine. I'm not done. Let me speak to Nora."

I looked across at Nora. She had been busy chewing her nails, and I almost wanted to get her a little salt and pepper for taste. When she heard her mother speak her name, she removed her fingers from her mouth and began waving both arms and shaking her head.

"Oh, sorry, I guess she left the room," I said. "I'll have her call you later."

"That's not necessary. I really wanted to know if Arthur Bainbridge is out there."

Despite Nora's silent *no*, Kit replied, "Yes, he is. Why do you need him?"

"Is he there right now?"

"No."

"I *need* to speak to him, Katherine. Do you understand me?"

I watched Kit nod silently.

"Katherine?" Beverly prompted her daughter. "Are you listening?"

"Yes, Mother," Kit spoke up. "I heard you."

"Good. So make that happen. It's very important."

"I will try—"

"See that you do. Bye, girls." The line went dead, and for a few seconds we all stayed in our positions, staring at the phone in the middle of the bed.

"Mothers," I said, as if they are all alike. I've always tried to pretend I can relate to Kit's exasperation with her mother's aloofness. Mine can be annoying, but it's almost always out of love and concern for me. Beverly Rudolph is another kettle of mom fish entirely. She's the wicked witch, or the icy queen, in any kids' movie. But still, she's Kit's mother, so I instinctively know she can criticize her all she wants. It doesn't mean I am free to agree.

"I have to just tell her what she wants to hear," Kit has told me a thousand times through the years. "Then I do what I want." And I have to agree that's the only way to deal with someone like Beverly Rudolph. But Kit has turned that ruse into a fine art and uses it on everyone.

Now she said, "Nice try, Val. Your mother and mine might share the title *mother*, but there the similarity stops. Mine is a selfish, controlling witch. Right, Nora?"

"That is, unfortunately, an accurate assessment. Why, you should hear the way she talks about Arthur. She hates him so much. And she's never even met him."

"Who *has*?" Kit raised her eyebrows at her sister. "I'm surprised she is aware of his existence, although I'm assuming you haven't told her that you are married."

Nora shook her head. "No, no, I mean to, or rather I meant to. I introduced his name a couple of times during our conversation when I called her, but she seems to carry some animosity toward him."

Kit gave a joyless laugh. "She's on his trail now, for sure, so if he's not dead already, he'll soon wish he was."

"She did indeed sound desperate to talk to him." Nora returned her fingernails to her mouth.

"Yeah, what was that about?" I wondered aloud.

Both girls looked at me briefly, and then Kit picked up the *C Magazine*. "Who knows, with her?" She flipped through the pages, stopping at a picture of an austere white kitchen. "Look at this. Sometimes I wonder if these Californians know the difference between minimal and jail cell. Ya know, Beverly probably had one too many last night and just realized her daughter is seeing someone older than her."

"Unfortunately, it's much deeper than that. Sometimes I think she hates me, Katherine. I know she'll just fly off the handle when I tell her . . ."

I pictured Beverly Rudolph on the handle of a broom, flying off to wherever witches fly and wearing the most fabulous velvet witch's hat covered in black feathers and sequins.

"She doesn't hate you," Kit soothed her sister. "At least not any more than she hates anyone else. But Nora, you should have told her you were married, just like you should have told me."

"I know. It was foolish not to tell you. Actually, I was planning to do so, and then I thought I would surprise you first, and then it felt anticlimactic to tell you after the fact . . . then I just blurted it out when we met Tom Haskins at the Briar that night. You know how awkward it is when you have a secret to tell, and the more you keep it to yourself, the harder it becomes."

"Okay, I don't even understand what the hell you're talking about. But right now, I think we have bigger fish to fry than worrying about Mother. Although I am curious why she wants to speak to Arthur—if we ever find him." She sighed deeply. "It's no wonder Daddy left her."

I knew it wasn't the first time Kit had expressed that notion to her sister. I'd heard it more than once. But somehow I'd never felt sorry for Kit about her mother *or* her parents' divorce. She always seemed too together, too confident, to ever need my sympathy.

Except for now.

I wanted to share with Nora that even if she felt she didn't have her own mother's devotion, mine at least thought she was the bee's knees. I'd never heard my mom apply such a high accolade to Kit, however, and it seemed unfair to leave her out. So I said nothing.

Kit changed the subject. "Nora, we have to know what was in Arthur's papers. But how? They're in the hands of some sorry son of—"

"Yes. It's unfortunate," Nora agreed, looking sad. Sad, but not necessarily hungry.

"Are you guys still up for breakfast?" I asked. Surely they were.

"Yes, yes, and for crying out loud, go put some lipstick on in case we see your boyfriend. Sheesh."

I wasn't proud of my shallowness, but I grabbed my most flattering pair of skinny jeans and a white T-shirt and headed into the bathroom, where I put on a lot more than lipstick.

The Juckett girls were sitting on the bed waiting for me, Kit tapping her foot, when I came back out. "Finally," she said.

I took my navy-blue blazer off a hanger and was slipping my arms into it when we all three froze at the sound of a loud knock on our door. We looked at each other questioningly, and then Kit went over and peered through the peephole.

"Oh hell." She turned and walked back toward me. "It's your dream boy. You better let him in."

***

I arrived at the Getty Villa first and realized that, once again, my mom—with the help of her gardening book—was right. This likely was not only the most beautiful *garden* in Los Angeles, but also the most beautiful spot, period. Which in the land of mountains, palm trees, and the Pacific Ocean, was saying something. I waited for Emily in the tranquil East Garden, under the shade of sycamore and laurel trees. As I watched the water splashing from a sculptural fountain, I felt the load of Nora's situation begin to lift.

After we'd finished with Culotta—or more accurately, after he'd finished with us—the sisters had insisted I call my daughter and arrange to meet her without further ado. They would begin looking through Arthur's things.

"For crying out loud," Kit had said, "who knows what's ahead? Go see Emily while you know you can. Find out more about her England move. And then book our flight." She gave a mirthless chuckle that sounded like she wasn't sure she'd be flying to England or anywhere else.

I could tell the circumstances seemed that grim to her, and I felt guilty leaving. But the pull to see my daughter was even greater than any guilt. Mine *or* Nora's. And I realized that focusing on the California freeway system for more than two hours, one way, would be better than thinking about the mess we were in.

But of course I couldn't help revisiting the scene where Culotta had barged into our room before I'd even opened the door fully. I'd stepped quickly aside, as it seemed he was about to run me over, and stood with my back pressed against the wall, feeling like I was in a police lineup. "Valerie," he said with a slight nod of his head, "good to see you."

I nodded, unable to find my voice. I had dreamed so often of seeing him again, but I couldn't recall any of the witty lines I had prepared. Instead, we remained silent, our eyes locked for several seconds, although it seemed much longer. I smelled a faint whiff of laundry detergent, something fresh and lemony, something very familiar, and I could see a crease at the shoulder of his shirt that was the result of bad ironing.

Finally, he broke the spell and turned toward Kit. "Mrs. James."

"Kit. Call me Kit." She looked almost offended, as if she assumed he hadn't remembered her first name.

"And you must be Nora Bainbridge." He walked over and stood before Nora, who was again sitting on the end of the bed biting her fingernails.

She rose, looking nervous. "Yes, sir. And you are—"

"Dennis Culotta. Detective Dennis Culotta."

"From the Chicago police?" she asked. "Why would the Chicago police—"

"I'm from Downers Grove, ma'am. But I'm here in an unofficial capacity. I can tell you, however, that the body found in your room has been identified." He stared intently at Nora, and I wondered if she was as mesmerized by his blue eyes as I was.

"Yeah?" Kit said impatiently. "Spit it out, Detective."

He took his eyes off Nora for a brief second to throw a sardonic smile in Kit's direction, then returned to his scrutiny of Nora before announcing the name of the dead girl. "Celia Decissio," he said at last.

Nora looked as if she were about to faint.

As I waited now for Emily to join me at the Getty Villa, I relived the whole scene yet again, a little ashamed of the tingle of excitement it gave me, considering the nasty circumstances. And then I heard her.

"Mom, Mom!"

I looked up from the fountain I'd been staring into and saw my daughter approach through the foliage along the well-manicured pathway. Suddenly I forgot all about Celia—and Culotta.

"Emily!" I hurried to meet her, wrapping her in my arms for a long hug. I could smell the rosemary of her hair product, a smell that always means *Emily* to me. Then I pulled back to get a better look at the younger, prettier, tanner me. She had her long blond hair in a casual knot on the top of her head. She'd probably taken all of ten seconds to form it, yet it looked so chic. Her miniskirt showed off her shapely legs—and also her flat, flat tummy. Nope. No grandbaby on the way.

Realizing I'd still harbored a slight hope, I put it to rest once and for all. "Should we take a stroll?" I asked.

"Let's do it." She grabbed my hand and smiled. "Say, did Tom get ahold of you?"

"Tom? No, why?" My boss is like another father to Emily. The loving feeling is mutual, so it didn't surprise me one bit that he would contact her if he couldn't reach me.

"Oh, he called all worried. You know how he can get. He's so caring." She smiled again. She's one of the few people besides me who see through Tom's rough, tough facade. We both know—and cherish—his loving side.

I felt touched to have it directed at me once again. I should have known he'd be troubled by my sudden departure and not hearing from me right away. I needed to phone him. But first I needed to visit with my daughter. "Yes, I'm sure he's worried. I'll call him soon. It's so silly, how he worries about me."

"I'm not sure it's you, Mom. He sounded awfully concerned about Kit's sister—Nora, is it? He even said he was calling a detective friend to check on things in Palm Desert. What's that all about? Surely that's not about *you*?" She stopped walking, as if to await my answer.

I stood still also, as if stalled by the unpleasant feeling in the pit of my stomach. I felt, well, almost jealous.

But why? I wondered, before assuring her it was not about me. Then I changed the subject.

CHAPTER THIRTEEN

After Emily and I hugged good-bye and I was back in the car, I called Culotta's cell. I expected to get his voice mail, the same message I'd listened to so many times, but he answered on the first ring.

"Valerie, glad you called. Where are you?"

"I'm in the car. On my way back to Palm Desert from LA. I met Emily at the Getty Villa."

"How is she?"

"Great. Look, I need to talk to you. In person and alone."

"Wow. How can I resist that?"

"Get over yourself, Culotta." The truth was, I did have a million questions for him, ones I preferred to ask without Kit and Nora around and with no danger of my going all gooey, as Kit called it. "Is there someplace we can meet close to the hotel in about an hour and a half?"

"Your hotel?"

"I'd prefer yours," I said. "Where are you staying?"

"I'm at the Desert Inn; there's a Starbucks about five minutes away on Monterey."

Well, that was close to both our hotels, but then anything in Palm Desert would be. "I know it. I'll call you when I'm about ten minutes away."

***

I was quite proud of the way I'd maneuvered around LA and the freeways and gotten back to Palm Desert, and when I eventually spotted the familiar twin-tailed mermaid of my favorite coffee shop, I pulled over and turned off the engine.

I took a few minutes to reapply lipstick, run a comb through my hair, and spray myself with a liberal amount of Chanel No. 5, a Christmas present from Emily. Normally, I don't wear perfume, but I'd tossed the barely used bottle into my suitcase at the last minute. I was, after all, going to California, and if the fragrance had been good enough for Marilyn Monroe, it was good enough for me.

Culotta was seated in the back of the coffee shop. He had the *LA Times* spread open, covering the whole table. He looked good. No, he looked great. Suntan; prematurely white hair a little tousled; blue, blue, blue eyes that caught mine and twinkled as a huge grin covered his face when I opened the door. He folded the newspaper, tossed it onto the empty table next to him, and stood up, arms outstretched. His whole demeanor was completely different from the one I'd seen earlier in our hotel room.

I fell into his hug. But when it lasted a little longer than I thought comfortable for two old friends meeting after a long separation, I released myself.

"Mocha?" he asked, and I nodded, watching him walk to the counter and order my drink.

"So we meet again, Ms. Pankowski," he said, returning with my coffee.

"Is that supposed to be a Goldfinger impression?" I smiled and took a sip.

"Was it any good?"

"It was awful. How are you?"

"How are *you?*"

"What are you doing here, Dennis?"

"I'm on vacation."

"At the Desert Inn?"

"It's a good hotel. It might not have a concierge level, but—"

"Okay. Don't tell me."

His smile disappeared for an instant. "I wish I could, Valerie. Please, let's just leave it at vacation. Tell me about Nora Bainbridge."

I could literally feel my stomach sink. So many of our encounters in the past had not been the dreamy dates I would have preferred, but brusque interrogations. "There's nothing to tell—"

"Come on. There's plenty to tell. What's her story?"

"Why? She's done nothing wrong—"

His grin reappeared. "Valerie, a dead woman was found in her hotel room. Her husband is missing."

"But she had nothing to do with either event."

"Are you sure of that?"

"Of course," I lied. "Do the police think she's involved?"

"Oh, she's damn well involved, all right. She's lucky they haven't locked her up."

I hurried to change the subject. "The dead woman . . . ?"

"Celia Decissio."

"Right. Who identified her?"

He leaned back in his chair until it balanced on two legs, and tapped the bottom of his nearly empty coffee cup on the table. It was a gesture I was familiar with. I could see he was debating how to respond.

"Who?" I urged him.

His chair snapped back onto all four legs. "Me. It was me. I identified the body."

"You knew her?"

"Yes. She was a friend. And a PI. That's a—"

"Private investigator," I said, my tone adding *don't insult me*.

"Sorry," he said, not looking a bit sorry. "I forgot who I was talking to. At any rate, she used to work on the force, then a few years ago she quit and went solo. Did pretty well, as I understand it."

Not that well, I thought, but of course didn't say. "I'm so sorry, Dennis," I said instead. "I had no idea she was a friend of yours."

He shrugged. "How could you?" he said, and he was right. I no more knew who his friends were than I knew what toothpaste he preferred or if he had cable TV.

"The police haven't officially told us who she was. Are you allowed to give out her name?"

He looked surprised. "*Allowed?*"

"Well, I mean . . . since you're not officially working this case, and the Palm Desert—"

"I don't need their permission."

"I just don't want you to get in trouble with them—"

"I don't give a damn about them. Celia was a pal. I'd like to know who murdered her, that's all. What do you know about Arthur Bainbridge?"

I took a long swig of my coffee, but even its hot deliciousness couldn't dissolve the irritation I was starting to feel. "Look, if you asked me here just to get information—"

"Stop right there." He held up the palm of his hand, warning me to shut up. "First, I didn't ask you here; you asked me. And more important, I'm really glad to see you. It's been a long time."

I suppose I could have asked why he hadn't bothered to respond to any of my texts or voice mails, but I let it go. "Okay. You're right. I did ask you here. I want to know what your involvement is with this case—"

"Ah, so in other words, *you* asked *me* here only to get information." He drained the last of his coffee in a single gulp. "Look, as I already told you, I don't have any official capacity here. But I used to know Celia well. Last I heard, she was contracting for a New York law firm. I had no idea she was in California."

"She was working for Arthur Bainbridge, perhaps?"

"Could be. So now she's dead, and he's missing." We remained silent for a few seconds, and then he spoke again. "Did you ever meet Bainbridge?"

I debated whether to be truthful, then decided why the hell not. It couldn't hurt, and it might help. "Okay, here's the thing. Kit and I had a drink with a man who presented himself as Arthur Bainbridge, only it turns out he was an impostor."

"How'd you find that out? Nora?"

"Well, Kit found photos of the real Arthur on a wiki site."

"And this impostor—what was that about?"

"I'm not sure. Seems like the only thing he gained from the time he spent with us was to stop our searching for Nora. And by the way, since the police never found him, the question is not just *who* he is, but *where* he is."

"So what you're saying is, you and your friend were the last ones to see the guy."

"Not exactly." I told Culotta about our meeting Nora at the mall, and her frenzied escape when she spotted the man who had posed as her husband. It came off sounding like an episode of *Laverne & Shirley*.

"Wow," was all he said, which only seemed to emphasize the insanity of the story.

"I really do think Nora is innocent in all this."

"Really? She seemed pretty shook up this morning when I told her the deceased's name."

He was right; Nora had been shocked when Culotta identified Celia Decissio, but after he'd left our room and

Kit and I questioned her, she claimed she'd never heard of her. "There's something else . . . ," I said.

"Go on."

"Well, have you heard of a couple named Dale and Louetta Powell?" I described our meeting with them and the fact that they weren't registered in the hotel even though they claimed to be.

"Want me to check them out? Give me a pen."

I dug through my purse and produced one I had taken from the desk in our room. *The Palms Hotel* was printed in gold lettering on one side.

"Did you steal this, Valerie?" he asked sternly, waving the pen at me.

"No, of course not."

"That's good. You should stick to gunrunning." He smiled as he wrote the Powells' names on a napkin. "You don't have a hotel bathrobe stuffed in that purse of yours, do you?" He folded the napkin and put it in his pocket before handing me back the pen.

"No little black notebook, Detective?" I asked.

"Nope. I told you, I'm on vacation."

After I'd filled him in on what else I knew, we lingered a little longer. I gave him the news about Emily. He seemed genuinely interested in my kid, and that pleased me. Eventually, we said our good-byes, and he promised to call soon. I told him I wouldn't hold my breath, and he agreed that was probably a good idea.

***

Back in the car I checked my phone for messages. I had six from Kit, so instead of starting the engine, I called her.

"Where have you been?" she asked.

"You know where I've been. I met Emily—"

"Yes, yes, how is she?"

"She's good—"

"Val, I need you to meet me at the police station—you remember where it is, right? I'm here now. They called Nora back for more questioning, and since we didn't have a car, they came and picked her up."

"How did *you* get there?"

"Those bastards wouldn't let me ride along, so I took a cab." She sounded breathless and a little frantic.

"Okay. I'm on my way." I put the car in reverse and backed out of the Starbucks parking area. "Why'd they want to talk to her? Did they say?"

"Hell yes," she said, as I eased the car into the traffic. "There's a problem," she repeated.

No kidding, I thought.

"It's the phone call," Kit continued.

"The phone call? You mean the one Nora got telling her Arthur was dead?"

"*Of course.*" Kit sounded indignant, as if that were the only phone call ever made. "According to that detective Tad Hunter—"

"You mean Tag Mason—"

"Whatever his effing name is, there was no phone call. They checked Nora's cell and all calls to her room. There's no record of any calls. Nora lied to us."

"Okay. Well, just sit tight. I'll be there in a little while."

"*Sit tight?* I'd like to wring her neck. What the hell is she thinking? Ya know, I hate to say this, but it might be a good idea for you to contact Culotta. If he's good for anything, he could at least find out everything the police have on her."

"I'm hanging up; I'll get there as fast as I can."

In Kit's emotional state, I didn't think I should tell her over the phone that I'd just met her least favorite detective for coffee, and even worse, that he wasn't betting on Nora's innocence.

***

With only one wrong turn, I arrived at the Palm Desert police station and pulled into the first vacant parking spot I found.

Kit was sitting in the waiting area, her iPad on her lap. As soon as she saw me, she jumped up and came toward me with arms outstretched for a hug.

"Hey." I led her back to the sitting area. "It's gonna be okay—"

"I can't get a signal for my iPad in here, and they don't have Wi-Fi; can you believe that? Didn't they invent it just up the road?"

"What are you trying to do?"

"I thought I'd check out Arthur's firm again on that wiki site. We may need to contact an attorney for Nora. Val, why would she lie?"

"Where is she now?"

"Being questioned, I assume. They haven't told me anything, other than she's here and not available. Call Culotta," she said. Then she added, "Please."

I left her seated and stepped outside to the starry night sky. Breathing in the scent of the fragrant jasmine that made me want to be dining al fresco with Culotta instead of calling him about Nora, I went to my list of recent calls and tapped on his name. As usual, I didn't expect to reach him, but for the second time that day he surprised me and answered on the first ring.

"Oh, Dennis," I said, realizing I sounded as frantic as Kit. "Nora has a problem—"

"That's the understatement of the decade."

"I'm at the police station. They called her back in for questioning. Apparently, there's a problem with the call she claimed—"

"She may have a bigger problem than that."

"What do you mean?"

"I mean that they found Arthur Bainbridge."

I held my breath, waiting for him to continue. When he didn't, I said, "So that's good, right?"

"If you consider it good that they found a dead body in the mountains, matching the description of her husband, then you got it."

CHAPTER FOURTEEN

I half expected the body in the mountains *not* to be Arthur's, the crazy way things had been going. *Arthur's dead. No, he's alive. No, that's not* really *Arthur.* But it turned out that Kit's brother-in-law, whom I'd never met—and *would* never meet—was indeed dead. But *murdered?*

That remained to be proved.

The general consensus, however, entertained no doubts. It would be just too much of a coincidence that in the middle of all these strange happenings, Arthur would go on a hike and *fall* to his death. No, the police, including Culotta, didn't believe in coincidences. Kit and I also felt certain he was pushed or dumped down the mountainside. And not much farther up than where we had ended our trek.

But neither of us was willing to admit this out loud, even to one another. Because then we'd have to also admit that Nora was a viable suspect. And certainly we didn't believe she was capable of murder.

I ended my phone call to Culotta and returned to Kit, passing a dilapidated coffee machine on the way. "Here." I handed her a Styrofoam cup of murky-looking coffee. Surprisingly, she took it without complaint and even sipped some of the brown liquid.

"How long is this going to take, d'ya think?" She indicated a door at the end of a long corridor to our right, where I assumed Nora was being interrogated.

"Hmm, not sure." I not only wasn't sure, I didn't have a clue. For all I knew, they could have taken Nora out a back entrance and she was on her way to San Quentin (wherever that was). I lifted my purse onto my lap and began rifling through it, not looking for anything in particular. I was just stalling while I decided whether to tell Kit what Culotta had said about finding a body. Another body. Arthur's body.

I glanced at Kit, who was holding the cup and its atrocious coffee with both hands. She smiled weakly at me, and I thought my heart might break.

"Val . . . I'm so glad you're here with—"

"Don't start that again."

I was thankful that before I had a chance to say anything more, we heard a door open and Detective Tag Mason stepped out into the hall. He raised his right arm, and his left hand beckoned us to come hither. Like a bouncer outside an exclusive nightclub giving us permission to enter. We gathered our things and hurried toward him.

Nora was sitting behind a long table in the bare room. Kit and I took the empty seats on either side of her. "Are you okay?" I asked.

"Did they torture you?" Kit asked. (*Really*? Torture? This was California, not Kabul.)

"I'm fine." Nora smiled. And surprisingly, she did look fine (well, certainly better than we did, and not in the least tortured). She grabbed our hands. "I asked Detective Mason if you could join me for a moment. Actually, he has just received some disturbing news."

We all looked across the table at Super Tag as he took a seat and ran a hand with professionally manicured nails through his thick blond hair. He was chewing gum again.

"Ladies," he said, opening a manila folder on his desk, taking out a sheet of paper and studying it hard, with all the seriousness of a student about to take an SAT test. "I'm afraid I have some bad news. Some *more* bad news. Er . . . um . . . looks like a body was found a short while ago." We watched as his blue eyes ran up and down the page. "Male. Appears to be elderly. Very possibly your husband, Mrs. Bainbridge."

"You don't know that." Kit leaned forward. "Could be anyone."

"Hmm," Tag Mason said.

I winced as Nora squeezed my hand tightly. "Can I see him?" she asked breathlessly.

"Not a good idea." Tag shook his blond head. "We'll get ID from his dental records. Ladies, if you would like to come this way," he said, indicating Kit and me. And a few seconds later I was in an identical room, but this time alone.

I shouldn't have been surprised that Kit and I would be questioned separately, but it made me appreciate how brave Nora was. (*She was, wasn't she?*) When I was finally released and joined Kit back on the bench in the waiting area, it didn't take us long to compare notes and realize they wanted anything we could tell them about Nora and her husband. I wasn't sure if they believed us when we insisted that was practically nothing as far as Arthur Bainbridge was concerned. But I was beginning to think we'd never see Nora again. I'd watched enough TV to know that she would probably confess to something she didn't do just to get out of the interrogation room.

***

We were all three back in our hotel room, long after midnight, when Culotta called. I put my phone on speaker and laid it gently in the middle of one of the beds so we could all hear.

"So," he began, "how are you ladies doing?"

"We're just peachy—" Kit said, but I put a finger to my lips to silence the tirade I felt sure was coming.

"I had a job convincing those guys to let Nora leave the station. So don't go doing anything stupid."

"Why shouldn't those idiots let her leave? She's done nothing—"

Before I could silence Kit again, Nora spoke up. "Thank you so much for that, Detective. That was so nice of you."

"I really called to tell you about the dental records. I thought you should know. The police aren't very forthcoming with their information out here."

I felt grateful once again that he was in the same state and appeared to be on our side. "So is it Arthur?"

"I gave them the name of Arthur's dentist," Nora cut in. "Dr. Gold in London. But actually he's a periodontist, not a dentist, which is quite different, and Arthur flies there twice a year to see him."

"I can confirm they positively identified the remains. And it's no surprise that you two didn't see the body. Even if you had hiked a little higher, a dead body in those hot mountains would not have been a pretty sight—" He stopped himself, probably in deference to Nora, who had moved to the second bed and lay on her back staring at the ceiling.

"So, it was definitely Arthur?" Kit asked.

"A hiker with a pair of binoculars hoping to find a rattlesnake spotted what remains of him. Of course they haven't yet determined time of death. Sorry."

Kit suddenly sat up straighter. "Wait just a minute there, Detective. I know the British aren't winning any prizes for their teeth, so how does a Brit have dental records so quickly accessible to a local police department?"

"Yeah, well, that's the crazy part." Culotta sighed.

"Go on," I said.

"Okaaaaay," he continued, in a you-asked-for-it tone of voice. "It has been confirmed that Arthur Bainbridge was not a Brit, but a California transplant from Oklahoma who'd had his dental work done compliments of the Golden State's penal system."

"What the—" Kit croaked.

"Oh noooooo," said Nora, from her supine position on the bed.

"Are we sure it's Arthur?" I asked. "I mean the Arthur we saw on the Internet? The man Nora married? Whatever his real name is . . . by the way, what *is* his real name?"

"Can't tell you that. But our Oklahoman definitely matches the description of Nora's husband."

So Nora, always the smartest girl in the room, had been duped.

***

Later, as we lay in our beds in the quiet of our hotel room, I wondered why the one in jeopardy was the only one able to sleep. I chose to believe it proved she had a clear conscience.

"How can she sleep at a time like this?" Kit asked me, obviously not expecting an answer I couldn't give her. "Sometimes I think she's . . ." She waved a hand at her sister, clad in pale-pink silk pajamas and lying on her back, her lips slightly parted, her chest barely rising with each breath. Matching pink slippers still covered her feet.

"What? Think she's *what?*" I asked, curious to hear Kit's assessment.

"Never mind. You know what I mean."

"Well, I'm glad someone can sleep." I took a bite of the huge delicious apple I'd snagged from the hospitality table on our way in. I was famished. "So who do you think this Arthur is? And the other Arthur? The one who *told* us he was Arthur. Surely they're connected." I took another bite of the crispy apple.

"Ya think you could possibly make any more noise with that?"

"Sorry," I whispered loudly.

"More important," Kit whispered back, "who lets their husband wander around with a top-secret file under his arm without finding a way to read it? Especially when it contains something about the first wife. I'd never let Larry get away with that."

"Well, the legal profession has strict confidentiality rules—"

"Did you learn that on *Night Court*?"

"All I'm saying is that attorneys stick to the attorney-client privilege thingy, and most wives are not as nosy—er, curious—as you."

As if she hadn't appreciated my clever insight into the legal world, Kit suddenly, and silently, sat up. "Where's her suitcase?" she mouthed.

"In the closet. Remember, she moved her things there after the police were finished in her room?"

Glancing at Nora, still sleeping like a pink satin princess, Kit swung her legs out of bed and beckoned me to follow. She gave my apple a venomous look, so I left it behind and followed her to the closet. Quietly, we opened the white louvered doors and each grabbed one of Nora's bags.

"Where to?" I asked, holding the larger of the two suitcases.

Kit glanced at Nora again and then pointed to the bathroom.

With the door of the spacious room locked, we sat on the floor, our legs stretched out and a suitcase next to each of us. We opened them and began rummaging in silence.

"Anything yet?" I whispered after a few moments had gone by. I kept my head bent, not looking across at Kit.

Going through another person's luggage seemed just plain wrong to me.

From the corner of my eye I saw Kit shake her head. "Not so far. *Hey*, is this one of those dildo things?"

My head jerked up, and I looked across at Kit, who was gingerly holding an object, a devilish look on her face. "No, dum-dum. That is a facial massager. Now quit messing around."

"*Oh really?* You answered that awfully fast, Val. How do you know so much about facial massagers? Looks like a vibrator to me."

"I think the brush is the clue. Pretty sure vibrators do not have brushes on the end."

"Hmm. How about this?"

"That is a toothpaste holder, obviously. Will you please be serious. And be quiet." I turned back to my task, running my fingers through Nora's neatly packed things, trying to be equally neat about it.

"Okay, this is definitely a dildo."

"I'm not even looking," I muttered, immediately doing just that. "Kit, that is clearly a shoe tree. And if you can't do this seriously—"

"I'll say this, Valley Girl, you sure know your sex toys."

"I've never even seen a so-called sex toy—"

"*Wait.* What's this?" She slid a brown leather folder with a zipper running around its edges across the floor to me. "Take a look," she said. "I think we found what we're looking for."

Crawling on her knees to my side of the bathroom, she unzipped the folder. Inside were three smaller manila files. The first one was labeled Keith Tippon. Kit opened it. "What in the . . . ?" She held up the photo of a man, the same man we had seen on the Internet identified as Arthur Bainbridge and apparently the same one they'd found dead in the mountains. But clearly written across the bottom of the photo in bold letters was the name Keith Tippon.

The file also contained various other sheets of paper, but before studying them too closely, we moved on to the next file, labeled Roger Carpenter and containing a photo of the man we'd had drinks with in the bar. Letters superimposed on the photo confirmed it: Roger Carpenter.

"This is bad," I said.

"At least we found out who these guys are. But this might be even worse," she said, handing me a copy of an e-mail.

I wasn't sure if I felt worse—but I definitely didn't feel better—when I saw that the files we were looking at did not belong to Nora. They belonged to Celia Decissio.

"So Celia wasn't *working* for Arthur; she was *investigating* him," Kit said, watching me read the e-mail.

I nodded my head slightly, reaching to grab the third and much fatter folder Kit was handing me. It contained printouts of bank accounts belonging to Keith Tippon and Roger Carpenter, listing some deposits the size of which would never show up on my own bank statements. More like something the Sultan of Brunei might deposit after a good day selling oil.

"Do you think," I asked Kit, my mind groping for how and why these men could be connected to Nora, "that the fifteen-million-dollar house she talked to Tom about could somehow be part of a swindle attempt?"

"Val," Kit said, "the only way Nora could have been considering a house that expensive is if she were hooked up with someone who *had* the fifteen million dollars to spend. *She* doesn't have that kind of money."

"How do you know? You barely have a Christmas-card relationship with her. My mom knows more about your sister than you do."

We froze as we heard a sound emanating from Nora in the next room. "Shhhh," Kit said, as we waited. But the sound had stopped. If Nora had rolled over and accidentally slid out of bed in her pink silk getup, it apparently hadn't awakened her.

"Hell," Kit said, as she grabbed the folder from me and began perusing it. "Why does Celia have to be dead? We need her to explain this."

"Yes, that was so rude of her to go and get herself killed."

***

When we finished our clandestine search of Nora's luggage, still not sure what to make of the gold nuggets it had produced, we returned all the files to the folder and zipped it up.

"What should we do with this info?" I asked Kit. "Should we wake Nora and discuss it?"

"Not yet. We need to mull this over for a bit."

"Okay." I started to return the folder to Nora's suitcase.

"No, no, don't put it back there." Kit looked shocked at my actions. "We should put it in *your* suitcase. That way, if someone really does come looking for it, the pink panther you dragged here would be the last place they'd expect to find anything valuable."

Totally insulted, but too tired to argue, I helped Kit return Nora's suitcases to the closet and attempted to stuff the folder into my bag. To my frustration, the zipper jammed, and I had a hard time sliding the goods inside.

I didn't even bother to mention that Kit's reasoning was faulty, as I thought of the innocuous-seeming can of peas with the fake bottom that stands on the top shelf of my kitchen cabinet. That's where I keep my own valuables. It sounds like a baby's rattle when I occasionally shake it and the paltry contents move around inside. That's the beauty of having so few valuables—and eating peas.

***

I tried to turn off the alarm clock when it woke me up. But my groping hand couldn't find it on the table next to my bed. In fact, my groping hand couldn't find the table. When I finally pried one eye open, I realized I wasn't at home. And then I remembered I was in a hotel room two thousand miles away from my apartment. Only when it was too late did it become clear that the ringing had come from Kit's phone, which was lying between us on the bed. She hadn't even heard it, although I noticed it had awakened her sister.

Indeed, Nora appeared *wide* awake, only her eyes looking as if they'd moved at all since she'd first fallen asleep. Her pajamas remained unwrinkled, and her hair looked freshly brushed. She sat up and stared at me quizzically, as if I could explain . . . what? Everything? Anything?

No, I wanted to tell her, the answer was *nothing*.

Instead, I picked up Kit's phone to see whose call she'd missed. Larry's. I began to shake my sleeping friend, gently at first and then hard enough to awaken her. "Kit, you missed a call from Larry."

"Wha—?" I watched her go through the same process I'd just experienced. Once she removed her sleep mask and seemed to realize where she was, a fleeting look of happiness was replaced by one of consternation. She rubbed her eyes with both fists.

"I said, you missed a call from Larry. Wanna call him back?"

"No. But I will." She pressed her thumb on her phone and was soon talking to her husband. She remained quiet, but I could hear his voice as it assaulted her ear. I couldn't decipher any words except for an occasional *what* and *hell*, as in *what the hell*.

Finally, Kit made some responses of her own. "Uh huh . . . oh? . . . hmm . . . uh huh." She sighed deeply. "Okay. Bye." She pressed her thumb on her phone again, without saying *I love you*. Something she always says to Larry, me, and their son, Sam, before hanging up.

I knew Kit wasn't going to have good news for us.

"How is Larry?" Nora asked from her side of the room.

"Who the hell cares how Larry is?" Kit yelled. "Nora, don't—"

Before we got sidetracked with a fight between the sisters that would no doubt be exacerbated by decades of unresolved sibling rivalry, I spoke up. "What did Larry say, Kit?" I grabbed the half-eaten apple from the bedside table and took a bite.

"Aside from what the hell are we doing out here and what the hell is going on with my sister and mother—my mother! like we need her involved in all this—he said he's been getting phone calls from someone who's desperate to get in touch with Nora. No, he said desperate to get *ahold* of Nora. And he's starting to worry they mean physically ahold of. He thinks we should go to the police. Ha!" she said, irony replacing her usual loving disdain at Larry's being half a step behind her.

CHAPTER FIFTEEN

I 'll have oatmeal and a small orange juice, please," I said, feeling self-righteous in my determination to eat healthfully—and lightly. With just a tinge of regret, I snapped the menu shut and handed it to the middle-aged waitress.

I had urged Kit to have breakfast with me in the restaurant of the hotel, and she had finally agreed to leave Nora, who had fallen back into a deep, undisturbed sleep.

"Just coffee for me." Kit handed her menu back to our server. She hadn't bothered to open it.

"So," I said, as soon as we were alone, "we should call the police."

"And tell them what?"

I rummaged in my purse and found a pen—two pens, in fact. The first one had no ink, and I threw it back. I clicked the end of the second one, which bore the hotel logo, and it worked. "Okay." I reached into my purse again for my checkbook and tore out a deposit slip. Then I started to write. "Arthur Bainbridge does not exist. Correct? The man Nora married, the man found dead in the mountains, is—was—Keith Tippon." I looked across the table at Kit, and she nodded wearily. "Okay, so far, so good."

"What's good about it?"

"Well, at least we know . . . something."

"We know Nora is as dumb as a box of nails."

"Because . . . ?"

"Because she married a man she clearly shouldn't have. Val, the police know all this. *Everyone* does. I don't think writing it down on your deposit slip serves any purpose whatsoever. What we have to find out is why Nora married a felon, why—if she's so smart—she didn't know he was a felon, and whether or not she's responsible for his death."

She took three packets of Equal from the ceramic container in front of her and ripped them open, making a tiny mountain of faux sugar on her place mat. "If the police can establish the time of his death, that might put Nora in the clear," she mused, suddenly swiping the miniscule granules off the edge of the table.

In California, who knew? Maybe that was considered littering.

"That's good," I said, ignoring her infraction and writing *time of death* on the deposit slip. "Detective Mason seems to think he'd been dead a long time. Possibly before Nora even arrived here. So, that would be excellent news." I drew two heavy black lines under the words I'd written, as if that answered all our questions.

"And what about Celia Decissio? Ya got anything on your deposit slip to explain Nora's involvement in *her* death?"

I scrunched it into a little ball. "I'm only trying to make sense of this—"

"Val, I'm sorry; I didn't mean to snap." She reached across the table and patted my hand. "I don't know what I'd do if you weren't—"

"Oatmeal, orange juice . . . and coffee." Our waitress had arrived at exactly the right moment. She placed my meager order in front of me and put an empty cup before Kit. After filling it with coffee, she placed the stainless-steel pot in the center of the table. "Can I get you anything else?"

"No, this is great, thank you." I unfolded my napkin.

"Er . . . as a matter of fact, there might be something . . . Marian." Kit's eyes were fixed on the brown plastic name badge pinned to the woman's white blouse.

"What d'ya need, honey?"

In a split second Kit whipped out her iPhone and swiped the screen several times. "Ever see this guy?" she asked, after locating the website that showed Keith Tippon, aka Arthur Bainbridge. She had enlarged the picture so that his head filled the screen and there was no sign of the tuxedo he seemed to be wearing in every picture.

Marian reached for a pair of reading glasses hanging on a chain around her neck, took the phone from Kit, and then smiled. "Sure, I know this guy. He was in a few days ago. Why do you want to know? Has something happened?"

"He's my brother-in-law," Kit said truthfully, taking the phone back. "And he's missing." *Not so true.* "I'm . . . we're just trying to find him. When did you see him?" She smiled sweetly at Marian, but managed to convey deep concern at the same time.

"Let's see." Marian put her hands in the pockets of the black pants she was wearing. "Okay, it was Friday, nearly a week ago. I was on the lunch shift."

"You remember that long ago?" I said, meaning to sound friendly, but it came out rather snotty. "What I mean is, I can barely remember yesterday, let alone—"

"Let me tell ya, I always remember a big tipper. And this guy . . ." She nodded at the phone. "He was nice. Left me a twenty on a thirty-eight-dollar tab. And the funny thing was, he was getting up there in years. Sorry; don't mean to be rude about your brother-in-law—"

"No problem," Kit assured her. "That's one of the things we all love about him."

"Right," Marian agreed. "He was impressive."

"Why was that?" Kit asked, as if looking forward to hearing something sweet.

"Oh, you know, him going hiking . . . at his age. Wish I could work up the energy—"

"A hike? On Friday afternoon?"

"Yeah, I was impressed."

Kit and I glanced at each other. With Marian still standing beside us, I didn't state the obvious: Nora had not arrived in California until Sunday, which didn't totally exonerate her, of course, but if time of death could be established . . .

"Don't tell me something happened to the old guy," I heard Marian say. "Hey, he's not the one I heard about this morning—"

"Not sure," Kit said. "Let's hope not. But you need to give the police this information."

"What about his friend? Have you spoken to him?"

"Friend?" I asked. "He was with a friend?"

"Oh, didn't I say that? There were two of them. Your brother-in-law and another guy. About the same age. Only this friend was wearing a suit—very formal, way too formal for California, if you know what I mean. I'm originally from Kansas myself—"

"So they weren't planning to hike together?"

"Didn't seem that way. The other fella acted like your brother-in-law was a little crazy."

"And this *other fella* . . . anything about him you remember? Any way I . . . we . . . can identify him?"

"He did have a really strong accent. I do remember that."

"Accent? Was it British?"

"Hell no. Sorry. I mean no. He was from the South. Texas, maybe, or somewhere out that way."

"Oklahoma, perhaps?"

"Yeah, coulda been. But honey, I can assure you he wasn't British. We get a few movie stars in here, and some of them are Brits. So I know a British accent when I hear it."

"This helps us so much, Marian," Kit said. "Do you happen to know if the other guy was staying here?"

"No idea. Sorry." She suddenly looked down at the sugary mess at her feet. "Look at this. I'll get a busboy over to clean it. Some kid probably did this deliberately."

"Yes, probably." Kit looked down at the floor in disgust. "They can be such brats."

We watched Marian walk away, and I unfurled the deposit slip and dug the working pen out of my purse. I drew a third line under *time of death*.

Kit decided to return to the room with coffee and a croissant for her sister. She insisted we had to get Nora up and talking. I told her I'd join her in a bit, but I wanted to call Tom first.

It sounded as though he was driving. "Hey, Kiddo. How's sunny California?"

I had walked outside the entrance of the building with my phone to my ear. There were two young girls sitting on the rim of a huge concrete planter, both on their cell phones. I found my own planter and sat down before answering.

"Not so sunny, Tom."

"Yeah, I hear you got a shitstorm going on."

I filled him in on what had happened since we'd arrived on Monday. He didn't interrupt and waited for me to finish. I wasn't sure if he was surprised or if he was already aware of all the events. "Tom?" I said, when I was done relating the drama.

He waited a few seconds before responding. "Is Nora okay?" he finally asked.

"Nora? *Okay*? She's a suspect in a murder, possibly two. Do you think she's okay?"

"That's what I'm asking *you*."

I took a deep breath. "Tom, you said Nora contacted you for help—"

"My opinion, Pankowski. I believe I said she wanted my opinion."

"Okay, your opinion then. But it was about more than just buying an expensive property. Right?"

"Yeah," he said thoughtfully. "It was a little more than that."

"Will you tell me?"

"Wait a second. Let me pull over. Geez, Pankowski, why can't you ever call at a normal time?"

I listened to the sounds of Tom driving, heard a few swearwords, and watched the two girls still sitting on the neighboring planter. They were both sharing one screen, laughing at something.

"Okay, I'm parked," Tom came back. "I'm only telling you this because I think Nora is in trouble and . . . because of your talent for getting mixed up in the same. Here's the thing. Nora did ask about a fifteen-mil property, but she wasn't planning to buy it. This Arthur Bainbridge guy—and his business partner—were in it together. Not her. Nora had nothing to do with it. She had an idea there was something else going on. Something wrong. She's really smart like that—"

"Oh yeah, she's really smart." I thought of Kit comparing her to a box of nails.

"I did some checking—anonymously—and she was right. The fifteen mil was dirty money; in fact, it was just the tip of an iceberg of dirty money—*what?* What are you talking about?"

"Sir," I heard a male voice that wasn't Tom's. "You can't park here."

"What the hell are you talking about?" I heard Tom say.

"Move it, sir."

"Listen, buddy, I—"

"Move it. Sir. *Now.*"

"Gotta go," Tom said. To me, I presumed. And then the line went dead.

***

136

Kit called me while I was in the elevator heading back to the room. "Where are you, Val? Get back here. Sleeping Beauty woke up, and she's ready to talk."

"I'm on my way," I said, exiting onto our floor and racing to our room. Before I even got there, Kit had opened the door and was waiting for me, one hand on her hip. I felt like a teenager being caught coming home late.

"Geez," she said, as I reached the threshold. "Get in here. We need to talk to Nora."

"Okay, I'm coming."

Nora was sitting on the edge of her bed, still wearing her pajamas. And they were still wrinkle-free, as if she'd just removed them from a hanger and was only trying them on. Was that the advantage of silk? Or was Nora—and for that matter, Kit—living in some kind of wrinkle-free alternate world?

"Are you listening, Val?" Kit grabbed my arm.

"Yes, of course I am. Just run that by me one more time."

"Nora," Kit said, "repeat what you just told us. Val here is a little slow sometimes; it's that daydreaming thing she does."

"It's called short-term detachment," Nora said. "I often fall prey myself. A mild form of dissociation with reality, usually to some more pleasant thoughts."

I didn't tell Nora that her smooth pajamas were not really my idea of pleasant thoughts.

"Will you shut up and tell us again what you just said." Kit was practically yelling.

I was pretty sure what was coming next from her sister.

"That's not really possible, to comply with both your requests at the same—"

"Argggh. Nora, I've just about had it with you." Kit threw herself backward onto the bed, as if she were a two-year-old having a tantrum. Then she sat halfway up and leaned on both elbows, which were buried in the heavy comforter. "You think this is some kind of a fucking game?

You are a suspect in at least one murder. Val and I are doing everything we can to save your skinny neck—"

"Even though I am so *slow* at times . . ." I couldn't resist throwing that in.

"Sorry, Val, you know I didn't mean it. Nora, tell me one more time—tell us *both*—what you said. About Celia Decissio."

We stared at Nora as she put her hands to her throat, as if feeling for an expensive necklace. "Very well. I did know Celia Decissio. In fact, I hired her. She was doing some investigative work for me. I had some major concerns about things Arthur was involved in. I gave her carte blanche to look into our lives. That was one of the reasons I went to Chicago instead of coming straight here. I wanted Celia to check things out without me around. She was the best investigator in New York. I trusted her implicitly. And . . ."

"Go on," I said.

"Oh, Valerie. I am so very, very sorry that she got herself killed."

CHAPTER SIXTEEN

*H*ow sorry?" Kit asked her sister. "Just *how* sorry are you that Celia, as you so conveniently put it, got herself killed?"

"I—"

"I'm thinking she maybe died with a little help from you," Kit interrupted her sister.

And then *I* felt the need to interrupt. "Kit! You know Nora had nothing to do with anyone's death—"

"I'm not saying she committed the act, but if Celia was working for Nora, it's very likely that led to her murder. And if my big sister here . . ." She paused to give Nora a penetrating look. "Nora, if you would be honest once and for all, we can maybe at least get *justice* for Celia."

I switched my gaze to Nora, conjuring up an image of her in court addressing a jury, wearing a simple yet elegant Calvin Klein suit and pleading for a defendant's life.

Her face took on a defiant yet confident look. "That always puzzles me," she said. "I mean people's need for *justice*. How does that help anything? It doesn't bring a loved one back."

"Nora," Kit said threateningly.

But threatening *what*, I had no idea.

"Of course if it keeps a perpetrator from taking any other lives . . ." Nora nodded her head slowly, as if it suddenly made sense to her.

Kit wasn't nearly so satisfied. "Nora, were there ever really important papers in Arthur's possession? Did anyone really take anything from your room?"

I held my breath.

"Actually, yes." Nora raised her eyebrows in seeming surprise that her sister would doubt her. But then her eyes shifted downward with a look of guilt, like a child about to confess she'd discovered her parents' stash of Christmas presents. Long before Christmas.

"What?" Kit and I asked at the same time, after Nora silently avoided our eyes for too long. "What are you not telling us?" Kit added.

"Actually, I did take a peek in the file Arthur carried around because it was so important. The one that contained the papers that went missing from our room. But only once. And only really fast, while Arthur was on a phone call." She paused and looked up, as if waiting to be chastised or congratulated.

I could tell by her confused look that she didn't know which reaction her sister would have.

Kit had none. She obviously wanted to know more before delivering her verdict.

"It's the reason I felt it was necessary to hire Celia. And I told her about it and even wondered if *she* might have been the one who broke into our room and took it. But when I talked to her last—on the phone—she told me she had done no such thing. And . . ." Nora teared up, and then her face crumpled. She obviously *was* so very, very sorry that Celia got herself killed.

I went over and sat by her on the bed, wrapping my arm around her and patting her shoulder.

As if wanting to take advantage of Nora's addled state, Kit pressed on. "What was in that file you *peeked* in?" Air quotes around *peeked*. "Nora, answer me."

Nora straightened up, and I withdrew my arm from her shoulders. She blew her nose and dabbed at her eyes with a tissue she'd removed from her pajama pocket. Then she spoke. "I don't know. It was beyond my ken. There were pages of, um, ledgers? You know, spreadsheets. Filled with numbers. But I did see on one of them the address of the house—there was a property Arthur was planning to buy, you see—"

"The one you spoke to Tom about?" I asked.

Nora scooted over and turned to face me. She looked startled—and then disappointed.

I knew I was in for it if Tom ever found out I'd broken his confidence. But I had bigger concerns at the moment. And one of them was to keep Kit from strangling her sister for *not* providing information, confidential or otherwise. "Was it?" I asked. "Was the property the one you consulted Tom about?"

She swiped at her tear-streaked face with the tissue and nodded her head. "But I saw there were many more properties listed, just as costly. And the columns seemed to show where money was coming from to purchase them. From various bank and investment-company accounts. Some overseas."

"That makes sense. Arthur *is* British, ya know," Kit said derisively, bringing out her air quotes again for the word *British*.

I wanted to tell her this wasn't the time to badger or ridicule her sister. It was the time to elicit information. Reading my mind, she moved to the other side of Nora and took her sister's hand in hers. "Nora, honey, go on. Tell us."

"Tell you what? Katherine, you act like I know what's going on, and I don't. That's why I hired Celia, and now she's—" A few racking sobs followed, heartrending in their sincerity.

But Kit was on a mission. She held fast to her sister's hand, and I had the feeling Nora wasn't going to be allowed to move until she gave Kit some answers, even if she had to fabricate them. "Nora, what sent you to Tom? What made you doubt Arthur? Was that the first inkling you ever had that something was amiss?"

Amiss? I doubted Kit needed to resort to Nora-speak to get answers, but I was glad to see her making an effort.

Nora made the stuttering gasp that comes from too much crying. "Let me be clear. The only thing I ever doubted about Arthur was his judgment or perhaps his naïveté. I wouldn't have married someone I didn't trust implicitly, Katherine."

"Speaking of poor judgment and naïveté . . ."

"*Kit.*" I opened my eyes wide, hoping to convey the message *shut up and let Nora talk*. I waited anxiously for Nora to continue.

Which she did, after another stuttering gasp. But all she said was, "I need something to eat. Some real breakfast, not that." She nodded her head toward the table and the untouched croissant Kit had brought her. "That is basically poison. The brain, you see, needs—"

Kit heaved a weary sigh. "Okay, I'll order room service."

Yay, I inwardly yelled. *Now I can have a* real *breakfast.*

Kit held the phone to her chest with one hand and pressed a finger from the other hand on the button that would keep the phone "on the hook," while her sister perused the menu. Knowing it would take Nora forever to determine just what brain food she should consume, I decided I'd try to complete my call with Tom. I figured he had no doubt finished his argument with whatever authority had been telling him where he could and couldn't park.

I grabbed my purse and stepped out into the hallway—after telling Kit to order me two eggs over easy, sausage, and hash browns. Then I dug out my cell and placed the call. When it went straight to his voice mail, I wondered if Tom were perhaps in jail. The thought made me smile, as I phoned the office.

Billie assured me Tom was in a meeting that was probably even worse for him than jail. Mrs. Battle-ax, as he called one of our most important clients. That elderly lady who bought and sold more properties and moved more frequently than someone climbing a corporate ladder had demanded to see him. Immediately, if not sooner.

"Well, he and I were having a rather important discussion when we got cut off. When do you think he'll be free?" I asked.

"Only Selma Fox knows the answer to that," Billie said, calling Mrs. Battle-ax by her real name. "I suppose he was calling you about Nora Juckett."

"What makes you say that, Bill? What did Tom tell you?"

"Nothing. You know Tom. But I've heard him on the phone a couple of times, and I've heard him say her name. It makes me wonder if he's ever gotten over her. Val, I told you Tom wouldn't be available forever, and now sure enough, Nora's single again, and he certainly seems to still have feelings. Of concern, at least."

"Billie, what in the world are you talking about? First of all, I don't care *who* Tom aligns himself with." *OMG*, I thought, *are we all going to start talking like Nora?* "And second of all, what do you mean *gotten over her?*"

"Didn't you know? Perry tells me Tom and Nora were pretty hot and heavy back in the day. I guess that was before you worked here. Seems they had a real romantic relationship going on until the distance got to them. Perry doesn't know who called it off, but he said his uncle moped around for weeks."

"Weeks, huh? Must have been real serious," I said, hoping to mask my shock with sarcasm. I made a mental note to ask Kit if she knew anything about Tom and Nora having been a couple. I still couldn't imagine such a thing. I convinced myself that was the only reason the very idea left me feeling unsettled. There wasn't even a hint of jealousy involved, and Billie was as off base as Kit always is to imply something more than friendship or a work relationship on either Tom's or my agenda.

"Want me to have him call you when he checks in?" Billie asked.

"No, I'll leave a message on his cell," I said, although I had no intention of doing any such thing. Suddenly I didn't care if I ever spoke to him again.

As I turned around and headed back in the direction of our room, my cell rang. I looked at the picture of Tom's face on the screen. "H'lo," I answered, not even wanting to speak his name.

"Pankowski, you called," he accused. "Leave a message when you call. Why didn't you leave a message?"

"Because I had nothing I wanted to say to you."

"Then why did you call?"

I sighed, realizing how childish I sounded. "I mean, I just wanted to hear what *you* had to say. We got interrupted, remember?" I put the key card in my pocket and walked back down the hall. I couldn't help but note that I still didn't see any room service on the way, and I wondered if Nora had even made up her mind yet.

"I can hardly remember my own name," Tom said, "after being with that Mrs. Battle-ax broad. If she didn't put so much money in our coffers . . ."

Coffers? Had he really said coffers? I pushed away an image of Tom and Nora reading the dictionary over candlelight. "Well, she does. So get over it. Tom, finish telling me what you know about Nora's . . . predicament."

"Predicament? How unlike you to understate something, Pankowski." He gave a grim laugh. "I'm coming out there. I'll text you my flight info and see you tonight."

"There's no need for you to come." I knew I sounded distressed. "Everything is under control."

"Yeah, right. You and Kit in the land of fruits and nuts. It would be hysterical if it wasn't so damn scary." And then he hung up.

Because my mind was simply too boggled to think of anything any deeper, I focused on the thought that he better damn well be sending me his flight info just for my, well, information. *Not* because he expected me to pick him up.

"Hi there, young lady," a loud voice came from behind me as I once again made my way toward our room.

It can't be, I thought, as I turned around. But it was. Dale Powell. And a half step behind him walked Louetta.

"Well, hi there, you two," I finally found my voice.

"You seem surprised to see us, honey," Louetta said.

"I was told you two weren't checked in here."

Dale looked startled, as if I'd just called him a liar. Which in a way I had.

"I mean . . . well . . . I wanted to find you so we could maybe have dinner or something one night," I said.

"That sure is a nice idea. And as a matter of fact, we aren't checked in," he added, rather defensively, I thought.

"But you said you were—"

"We stayed here three days and then moved to a different hotel. When we met you, we'd just finished checking out and were trying to enjoy a last hour or two here while we waited for our room in the other hotel to be ready."

"Why did you check out?" I tried not to sound accusatory but felt I failed again.

Dale proved me right. "I'm not sure what you mean. We found it hard to relax with all the ruckus caused by that little ol' murder. Louetta here couldn't get any rest." As he spoke, he put a protective arm around his wife's shoulders. "You need your rest, don't ya, honey?"

I didn't wait for her to answer. "Yes," I said, "that makes sense. But what are you doing back here, then?" Once more it came out all wrong, and I sounded like a bad detective trying to trip up a suspect.

145

"Ma'am, why don't we start over? Maybe where we left off that day in the lounge, when we were being polite to each other."

"Daaale," Louetta chastised her husband. "Quit being so uppity."

He grinned at her. "Sorry, sugar." Then he turned his attention back to me. "We didn't realize it when we met you the other day, but it seems we have something in common. And we need your help. Or rather the help of your friend, I think she is? Nora Bainbridge."

"Well, she's a little busy right now. Not even dressed. How about I get your number and have her call you."

I watched Louetta raise her wrist and glance at her Rolex Oyster. "Hmm," she said, as if questioning why someone wouldn't be dressed at this time of the morning. "I suppose we could do that. Perhaps she'd let Dale and me buy her lunch?"

"Um, I'm sure dinner would be better," I said, thinking of my second breakfast that was on its way. "Yes, that would probably be okay, an early dinner." *If she hasn't been picked up by the police and charged with murder,* I didn't add.

"Okay," Dale said, "here you go." He fished a card out of the inside pocket of his jacket. "We're only ten minutes down the road, so we can scoot back here whenever she wants."

"Good deal." I looked around them as the elevator doors opened, and I saw the blessed room-service cart being wheeled into the corridor. "Leave it with me." I took his card and stuck it in my purse. "I'll have her call."

146

CHAPTER SEVENTEEN

I scooped the shredded potatoes from a side plate into my mouth. "Thanks for ordering this, Kitty Kat," I said. My other plate was brimming with eggs and sausage links.

Kit was leaning against the dresser, holding a cup of coffee with both hands.

Nora was daintily chewing on a spoonful of grapefruit with as much relish as if it were a juicy steak. "Mmm." She pointed her spoon at the pink fruit. "This is so good."

"Nora," Kit said. "I don't think you've told us everything."

Nora gulped on her mouthful. "Really, Katherine, you need to know *everything*—"

"Yes. But how about I start. Last night, while you were asleep, Val here went through your suitcase and found—"

"Whoa!" I waved a sausage link on the end of my fork in her direction. "She says *me*, but it was both of us; in fact, it was her—"

"The *who* is not important." Kit took a dismissive sip of her coffee. "What's important is what she—okay, we—found. Nora, it appears that your darling husband was not quite the same man you led us to believe. Wanna explain that?"

The room was silent. Kit and I watched Nora pick up a blackberry from her side dish of fruit. (*Really? Fruit to accompany* more *fruit?*)

"You better come clean," Kit broke the silence. "We know your husband's real name, and Culotta already spilled the beans about the American teeth. So it's time for you to tell us everything. I mean it."

We watched Nora take a deep breath. "Very well." She rose from the table, patting her mouth with the linen napkin, and moved toward the bed. "I owe it to you both. You've been so magnificent, flying out here and being so supportive." She sighed. "Here goes."

She proceeded to tell us that Arthur Bainbridge had come to the United States when he was fourteen. His father, an oil executive, had moved his family from England to Oklahoma.

Arthur attended high school in Tulsa and then went to the University of Oklahoma. At that time he still went by his birth name, Keith Tippon. After graduation from college, he married his longtime girlfriend, Elizabeth, and moved to New York to study law at Columbia. Money was never a problem for the Tippons, and after law school, Keith and Elizabeth moved to Los Angeles, where he passed the bar and hung out his attorney's shingle.

For several years things went well for the young lawyer. He took on a partner, Roger Carpenter, an old friend from Oklahoma, and they slogged along, making a decent living. By the time Keith was in his midthirties, however, he found himself in a financial bind. A flood of lawyers had moved into the state, and clients and money were becoming scarce. To make matters worse, he had made some unwise investments in the stock market.

Then, in a last-ditch effort to salvage his portfolio, he invested in a nursing home development. He had no idea it was understaffed and poorly constructed—or that the other partners, none of whom Keith knew well except for Roger Carpenter, were using the project as a way to launder money. He was also unaware that the operation was being scrutinized by the federal government, which eventually seized all the assets and targeted the scapegoat Keith Tippon with their charges.

In a messy trial where he was convicted of fraud and tax evasion, he proclaimed his innocence. Nevertheless, he was sentenced to two years and served the maximum. Not too long after he was released from federal prison, he moved to New York, where he reinvented himself, changing his name from Keith Tippon to Arthur Bainbridge and resurrecting the clipped British accent he'd brought to America with him.

"Wait just a damn minute," Kit interrupted from her place on the bed, her iPad open on her lap. "Presumably, he was kicked out of his profession, right?"

"Yes. He couldn't practice law," Nora agreed sadly. "Actually, he spent the ensuing years trying to prove his innocence. But eventually he moved on and built a successful new life."

"So how did he get to be a lawyer?"

"He didn't practice," Nora said, with a little satisfaction on her face. "He was the *founder* of Bainbridge, Littlefield and Stein, but not a litigator. More of a Svengali, if you will. A *good* Svengali," she hastened to add.

While I pondered the oxymoron, she came up with another term. "A mentor," she said.

"Riiiiight," Kit said. "Because who wouldn't want a mentor who's done time?"

"Kit," I said, "that could make some sense."

"A lawyer who's also a felon? Are you nuts?"

"It gave him a unique perspective," Nora answered for me.

"So," Kit moved on, gathering her thoughts, "you are really Mrs. Tippon, not Mrs. Bainbridge?"

"Absolutely not. Arthur changed his name legally, long before he met me."

Kit moved across the room to the service cart and poured herself a fresh cup of coffee. "Okay. Glad we got that established. So, this Roger dude, the one who was following you, the one who posed as your hubby when we first got here: who is he?"

"I'm not certain, but I think he's Roger Carpenter. I know very little about him, other than he testified for the government against Arthur at the time of the trial and was never charged. To my knowledge, Arthur had not spoken to or seen Roger Carpenter for over forty years."

"So, why show up now? It's been like a *hundred* years since Arthur was in the pokey."

"I don't know. Arthur refused to talk to me about his past dealings with Roger, so I was actually hoping Celia would find out. Among other things."

"Too bad your Keith Tippon got himself bumped off—"

"*Bainbridge*. His name is—was—Bainbridge. Arthur Bainbridge. I've never referred to him as Tippon."

Suddenly the name **TIPPON** flooded my brain in big, bold letters, just like the ones on the photo in the file Kit and I had stolen a look at. I could not only *see* the name, but hear it, like a shout.

That was the name I'd overheard at the front desk just two days earlier.

"Did Arthur have any children?" I asked, remembering that the guy was about my age.

"He and Elizabeth were unable to have children of their own, but they did adopt a child. A boy. That was when they were living in California and their lives seemed settled. Unfortunately, Elizabeth was run over by a car shortly after Arthur's release from prison."

"So, Arthur and his son moved to New York without her," I said.

"Of course, Val. Since she was dead," Kit stated the obvious, kindly clearing it up for me.

"Give me a break. I was thinking out loud. Nora, are you in contact with his son?"

"No. That was one of the many tragedies of poor Arthur's life. When his son graduated from college, he chose to sever all ties with his father. Arthur searched in vain, but he was never lucky enough to locate him."

"What name did he use?"

"Name? You mean his son's name?"

"Yes, that's what I mean. Does he go by Bainbridge or Tippon?"

"I'm not sure. Why do you ask?"

"Well, I think we just might have found him."

***

When Nora left us to take a shower, I chewed slowly on the last piece of toast, and Kit poured another cup of coffee.

"So, what do you think?" Kit asked, as soon as we heard the bathroom door close.

"Well—"

"I think she's full of it."

"Why do you say that?"

"Because I checked out Keith Tippon online while Nora was babbling. I didn't find anything on him."

"Is that conclusive?"

"What do you mean?"

"Well, it was a long, long time ago."

"True. I may have to check with my sources."

I laughed. "And who, exactly, are your sources?"

"I have sources."

"Well, I have no doubt that you and your sources will get the scoop on Keith Tippon. But I don't think it's true that Keith, or Arthur, or whoever he was, didn't see Roger Carpenter for over forty years. I think Marian saw them together a few days ago."

"Riiight," Kit drug out the word, giving it extra meaning. But meaning *what?*

"Are you just latching on to anything I say?" I asked her.

"First, tell me this: who is Marian?"

"*Marian.* The waitress. She cleaned up your sugar mess."

"Oh, right."

"Also, I'm curious as to why the Powells want to have dinner with Nora."

"Don't worry; we'll find out soon enough. We'll invite ourselves along to that little shindig."

"There's one other thing you should know."

"Oh great. What else is there?"

"Tom. He's flying in tonight."

"What?" She jumped up from her chair. "Why the hell is he coming? Did you invite him? Because he's the last person we need here."

"No, I didn't invite him, but while we're on the subject of Tom, did he and Nora ever have a thing?"

"A thing?"

"Yeah, a thing. Were they ever involved? Were they ever seeing each other—"

"As in dating? Have you lost your mind? Look, Nora may not have the best taste in men, and certainly she seems to lean toward the older types like Tom Haskins—"

"Tom's only a year older than Nora, for heaven's sake—"

"Whatever. But to answer your question, no, never, not in a million years. It's unthinkable. Nora is an extremely intelligent woman. She belongs to Mensa, for crying out loud. She's far too smart to ever be interested in a moron like Tom Haskins."

And then we both looked toward the bathroom door, where Nora had emerged, a towel wrapped around her body, a shower cap covering her hair. "Sorry to be a bother," she said. "But I can't seem to figure out the faucet on the tub. How do you make it into a shower?"

I looked at Kit. "Mensa is calling," I said under my breath. "Go show your big sister how a bathroom works."

***

"Let's take this larger table." Kit laced the strap of her purse over a nearby chair.

The hotel restaurant was almost empty. The Powells were already seated and clearly not happy to see Kit and me flanking Nora.

"We had hoped to have a private conversation with Mrs. Bainbridge," Louetta spoke up, obviously not in the mood to move.

"Ah." Kit took a seat at the larger table and beckoned Nora and me to sit with her. "I'm afraid Nora is not feeling one hundred percent today. I have to keep an eye on my sister. Nora, honey, I think you should eat something." Kit stared Louetta Powell down, her look conveying *take it or leave it*.

"I guess it won't hurt us none to move." Dale stood and put a hand on the back of his wife's chair. "We've come this far, Lou." He held out a hand to help his wife stand, and she moved slowly to our table. She didn't look pleased. Of course it was hard to read her stretched face, so maybe she *was* pleased, or maybe she didn't give a flip.

Before we could say another word, Marian the waitress appeared and handed us all menus. "The quesadilla is good," she said. "Homemade guacamole."

"Really!" Kit took the menu and opened it, not making eye contact with our server.

"I'm sure it's delicious," I said quickly, before Kit could remark that the very least she would expect of guacamole is that it be made from scratch. We didn't want to offend Marian. We might need to jog her memory again.

Nora remained mute, and I was willing her to put on her game face, her *delivering a brilliant closing argument to a mummified jury* look. Instead, she opened her three-page menu and began reading from page one. "Valerie said you needed my help," she muttered, not looking at the Powells, but I was relieved to see her court face appear.

"We do." Louetta turned to her husband. "Oh, Dale, I'm suddenly lost for words. Perhaps you could . . . explain to Mrs. Bainbridge our situation. You know, so we don't sound like a couple of crazy loons."

Her husband patted her hand. "I got it, honey." He put his menu down flat on the table. "Here's how it is, Mrs. Bainbridge. Lou and I are after some information, and we thought your husband could help us. Of course now it seems like he can't help anyone. We sure are sorry about what happened."

"It *was* your husband they found in the mountains, wasn't it?" Louetta asked. "Like Dale said, we sure are sorry about that. Terrible thing to have happened—"

"Perhaps you could just tell us why you need my sister's help," Kit said. "We're all curious."

"You betcha." Dale smiled. "It's gonna sound strange, but we believe Mr. Bainbridge is the same man Louetta here had some dealings with a long time ago. Seems like your husband—although he wasn't going by the name Bainbridge at the time—was, er, instrumental in a situation Louetta was in . . ."

"And?" Kit prompted him, since he had stopped talking and was once again patting his wife's hand.

"Seems like Louetta was in somewhat of a jam when she was just a young gal," he continued, "and . . ."

"Oh, for goodness' sake, Dale, it's gonna take you a month of Sundays to spit it out." Louetta withdrew her hand from underneath his. "Mrs. Bainbridge, we've been searching for your husband for a long time. It wasn't easy, especially since he changed his name an' all. But we did a lot of research, with help from some professional people—"

"Which don't come cheap," Dale said.

Louetta gently tapped her husband's arm. "Hush up, Dale. As I was saying before Scrooge here interrupted, we were looking for your husband, and then he found us."

"But why?" Kit asked. "What could you possibly want with Nora's husband?"

"Very simple." Louetta attempted what I thought was a wide grin, although it held no joy. "Hold on to your hat, honey. Her husband stole my child."

CHAPTER EIGHTEEN

As I sat in the cell phone lot at the Palm Springs International Airport, awaiting Tom's call that he was out front and ready to be picked up, my thoughts flitted from all Nora had told us before her shower to Louetta's claim that Arthur had stolen her child. I wondered how I was going to explain it all to Tom, who of course had texted me in the middle of our dinner with the Powells that it was urgent I pick him up. He needed the time alone with me to explain some stuff.

That's what he called it. *Stuff.* Well, I was willing to bet that my stuff was more serious than his. Not that I'd ever make a bet with Tom. Not unless I wanted to lose.

Nora, it seemed, not unlike Kit and me, still had more questions than answers when it came to her husband. Or so she said.

When she first began working for his law firm, she told us, she confronted him with questions no one else had ever raised. No doubt because of her Mensa brain. She couldn't understand why he didn't practice law and pressed him for more answers when he tried to explain. So even before she became romantically involved with him, she knew of his jail time and name change.

"After careful consideration and due diligence, I decided it had nothing to do with the here and now," she'd told Kit and me. After they began courting, as she called it, he told her about his son, although she always felt unsettled about *why* his son had severed all ties. If Arthur knew, he wasn't telling. But Nora had made it her mission to locate Arthur's son and attempt a reconciliation between them. That was another reason she'd hired Celia. That and all those property transactions she'd found out about.

"So why, if you could so bravely confront him when you were a new employee of his, could you not, as his wife, demand answers about those transactions?" Kit had asked her sister before Nora finally insisted she just had to take a shower—it was actually the best way she knew to clear her head.

"Katherine, it's not unusual to be more straightforward with someone you don't love, someone you don't have a vested—"

"Fine. Never mind. So let me get this straight. You knew about Arthur's past. It was his current goings-on that led you to mistrust him. This was after you'd already married him?"

"Of course." She sounded shocked that Kit would think otherwise. "But just barely," she added, rather sheepishly. "We were, in fact, on our honeymoon. At Niagara Falls. It was all we had time for, a quick weekend there, because of Arthur's important case."

"But he wasn't a litigator?"

"No. Many of the cases were actually handled by him, not the attorney assigned to them, the one supposedly doing the litigating. Everyone in the firm was used to that. But Arthur was acting so . . . so mysterious that I just had to look at the file when I had the chance."

"But why didn't you confront him right away?" Kit asked.

"We were just newlyweds," Nora said, as if that should explain it to Kit's satisfaction.

Ha! Not even close. "I still think that because you were married to him, you had all the more right to get to the bottom—"

"I just wanted to be sure there was really something to worry about. I didn't want to start our marriage with him thinking I didn't trust him."

"Even if you didn't?" Kit was relentless.

Nora looked at her almost defiantly. "Yes, even if I didn't. I had to be sure first. And when I saw what was in the file, I was alarmed. It appeared he might be back into money laundering, not that he ever was into it in the first place . . . I just had to . . . that's why I hired Celia . . ."

"I understand the pickle you were in," I said to Nora, because *someone* had to. She was turning red and practically hyperventilating. All while her little sister looked on, wanting to know everything. Well, so did I, but just not at *any* price.

"I have to take a shower," Nora had said, which for anyone else would have been a total non sequitur. With her, it came as no surprise.

Kit, it seemed, had other ideas. "Not yet, you don't," she'd said.

"Very well." Nora sighed. "I will share with you what Celia uncovered."

And even Kit didn't speak again until Nora had finished her horrific story. By the time she was done, I think we all needed a shower. No wonder she couldn't figure out how to work the faucet.

***

My cell phone began vibrating, and I remembered that I'd silenced it during dinner with the Powells. *Damn.* Tom would kill me if I didn't answer. "Tom?"

"You were expecting maybe George Clooney?"

"A girl can dream."

"Sorry to disappoint you, but yeah, it's only me. Where the hell are you?"

I started my car and pulled into the lane that would lead me to Tom. The sound of his voice and the laughter that accompanied it flooded me with relief. Not because it meant I hadn't missed his call—as furious as Tom can get, he doesn't scare me a bit—but because maybe it meant his urgent news wasn't going to be as chilling as the news I'd already heard from Nora and the Powells.

"How's Nora? What the hell's going on? Who's trying so hard to find her?" Tom asked as soon as I'd pulled up by the curb and he'd climbed in, tossing a small bag onto the back seat. I knew he would be just as dogged as Kit when it came to uncovering every single truth about Nora's husband. But he could damn well start with a few truths of his own.

"Tom, why didn't you tell me you and Nora were lovers?" We were making the half-hour drive to Palm Desert from the airport in Palm Springs.

As predicted, a sandstorm had started, if only barely, before I'd even headed out to pick Tom up. I found myself vaguely wondering if insurance would cover any dings the rental car might sustain when we got out in the open area between the two desert cities. There the wind could whip the sand around with enough force to cause some serious damage, not to mention how it could reduce visibility. I was glad Tom was with me. Somehow it made me feel safer.

"What the *hell* are you talking about? Nora and I are not lovers."

"Well, *were* you? Ever?"

He grunted. "That depends on what you mean by *lovers*."

I paused, as if waiting for him to follow the word with belated air quotes. "Um, lovers? As in being in love? Oh, I suppose *you* think it means having sex."

"Whatever. I don't kiss and tell, but yes, it might have been love. Or we thought so at the time. You got a problem with that?"

"Well, if you thought you were, then you were." I knew I sounded churlish. Why did I have such trouble with Tom and other women? Even Nora, who was clearly not Tom's type, no matter what he thought. "And no, I have no problem with that, or any other woman in your life." *Okay, Val. Get a grip. You and Nora both have far bigger issues to deal with than her* or *Tom's love life.* I literally shook myself in an attempt to gain some composure.

"Are you having a seizure, Pankowski?" Tom asked, his chuckle indicating that if that was the case, I was on my own.

"So, when was this? This so-called love affair? And how come I never knew—"

"It was before your time, and why do you have to know—"

"Before my time? You're only three years older than me. Are you talking high school, college, what?"

"If you must know—and apparently you must—it was long before you came to work for me. Just a little sojourn after Nora first moved to New York."

"Sojourn? What does that even mean?"

"It means we had a fling—"

"I know what *sojourn* means, and—"

"Then why'd you ask—"

"Forget it." I took my eyes off the menacing road and stole a glance at him. He was posed like a Buddha, the kind you see in Chinese restaurants, his clasped hands resting comfortably on his stomach, a knowing smile on his face. "Oh, Tom, I don't even know where to start with all I have to tell you."

"How about we start right there. Take that exit. Hurry. Get over. There's an In-N-Out Burger."

Well, I had been forced to leave dinner early, so the least he could do was buy me a Double-Double

Cheeseburger. I turned off Ramon Road onto Varner and parked in the In-N-Out Burger lot. We were going to sit inside, where we could talk and I could enjoy my food without worrying about crazy California drivers.

***

"So what you're telling me is that Nora's husband sold babies on the black market?" Tom had wolfed down his Double-Double in half the time it had taken me, no doubt because I had done more talking than eating as I shared what I'd learned. All Tom had done besides eat was grunt occasionally.

I'd just finished my last bite and was attempting to polish off my fries and vanilla shake. As full as I was, I hated to waste even a morsel of my favorite food in California. "That's the long and short of it, according to Nora. And the Powells."

"Could there be a bigger asshole than that?" Tom shook his head.

"Well, Nora claims he did it for the good of the babies. And children. He said the mothers of the babies were mere children themselves. He and his partner would pay their way to Canada, where they'd give birth in a facility the men had made arrangements with. Then the young mothers would be told their babies were born dead or given to good homes. Then Arthur saw to it the babies *were* placed in good homes."

"Yeah, right. And earn a bundle doing so. None of which, I'm willing to bet, he spent on screening those *good homes*."

"Well, we might never know, since he's dead. It took forever for us to get Nora to tell us all this. She wants to think Arthur . . . Keith . . . whatever . . . she wants to think him innocent. But this is all a moot point, isn't it? I mean, what's important is finding out who killed him, who's trying so hard to get ahold of Nora, and making sure she isn't in jeopardy." I shook my head and upper body again to try to clear my head or at least sort out my thoughts from the jumble they were in.

"What's this new seizure thing you have going on?" Tom asked, this time without a chuckle. "You okay?"

"Not really, Tom. No, I am not okay. But I will be. Now what is it you have to tell *me*?" I asked, almost daring him to top *my* stuff with his.

He swiped one of my fries, and after slowly chewing and swallowing it, he addressed my question. "Valerie—"

When I heard the ring of my phone interrupt him, I figured it would be a call I would have to take—what with all that was going on. I just didn't figure it would be my ex-husband, David. For a few seconds I debated whether to answer, but since he never calls me, and our only link is Emily, I knew I had to.

"Sorry, Tom, it's David," I said, and then silenced my phone by answering it.

"Speaking of assholes," I heard Tom mutter, although he was almost drowned out by David's loud voice.

"What the hell is this about Emily moving to England? You can't let her do that. What's in it for her?"

"That's how marriages work, David," I started the lecture I'd given him a million times. "Compromise." What I wanted to ask was, *what's it to you?* But I didn't want to sound too adversarial, for fear Tom would grab the phone from me to set David straight. Even though David deserved just that, I was tied in enough knots of conflict already. I wasn't wanting to add any. Since I felt certain David didn't have an emergency that involved Emily, I just wanted to get off the phone.

But David, it seemed, felt that was exactly what we had on our hands: an emergency involving Emily. "Val? Are you there? Do you hear me? She's only in her twenties. What does she know about living overseas?"

"Um, I think that's the point, David. She's in her twenties. She's married. She and Luke can damn well live wherever they want." As much as I hated the thought of her moving so far away, I suddenly felt forced to defend the decision. Just as I would defend anything that went against David. Especially since he certainly hadn't worried about Emily when he was chipping away at our marriage until it broke to pieces.

"I can see this was a waste of time. I should have known." And click. He was gone.

"Emily's moving to England?" Tom asked, as I stared at my phone.

"How did you know?"

"I just heard Asshole say so. I think they heard him clear down in Mexico."

"Yeah." A feeling of sadness enveloped me. But I shook it off—just mentally, not physically; I was already tired of hearing Tom comment on my "seizures." "Tom, tell me what it is you came to tell me."

"Did you know Nora was adopted?" he asked.

CHAPTER NINETEEN

How do you know this, Tom? Did Nora tell you?"

We both stared out the restaurant window at the sand whipping across the parking lot, swirling around the tires of the cars belonging to the other patrons who had come inside for some relief, or some of the famously fresh French fries. Or both.

"Nora?" He turned to look at me. "She doesn't even know."

"Then how do you know?"

He reached over and picked up my vanilla shake, taking a sip. "How d'you drink this stuff, Pankowski?"

"It's good." I grabbed my beverage back.

"Yeah, if you're six."

"Don't change the subject. Obviously, you want to tell me."

"Okay. I got a call from Beverly Rudolph. By the way, she's as sweet as ever."

"Why'd she call *you*?"

"She was trying to reach Arthur Bainbridge and when she didn't hear back from him, she called me."

Hmm. That puzzled me. I mean, *I* know that Tom's famous for knowing things, but was Beverly Rudolph aware of that?

"To be fair," Tom was saying, "the woman sounded a little panicky. Anyway, she asked me to meet her. She was in Chicago on an overnight trip, on her way to somewhere. I forget where. But she said she had something to discuss. Concerning Nora."

"Oh, so she knew what button to push to get your attention."

"What's that supposed to—never mind. I was curious, so I met her at a bar close to O'Hare—and before you ask, you don't know it."

"Or care. Go on, what did she say?"

"You know, she's still a good-looking woman. Of course I haven't seen her for a long, long time, but she looks great."

"Glad to hear it. But I asked what she said, not what she looked like."

"Oh, she rambled on through a few martinis, but the long and short of it is, she and her first husband adopted a baby—a baby girl—after they'd been married a few years. They were told they'd never be able to have kids of their own, and so they hooked up with a guy named Keith Tippon, who was known for speeding up the adoption process for a hefty fee. He helped her take care of the situation."

I have to hand it to Tom. He never minces words, always straight to the point. How had he ever kept his patience with Nora, who seemed to swallow a dictionary before she answered a simple question?

"And this baby girl was Nora?" It sounded unbelievable when I said it out loud.

"Gee, you're quick, Pankowski. Yeah, he fast-forwarded them through the whole thing."

"So what's the problem? Nora isn't the first child to be adopted." But as the words came tumbling out of my mouth, I felt incredulous.

"Apparently, most people tell their kids they've been adopted. Seems like, for her own reasons, this slipped Beverly's mind. She never did mention it, so Nora doesn't know. Neither does Kit."

"Wait—Kit isn't . . . I mean, Kit is—"

"Beverly's biological child? You bet. The second Immaculate Conception. Seems like the doctors were wrong about Beverly; a coupla years after the adoption, along comes Kit. Haven't you noticed that she has all the charm and warmth of her mother?"

"That's rude. Kit is nothing like her mother," I argued, but I know she does have some Beverly in her. "So," I said, trying to wrap my mind around the situation, "are you saying the whole thing was illegal? And that Nora has another mother—a birth mother—out there somewhere?"

"Yeah, of course it was illegal. And who knows if Nora's biological mother is still alive, or what the circumstances were, but as far as Beverly is concerned, she and her husband gave this Keith Tippon a bag of cash, and he gave them a baby."

"And probably they didn't want to tell Nora because it was against the law?"

"There goes that razor-sharp mind of yours again."

I drained the last of my shake, ignoring Tom's comment. "So, then Beverly finds out her daughter is about to be married to the man who arranged her adoption? It sounds a little like incest."

"Yeah, it's a little Beverly Hillbillies. And when she found out Nora *had* married your Arthur, it sent her into outer space on a martini-fueled spaceship." He stopped to chuckle at the image he'd created.

"But how could she know? Oh, Tom, did you tell her?"

"Calm down. It wasn't me."

"But you were the first person Nora told. The only person, in fact."

"Apparently not. I'm telling ya, I never said a word. You think I wanted to be in the middle of that little family drama?"

"Then who?"

"It was your mom. She called Beverly to congratulate her."

***

When the sandstorm subsided, we headed back to the hotel. On the drive there, I was plagued by the knowledge that Nora was adopted. Not to mention the anguish of Beverly having to keep it a secret all these years. It almost made me feel sorry for her.

Even more startling was the fact that Nora had somehow managed to find the only other person on the planet, aside from her parents and her birth mother, who knew the truth. Unless, of course, she had known of Arthur's involvement all along. Or unless *he* had sought *her* out.

"Lovely weather you got out here," Tom said, gazing out the window at the highway, which the sandstorm had turned into a minibeach.

"I think it's kind of wonderful."

"Yeah, you would. Give me a six-foot snowdrift any day. You know where you are with snow."

"Believe me, our snowstorms back home happen a hundred times more often than a sandstorm here."

"If you say so."

"As a matter of fact, it was Nora who pointed out the near perfection of the weather here in—"

"Okay, if *Nora* says so."

"So, Tom, you came all this way just to tell me Nora is adopted? You know, they have these things called phones. You press a button—"

"I came to make sure you're okay."

"Me? Or Nora?"

"You. All right, both of you." I glanced over at him and noticed he had struck up his Buddha position again, looking very content. "Two dead bodies," he suddenly mumbled, the contented look vanishing, "and a lunatic on the loose. That's bad, even for California."

I chuckled, but kept my eyes on the road ahead. "That sounds like something my mother would say. Especially the lunatic part. Can you imagine Jean out here in the middle of this—oh no; wait just a minute. Did you speak—"

"She gave me a call, okay? No big deal. She was worried. She asked me to just keep an eye—"

"An eye on me? I can't believe it. No, I can. Well, I guess it's better than *her* flying out here to check on me."

"Exactly. And it's been a long time since I've been to California."

"You hate California."

"Maybe it's changed. Look, I'm only here for a couple of days, doing a sweet lady a favor. I'll just check on you girls; then I'm headed to Reno."

"Girls? Did my mother ask you to check on me, or Nora?"

"Both, of course." He was fiddling with the lock on the glove compartment. "Mainly Nora," he added quietly.

"I knew it!" If there was any justice, I'd find out I was adopted too.

***

When we got to the hotel, I stood with Tom while he checked into the room that Billie had reserved for him. "I have a few calls to make," he said. "How about you meet me in the bar in twenty minutes for a nightcap."

"Okay." I looked at my watch. It was close to ten o'clock. "I guess I can stay up for one drink."

"Yeah, live it up, Kiddo. And bring Nora with you."

"And Kit?"

"Ah geez, do I really have to see her?"

"Well, of course you do. You think she's gonna let Nora meet you without her?"

"Okay. But don't go blabbing about what I told you."

I nodded silently as we walked to the elevators. That was going to be hard for me. Kit and I share everything, and I really didn't know how I was going to keep something that big from her.

"Valerie?" Tom pressed the button on the wall. "I'm not getting a good feeling from you. Promise me you won't say anything."

I watched the red button that showed the elevator was on its way. "I promise I won't say anything. But on one condition."

"No conditions."

"Yes, there is a condition. *You* must tell Nora."

He dropped his bag to the floor and took both of my arms in his big hands. "Are you nuts? I'm not saying a word."

"Yes, you will. Nora is not a child, for heaven's sake. For one thing, she has a right to know, and for another, it may be important. It may have something to do with her husband's murder."

He let go of my arms and grabbed his bag again, stepping into the elevator as soon as its doors opened. "I don't like this, Valerie, not one little bit."

"You think I do? But it's got to be done. Preferably by you, but if not, then by me. And that's my final word." When the doors opened on our floor, we walked down the corridor in silence.

He stopped four rooms before ours. "This is mine. I guess I'll see you in the bar." His back was turned to me, and he didn't look around. He unlocked his door. After he closed it in my face, I took a deep breath and headed to our room.

"What's up with you?" Kit asked, as soon as I let myself in. She was sitting at the table, her iPad open before her.

"Nothing. Why? What would be wrong?"

"You look like there's something on your mind. Was it Tom? Has that idiot upset you? I still don't understand why he came out here."

"For heaven's sake. He's worried about us. Plus, it's just a stopover on his way to Reno. He wants to meet us in the bar."

"Is there anything you want to tell me? You look strange." She was gazing directly at me, her eyes boring into mine, causing me to look away.

"Of course not. Where's Nora, by the way?"

"Downstairs having a massage. She should be back any second."

"Oh good." I threw my purse on the bed and took a seat at the table across from Kit. "So, tell me what happened with the Powells after I left. Do you really think Arthur stole her child?"

"I think it's quite likely." Was it my imagination that she was staring at me too hard, her eyes unblinking? She slammed her iPad shut. "Louetta couldn't say for sure it was Arthur, but she's working on the theory that it was him. But let's face it; it happened a long time ago, and they discovered America since Arthur was a young man."

"Yeah, as I think you mentioned a few times already, he was old."

"Plus his appearance changed—"

"Not as much as Louetta's, that's for sure."

"The point is, she lost her baby, and she's not even sure if it was a boy or girl. Apparently, Louetta never even got to see it."

"But surely she had to sign documents and stuff."

"That's just it, Val. She didn't sign anything. The baby was delivered via C-section, and after she awoke from the anesthesia, she was told the baby had died. But Louetta never believed them. She's spent the remainder of her life looking for her child, and with the help of a few expensive detectives, she found out about Arthur's scam. Obviously, she is hoping that her baby did not die, but was merely adopted."

"That's so terrible. Are you thinking Arthur and his wife Elizabeth took it?"

"Not sure. And by the way, apparently there was another man involved. So, I'm thinking this fake Arthur guy, this Roger Carpenter, was in on the scheme. You're acting weird, Val. Are you sure there isn't something you need to tell me?"

"Nothing. What do you think the Powells plan to do now?"

"I told them to go to the police with their suspicions. We know Arthur/Keith can't help them, but Roger is still around somewhere. Are you sure Tom didn't upset you? You're as white as a ghost."

"Let me just change clothes and put on some lipstick. As soon as Nora gets back, we should go meet Tom in the bar. He really wants to see her."

"Is he planning to take her surfing?" She stood up and went to the closet to find a jacket to wear with her white skinny jeans and coral-colored T-shirt. "I still don't understand why he felt the need to fly halfway across the country to somehow save Nora. What's that about? It's not as if they have any real connection. Wait a minute. When you asked me earlier if those two ever had a romance . . . do you know something?"

I tried to gauge what would be worse news for Kit, that her sister was not her sister by blood, or that at one time Nora and Tom had had a fling, even if Tom elegantly dubbed it only a *sojourn*. Since I was sure the *sister* was the worst of the two evils, and I definitely wanted Tom to be the one to share that bit of news, I plunged into the Tom/Nora romance.

Kit stopped at the closet as I gave her the brief details, and I was shocked to see she didn't at least feel the need to burn down the hotel.

"Oh. Is that all?" She pulled out a soft brown leather jacket.

"Kit, you blew a gasket when I merely hinted at it before."

"I know. She's far too good for him. But that was a long time ago. I was afraid you were going to tell me something else."

"Really?" I was only half-relieved. "What else is there?"

"Nora's adoption, for one thing."

I took off a sandal and threw it across the room at her. It missed by a mile. "You knew?"

Kit retrieved my sandal and laid it—and her jacket—on the bed next to me. "Yes. I knew. Of course I knew. But Nora doesn't. At least I don't think she does."

"So how did you . . . I can't believe you never told me."

Kit sat next to me on the bed and put her hands on her knees. "Val, I found out when we were teenagers. My mother, in one of her talkative drunk modes, let me hear all the sordid details. The whole thing. How she and Daddy were able to get Nora so quickly. Of course Mother made me swear not to say anything, because . . ."

"Because it might have been an illegal adoption?"

"Oh, it was illegal, all right. And yes, that's why I never breathed a word. I was scared they—someone—would take Nora away and my parents would be in trouble."

I nodded numbly. I could understand that. "But Kit, don't you think it's crazy that Nora ends up marrying the man who arranged it?"

"Arranged what?"

"The adoption, of course. Arthur Bainbridge was Nora's baby broker."

172

"Yeah, that part is crazy. Unless, of course, Nora knew his role and married him for some reason, anyway."

"But why?"

"There's even more stuff you don't know." She stood and walked to her iPad lying on the table. "While you were out picking up Superman, I did some checking on Roger Carpenter, also known as Arthur's partner in crime, also known as the world's biggest asshole . . ." She had switched on her iPad and was waiting for it to boot up. "It's not pretty, Valley Girl."

"Oh crap. I was hoping Arthur was the only one involved, and he was acting like some sort of Santa Claus helping pregnant women find good homes for their babies."

"Yeah, that might make a good Disney movie. However, there's more to it. Take a look at this." Using both hands, she turned the iPad in my direction. "I used one of those sites where you can get criminal records and stuff—for a fee, of course."

I hesitated before joining her at the table, and on the way, I took my reading glasses out of my pocket.

"Seems like Arthur's—or Keith's—buddy Roger Carpenter, or maybe both of them, offered a full range of services. Like I said, it's not pretty, Val."

I saw just enough of the headline to make me stop in my tracks: ROGER CARPENTER CHARGED WITH HUMAN TRAFFICKING.

CHAPTER TWENTY

E m, Em, slow down. Honey, don't cry. I can't understand what you're saying." I felt a lump form in my own throat and knew tears would soon follow if I couldn't get a grip.

But that's always hard to do when Emily is distraught and incoherent.

I heard her take a deep, shuddering breath. "Mom, why is Dad being this way? What is so bad about us moving to England? He can afford to fly and see us as much as he wants—"

She interrupted herself with sobs, and I wrenched myself away from the crisis of the Juckett girls so I could try to soothe my daughter. "Honey, you're just going to have to ignore your father. He likes to be in charge—"

"Mom." My daughter seemed to have gotten control of herself, judging by her tone of voice. The one that indicated she was ready to take control of *me*. "This isn't the time for you to unload about Dad. This is *my* problem with Dad."

When have I ever unloaded to you about your father? I wanted to demand. *Or had I?* I had certainly bitten my tongue a million times *not* to, but I suddenly recalled a few subtle, or so I'd thought, jabs I'd managed to sneak in.

There was the time he'd been overseas and was only minutes late in calling, but nevertheless missed her actual birth date: *How unfortunate your dad is too busy with his own life to call you on your birthday.* And another time: *Oh, that miniskirt reminds me of the one I saw your dad's date wearing—she's probably almost as old as you.*

There were probably many more, if I could bear to make myself recall. I did remember that each such remark from me caused Emily's face to cloud over in sadness. And each time, I vowed *no more.* And I did believe I'd all but stopped, the sting of our divorce and its causes lessening with every passing day.

But it was almost as if Emily had resolved that *next time Mom says something like that, I'm calling her out.* And I guessed that time had arrived. But I hadn't ever *unloaded.* Emily can be so dramatic. Well, she *is* an actress.

My anxiety was reaching a dangerous level. Nora had returned from her massage just as my phone started to ring. "It's Emily," I'd told the sisters. "I'll make it quick and then join you. We don't want to keep Tom waiting. Who knows what—"

"Yeah, yeah, we'll put a stop to his usual showboating," Kit had said.

"Kit!" Nora protested, as they went out the door and I returned to my sobbing daughter.

I decided to take the high road, one I always prefer and feel better for afterward. Sometimes I just need to be forced into it. Like now. "I only meant it's understandable that your dad worries about you moving overseas. But we'll—he'll—get over it. Just gently remind him that this is something you and Luke *are* going to do—"

"That's the bad part, Mom. He doesn't seem to *trust* Luke."

That was a shock. But a little clever, too, I had to admit. Making innocent Luke the bad guy. "What in the world is not to trust about Luke? What in the hell does your father think? That sounds like the time he—"

"Mom, don't fuel my frustration. I just mean I don't think Dad trusts Luke to *take care of me.* Like a world event or some natural disaster is going to take place with Dad too far away to help me, and Luke incapable of it. That's what Dad sounds like."

I was unable to muster any sympathy for my ex-husband and was even suspicious of his motives. He'd had no problem letting his little girl sail off to various camps in the summertime when she was growing up. I didn't recall any separation anxiety on his part; in fact, I took her and picked her up alone since he was too busy doing whatever the hell it was he did that kept him from his wife and child. This sudden burst of fatherhood was just too annoying.

"Well, he has no right to be so mean—"

"He *wasn't* mean, Mom." By now Emily sounded rather mean herself. "He's sad and worried. And that's what makes it so hard."

When would I learn to just shut up and listen? "Sorry, Em. I misunderstood. I thought—"

"It's okay, Mom. I think this move is scaring us all."

Scaring us? Really? She wasn't going into combat, and she was unlikely to get kidnapped or contract an incurable disease. I guess that's what all those theater camps and drama lessons got me. Still, I didn't like the idea of her moving any better than David did.

"Oh, honey, it's not forever," I said. "It's good for Luke's career, right? And it will be an adventure." *No doubt about it. Emily got her acting skills from me.*

"Right. Hey, Mom. Can we finish this talk later?" She sniffed, but her crying seemed to have stopped. "Luke just got home, and we need—"

"Sure, honey. Call me." I think I hung up before she could say good-bye.

I had to hurry down to Tom and the girls. I felt certain I had to save someone. I just wasn't sure who.

***

The three of them were huddled over the table talking feverishly, at least two at a time, like scientists examining slides of some lifesaving cells they'd just discovered. But as I approached, it became apparent the talk was of death, not life. Arthur's death. Rather, *Keith's* death.

"Okay, this is a lot to grasp on just one drink," I heard Tom say, as he sat up straight and snapped his fingers toward the bar. When he had the bartender's attention, he ordered a scotch. "You sure you ladies aren't ready for another?" He motioned to their half-full wineglasses. "Val, sit down. What can I get you?"

Nora answered first. "Tom, I must go to bed soon. And it is not good to have too much alcohol before retiring—"

"You're right." He smiled at her as if she were a two-year-old who had just recited the whole alphabet. Like he thought she was adorable and very smart. But he welcomed the scotch the bartender delivered by taking a big swig. Obviously, he thought Nora's recommendation was wise for her but didn't apply to him.

I ordered a glass of wine, and then once I realized Nora and Kit had brought Tom up to date, I pushed for our next step. "Can you talk to Dennis, er, Culotta, Tom? See if they're making progress?"

"I want to find out if they know who is trying so hard to get ahold of Nora—and why," Tom said.

"What I want to do right now is go to bed," Kit weighed in. "This day has been about twenty-four hours too long."

She rose from her chair to a duet of agreement from Nora and Tom. "It's two hours later back in Chicago," Tom added, "so if you think you're tired—"

"Yeah, Tom, we all know you're the best at everything. Even being tired." Kit sighed.

I seemed to be the only one ready to stay up, no doubt because I'd just joined them. I wanted to get something accomplished, besides drinking a glass of wine. I wanted to get Kit and Nora *fixed*, so I could turn my full attention to Emily. Even though I knew I'd been correct when I'd reminded David she was a married twentysomething who didn't need her daddy—or mommy—fixing a dern thing.

But I realized I'd have to wait, when I saw Tom gulp his drink down and then stand up to leave with Kit and Nora. "I'll be up in a bit. I'm just going to enjoy this." I held up the glass of wine the waiter had just set on the table.

***

"I'm feeling landlocked." Those were the first words out of Kit's mouth the next morning.

My eyes weren't even open yet, although I *had* peeked at the clock. I supposed Kit had seen that and taken it as an indication she could talk. No, Kit wouldn't feel the need to wait for that. Maybe she'd been speaking for a while and I just hadn't heard her. Either way, I thought *what the hell*. And then I said it out loud. "What the hell—"

"I said I'm feeling landlocked. I need to get to some water."

"Kit, you're hardly near water back home. It's not like Lake Michigan is close enough to Downers Grove to do any good. And if you're hinting we go to the ocean, *I'm* not driving. That LA area—"

"We don't need to go to the ocean. I've been googling, and the Salton Sea is only about an hour from here."

"If you would google a bit more," Nora piped up from her bed, where I'd thought she was still asleep, "you'd know you don't want to go to the Salton Sea."

"Why do you—"

"Katherine, it was once a beautiful resort area, but now it's rather . . . it's not what it used to be. Actually, at one time there wasn't even any water there. Now, of course, there is, and it looks beautiful when you drive by, but the pollution and the salinity of the water have killed off fish, making it extremely malodorous. There is an effort to restore—"

"Oh, forget it," Kit said. "We don't have time for a side excursion, anyway. We have to save your butt. Val, how do *you* propose we go about answering Tom's question?"

"Tom's question . . . ?"

"*Who* is trying to get ahold of you, Nora? And *why*—"

"Technically, that's two questions."

"Nora! You lied about that threatening phone call. The police can find no evidence—"

"The police, as it happens, didn't look at the right phone records."

"What does that mean?"

She sighed. "It means I acquired a separate phone to handle all this . . . business."

"Humph. Some business. I'd like to be on the board of directors of this business. Maybe then I'd get the facts. Maybe then you'd be so kind as to just tell the truth."

"Katherine, the truth is, our mother surrounded my life in a lie. In fact, lie upon lie. And it's all crumbling apart now. Oh, I don't know why I even started—" And then Nora herself crumbled. She slumped onto the bed she'd just left and the tears flowed.

"Oh no, you don't, sistah." Kit had had her back to us while standing before the dresser mirror applying some ridiculously expensive cream to her neck. Now she whipped around. "Details," she said. "Right this minute. And make sure they are the truth."

"With our mother, I'm not sure truth is in my DNA," Nora said. "Then again, her DNA and mine . . ."

Kit stared at Nora for a few seconds and then said, "So . . . so you . . ."

"Know? Yes. I didn't realize that *you* did, but I know I was adopted. Or more precisely, I'm told, I was kidnapped and sold. And Beverly was the purchaser."

"When did she tell you?" Kit asked, more quietly than I would have expected. She put down her jar of cream.

"Actually, *she* didn't tell me. Truth is *not* in her DNA. It was Arthur's *business partner* who told me." I wondered if in fact she and Kit *did* share some DNA, the way she formed air quotes when she said *business partner*.

"And he told you he'd killed Arthur and that you were next?" I asked.

"No, no. Not exactly. He didn't say *he* killed Arthur. He didn't say he didn't, either. He just said Arthur was dead. Actually, I thought he sounded regretful, if not downright sorry. Of course that doesn't indicate he was—or wasn't—the one who killed him."

"Wait a minute." Kit took a seat on the edge of Nora's bed. "You never told anyone you had identified the man who called and threatened you as the dude you saw in the mall when you ran off like a fu—like a scared rabbit."

Nora scooted down farther in the bed and pulled the covers up to her chin, shaking her head. "No, I didn't mention it," she finally whispered.

"But why not?" I asked, before Kit had a chance to. "Why would you keep something so important a secret?"

"Because . . ."

"Because you were afraid of him?" I took a spot on the other side of the bed. "But even so, don't you realize that's information we need? Not to mention the police?" I said.

"Yes, of course. And yes, I felt threatened by him. But not so much by what he said as by what I know about him. He actually spoke rather kindly to me. But I knew how he'd lied to Arthur. And he knew Arthur was aware of that."

"What is it you know?" Kit asked.

"I know that Arthur knew only *half* the story, back when they were running their adoption business. And recently Arthur found out the *rest* of the story."

"Which was . . . ?"

"The young mothers who gave birth were often spirited away by Roger to become prostitutes. Arthur really did try to provide a service he felt many people needed, people who wanted to adopt but, for whatever reason, were having trouble doing so. Like he and his wife Elizabeth. But he did not know that Roger used *that* program as a way to get young girls for his *own* enterprise."

"Business. Enterprise. You slay me, Nora. Your words really whitewash a nasty, nasty underworld."

"Kit, let's not forget Nora was a *victim*, not one of the perpetrators," I said.

"I don't know about that. How long have you known all this, Nora? How long did you cover up for Arthur?"

"I didn't *cover up*, Katherine. I was *undercover*. And that's why I didn't tell you—or the police—that I knew this man, this Roger, was tied to Arthur. I was hoping, with the help of Celia, to get more information, to procure proof. And not just about their business dealings—about me."

She stopped speaking again, and I noticed Kit had squeezed her fists into two balls. Surely she wasn't going to punch her sister?

Luckily, Nora continued. "About how I came to be adopted and who my birth mother was. Even with poor Celia's demise, I've felt determined to get to the truth. I had spoken to Roger Carpenter before, in New York. In fact, that's why I had a separate phone that I used to call only him. So when I got the call that made me feel threatened, I knew it had to be from him."

"I still don't understand why you didn't come clean about his identity."

"Because, with Arthur gone, and Celia too, he was my only link . . . the only way I could ever hope to find my birth mother."

CHAPTER TWENTY-ONE

It's Tag What's-His-Name," Kit whispered, as she turned her face away from the peephole in the door. "And he's brought a helper." She looked alarmed.

"Oh no," I said, although I wasn't really surprised.

"What should we do?"

"Well, for starters, let them in."

"Just a moment," Kit called through the door. Then she spoke to Nora. "Get up and put on a robe; the fuzz are here."

Kit dashed into the bathroom and grabbed a heavy cotton robe embroidered with the hotel logo on the breast pocket, throwing it onto Nora's bed. She then slipped into its twin, running a hand through her auburn hair. Since I was wearing my knee-length T-shirt, I guess I didn't need further covering up.

Detective Tag Mason and the other cop, an older guy, stepped into the hotel room. They looked like father and son headed out for a day of bonding. They were both chewing gum.

"Good morning, Detective," Nora said, standing at the edge of her bed and tying her robe at the waist.

Before answering, Detective Mason eyeballed the room, taking in everything. His shadow cop turned his head to inspect the bathroom.

"Good morning, ladies," Tag said, when he had finished his visual survey. "I have the results of the autopsy. Thought I'd deliver them in person."

I felt my involuntary intake of a deep breath, relieved that they weren't swinging handcuffs in Nora's direction. Yet.

"Please, sit down." Nora had moved swiftly across the room to the table and chairs by the window that looked out onto the balcony. "Can we order some refreshments? Coffee, perhaps?"

"No, thanks." Tag waved a hand. "This won't take long." He didn't move from his spot just inside the door; his companion stayed a step behind him, although his eyes were still sweeping the room. "Autopsy reveals that Keith Tippon, the man who was calling himself Arthur Bainbridge, died from blunt-force trauma to the back of his skull. It appears a large, jagged rock was the weapon—"

"So it was murder?" Kit was leaning against the dresser, arms folded across her chest.

"Hmm," Tag said.

I assumed that meant yes.

"And time of death?" Kit probed.

"Between noon Friday and the early hours of Saturday."

"When Nora was in Chicago." Kit looked triumphant.

"Right; we've verified Mrs. Bainbridge's alibi."

"A million people saw her in Chicago—"

"Yes, Katherine, that's what an alibi is," Nora said. "Detective Mason has verified it."

"And has he found out who killed Arthur?" Kit stared hard at her sister, but the remark was clearly aimed at the young detective.

"Not yet, Mrs. James, but we have some leads we are following up on. I just thought I'd stop by and give you an update. *Per your instructions.*" He looked amused.

"Well, thank you," I said, hoping to ward off any antagonistic words from Kit. "We appreciate it."

"So, my sister is in the clear?"

"Hmm. I wouldn't go that far. There is the little matter of Celia Decissio."

Kit unfolded her arms and walked across the room to her sister. "Nora, tell Detective Mason about the phone."

"The phone . . . ?"

"Yes, tell him that the warning call you received was to a second cell you have."

Nora went to her purse and produced a phone. She offered it to Detective Mason, but he moved slightly and his partner took it from her as if it were a hand grenade about to explode.

"What is this?" Tag asked.

"It's another phone I keep."

"Really? Why? And why didn't you mention this before?"

"Actually, I wasn't aware you would be checking phone records. If you had told me, I would have broached the subject then."

I wasn't sure if Nora was the dumbest or the smartest lawyer in the world. I knew she didn't handle criminal cases, but surely she should have offered this little tidbit to the police earlier, if for no other reason than to confirm she had received a warning call that caused her to flee.

"We'll need to keep it for now," Detective Mason said.

"Of course." Nora smiled weakly.

"Anything else?" Kit asked.

"No, that's it for now. Stick around; I'll let you know when we can release the body. Have a good day, ladies."

"One other thing, Detective," Nora said. "I should tell you who the caller was."

***

As soon as Kit shut the door on Detective Mason and his silent henchman, she threw off her robe. "I didn't like that one bit," she said.

"What did you expect? That Arthur died of natural causes?" I asked.

"Hell, he could have, since he was older than—" She looked defeated. "Oh, Nora, what is it?"

We both looked across the room where Nora was standing at the balcony window, her shoulders shaking. When she turned, I saw her face was wet with tears. We watched as she rubbed her cheeks with the palms of her hands before speaking. "Blunt-force trauma. Poor Arthur. He was a good man."

Kit gave me a raised-eyebrow look, then went to her sister and put an arm around her. "Don't think about it. He's gone, and he didn't suffer."

I didn't challenge Kit's logic that being whacked on the back of the head was painless. "Nora," I asked, "is it possible that Arthur was meeting someone there, or would he really just go for a hike?"

She rubbed her wet face again. "It is very likely he was just going for a hike. That would not be a good meeting place, surely, and we both did love hiking. Once, before we were married, I accompanied him on a trip to Europe where we hiked Mont Blanc. It is considered the rooftop of Western—"

"I know," Kit said, before Nora could launch into a travelogue. "Let's get out of here. Why don't we go shopping? We can have breakfast somewhere wildly expensive, then hit the shops."

I didn't share her enthusiasm. "I don't think I feel like spending any—"

"You don't have to. This will be on Larry."

In a flurry of activity, the sisters got ready for a day out, but I decided not to join them. Apart from the fact that shopping, even using Larry's credit card—again—was not appealing, I thought they might need some sister time alone, now that their family history was out in the open.

As soon as they left, I took my turn in the bathroom and showered, taking a long time and enjoying the solitude. When I emerged, towel-drying my hair, I heard my phone ringing. I saw David's name on the screen and debated whether to answer, but it was a call I'd have to handle at some time or another, and this was as good as any. "Yes?" I said, sitting on the edge of the bed.

"What the hell, Val?" I heard my ex-husband yell.

"Is that a question?"

"Yes, it's a damn question. What are you thinking, encouraging our daughter to go halfway across the world?"

I didn't respond right away. We'd already been through this, but I did rather like the idea that he thought I had such power over Emily. "What of it?" I finally asked.

"Oh . . . oh . . . *you*!" he countered, proving he was no wordsmith.

This thrilled me so much I decided I didn't even need to bolster my argument that it was our daughter's decision, not mine, not his. I took my time replying. "Yes, *me*," I said at last.

And then I heard his exasperated sigh before he hung up.

I tossed my phone on the bed, exhilarated by his frustration.

***

I put on a fresh T-shirt and jeans and applied a little makeup. Still jubilant from David's call, I was planning to take advantage of my alone time to call Emily and see if *her* spirits had lifted. After that, I thought I'd call Tom—who I figured was still dealing with the time lag and not awake yet—and let him buy me lunch. I would give him the good news that Nora already knew she was adopted and he didn't have to be the one to spring it on her. Before I had a chance to place my first call, however, my cell rang and Dennis Culotta's name appeared on my phone screen.

"Well, good morning, Detective," I said.

"Good morning. Reporting back."

"Huh?" I laughed a little. "Reporting?"

"Yeah, you asked me to check out the Powells, remember?"

"Oh, right." So much had happened since I'd given Culotta that mission, I'd almost forgotten I'd ever solicited his help. "I may have information for *you*. At least we did find out what they're doing in California. What do you have?"

"Not so fast. I should at least get to see my favorite Midwestern girl before I spill my guts. Wanna meet me for coffee? I'll come to your hotel, be there in ten minutes. See you in the restaurant."

He hung up before I could respond, but I latched on to his Midwestern girl comment and took the ten minutes to change into a dressier shirt and black pants. Oh, and I applied a little more lipstick.

***

Dennis Culotta's clothing was similar to what I had just discarded. Jeans and a T-shirt. I was a little thrown off by his appearance since I'd never seen him quite so casual. His T-shirt was sparkling white and a little wrinkled, as if he'd just taken it out of a suitcase. He had a pair of sunglasses hanging from the pocket.

"I ordered coffee and toast and eggs," I said, as he sat down at my table.

He smiled. "Good. And let's get bacon or something," he added, much to the delight of my tummy.

I signaled our waitress (a young woman had replaced Marian) and gave her the happy news. "So," I said when she left, "Tag Mason was here this morning with the autopsy results on Arthur."

"Yeah." He picked up the menu, glanced over it, and then put it back down on the table. "Someone smashed his skull in."

"Unfortunately. But it looks like Nora is in the clear for that."

"How so?"

"Well . . . time of death. She was in Chicago when he was attacked."

"Riiight," Culotta said, with very little enthusiasm. He had his elbows on the table and held his hands clasped in front of his face. I looked at his forearms, noticing they were covered in fine blond hairs, which gave a hint as to the original color of the thick, prematurely white hair on top of his head. His deep-blue eyes scoped the restaurant in a manner similar to Tag Mason checking out our hotel room. I wondered if that was something all cops do wherever they are.

When his eyes returned to me, he gave a satisfied smile.

"You don't sound convinced," I said.

"Frankly, I'm more concerned with Celia than this Arthur/Keith guy." His face took on a look of genuine sadness, breaking the spell his blue eyes had cast on me.

I reached across the table, putting my hand on his forearm. "Dennis, I'm really sorry about your friend. Celia. This must be very hard for you."

"Yeah. I guess it kinda goes with the territory. She was a good woman." He unclasped his hands, picking up the menu again, and it was clear he had nothing more to add.

"So, what did you learn about the Powells?" I asked, glad to change the subject.

"Not much. You?"

I debated for a brief second before replying, struggling to decide just how much information to give him. But I reminded myself it wasn't his case and surely he was there to help Nora. "Well, it seems like Louetta had a child when she was very young, and apparently she decided to give it up—"

"For adoption. Right. Bainbridge's baby dealing at your service."

The waitress appeared with our orders, and Culotta sat back in his chair, his hands on his chest as she placed his food before him. She was pretty, with curly chestnut hair and big brown eyes. I noticed she gave him a smile, although she never looked at me once.

"Thanks," he said, smiling back. Then, as soon as she left, he returned to me. "Nice blouse," he said, not taking up his knife and fork but nodding his head in my direction.

"Huh?" I dug into my scrambled eggs.

"Your blouse, or shirt, or whatever you call it. It's nice."

I reached for the salt at the same time as he did, and our fingers briefly touched. I pulled my hand back as if it had just landed on a cactus. "Really? You like this old thing?" The *old thing* part was true.

"Yeah, you wore it once before." He picked up the saltshaker and liberally tossed some of the contents over his plate. "One of the many times you stopped by the station uninvited."

"Well, er, thank you, I guess." I was thrilled he had remembered. When I last wore the shirt in his presence, it had been newly purchased online from one of those websites where everything's seventy percent off. I'd thought I'd gotten the deal of the decade; his compliment was proof the twenty bucks I'd spent was well worth it.

"So, I hear Tom Haskins is in town." Dennis was eating his eggs, quickly and without taking proper time to chew. My mother would be appalled.

"How'd you hear that?"

"Police scanner." He smiled. "No. He gave me a call last night."

"Okay, then. Yes, he's here. I'm not sure why, but he's here, all right. So, back to the Powells." It occurred to me I was a little nervous, as I generally am in his presence. But in a good way. "You don't really know anything shady about their past?" I asked, sounding like a character from a fifties murder mystery.

"*Shady*?" He stuck another fork loaded with eggs into his mouth. "By shady, do you mean—"

"I don't mean anything. That was the wrong choice of words. Sorry. It's just that you said you might have information. I assumed it was about them."

"No, not really; you seem to already know as much as I do."

"Then what? Of course I guess we don't need to have a reason to have breakfast, right?"

He leaned back in his chair again and then picked up his coffee cup. He took a long sip, his eyes never leaving my face, before responding. "None that I can think of."

"Good."

"So what do you know about this Bainbridge?" he asked.

"Well, just that he isn't Arthur, he's really Keith Tippon, and he was married to Elizabeth. He spent some time in jail for tax evasion or something."

"And Nora knows this?"

"Yes, he told her. Plus, she hired Celia to do some investigating."

"So what do you know about his wife? His first wife."

"Not much; just that she died before Arthur—I mean Keith—left California and moved to New York."

He was nodding at my little recitation, but his baby blues had taken on a thoughtful look.

"What?" I asked. "Is there something else?"

"Maybe."

"Tell me."

190

"I did some checking on the first Mrs. Bainbridge. Sorry. She was Mrs. Tippon—Elizabeth Tippon. She was the victim of a hit-and-run. No one was charged."

"Oh my, I didn't know that. Is it significant?"

"Possibly. Seems the car that hit her was never located, but a police report I saw mentioned a witness statement."

As I tried to digest that news, the smitten waitress refilled Culotta's coffee cup (but not mine), and then my cell began singing from inside my purse. "Excuse me." I held a finger up to Dennis, but he was busy listening to his new admirer and seemed not to notice me. "Hello, Larry," I said. I felt an involuntary smile appear on my face, as it often does when I speak to Kit's husband.

"Hey, Val, how's it going? I really wanted to talk to Kit, but she's not answering her cell. Everything okay there?"

"Oh yes; she and Nora went shopping. She probably didn't hear it ring." I glanced at the waitress, who was marveling at something Culotta had said. He was shrugging, like he'd just told her gold had been discovered in the California hills again. A sort of *check it out for yourself* look.

"I had another call from someone trying to reach Nora," Larry said. "This one left her number and wants a call back."

"Her? So it's a woman?"

"Yeah, this one was. And not just any woman. Sister Theresa Magdalene."

"Sister? You mean like a nun sister?"

"That's what I mean."

CHAPTER TWENTY-TWO

They weren't related by blood and didn't share the same DNA, but—maybe because they were raised by the same mother—Nora and Kit obviously did share a love of shopping for elegant and unusual clothes. Granted, they each had their own kind of unusual. No one would guess they were sisters when it came to their choices.

They returned from their shopping trip on a retail high, eyes aglow as they showed me their purchases. I was just beginning to wonder if maybe they'd capped their shopping spree off with a drink, when Kit said, "That was exhausting. I need a drink. How about you, Nor?"

Nor?

"Yes, that would be fabulous, Kit." *Kit*, not *Katherine?*

I decided they had indeed bonded. I felt almost jealous.

"Valley Girl, you should have come with us," Kit said, as if realizing I felt a tad left out. She hung up the last of her purchases—a gray silk shirt with long flowing tails, the kind

I needed, to camouflage my little (okay, not always so little) pooch. Certainly nothing Kit and *her* flat tummy needed.

"Well, I'd really like a drink," I said, deciding it would be easier for me if they had a cocktail in hand when I reported what I'd managed to drag out of Larry. I also figured a public place might keep Kit more mellow. Then again, alcohol might make her come unhinged. Oh well, I concluded, *I* needed the fortification of a glass of wine. "Let's go."

Nora finished folding her brand-new silver-sequined sweater back into its tissue and placed it in a drawer. "Let me cut these tags off first," she said, snipping at the plastic that was used to fasten them to the new red-and-purple-paisley tunic she'd left on after the mini style show she and Kit had put on for me. By comparison, the shirt I was still wearing, the one Culotta had so admired, seemed positively dowdy.

I was vaguely aware of them chatting about their exquisite finds from the shops that lined El Paseo as I followed them to the elevator. "Let's not go to the hotel bar," I spoke up, surprising myself. "I don't want to see a familiar face."

Kit turned and looked at me, and I knew she was about to ask me if anything was wrong. But then she said, "No problem; I saw a charming place around the corner I'd like to try. We can get a bite to eat, too, and sit outside."

"Oh, marvelous," Nora said.

Do these sisters forget what's going on? I wondered.

No doubt about it. Shopping *is* a drug. Well, before their high had a chance to wear off gradually, I was about to make them crash. And I wasn't happy about it.

***

"Why the long face, Valley Girl?" Kit asked, after we'd told the waiter what we wanted for our late lunch and had all taken a few sips of wine.

I wanted to tell her *she* should have a long face, but I decided it was good *someone* had been able to forget our problems for at least a while.

But her *while* was up.

"Kit. And Nora . . . ," I began.

"Gee, Val." Kit put her glass to her lips and raised an eyebrow in her sister's direction. "Now you sound like Beverly." She held up her right hand as if taking an oath. *"Sorry, Mother, I swear there wasn't a dent in the car when I drove it home from the drag race."*

"And I promise I never put your Cartier earrings on the cat," Nora mimicked her sister's imitation.

"Oh, I forgot about those earrings." Kit looked wistful.

"Yes, they were exquisite."

"Will you both shut up and listen," I said, loud enough to break their reminiscing. I had their full attention, but in a way I was sorry to spoil their fun. I couldn't remember the last time I'd seen them so chummy. If ever.

"Larry called me while you were shopping."

"He called *you?* That SOB hasn't returned *my* last call." Kit shook her head and took a sip of wine. "What's up with *that?* Oh, wait. You don't think that last store called him about the charges for those damn shoes—"

"Is your ringer off?" I asked her, my tone implying that of course it was.

She picked her phone up from where she had it placed next to her water glass as if it were part of the Emily Post–recommended table setting. Not unlike most people nowadays. "Oh yeah." She had the decency to look chagrined. "So what did he want?"

"He wanted to tell us about a phone call he received. From someone who has information she wants to share with Nora about her birth."

"Say *what?*" Kit asked, her words matching the "O" of shock Nora's mouth formed.

I recounted Larry's report, starting with how the caller, a nun of all people, wasn't even alive when it all went down about five decades ago. I smiled, all of a sudden wondering if *when it all went down* was Larry's word choice or the nun's. She *was* young, Larry had repeatedly reminded me whenever I'd asked him a question he couldn't answer.

"I'm guessing that's why she told me everything," he'd said. "Everything she can, that is."

When Larry had called, I left the table, even though Culotta didn't seem to notice my signal that I needed to find a better place to finish my phone conversation. He just continued listening to the waitress, who appeared to be babbling on about the glorious California weather. Like we couldn't figure *that* out for ourselves.

"And just why the hell didn't Kit tell me any of this?" Larry asked me. "Or Nora? Or for that matter, *you*?" I'd never heard his voice sound so stern.

"Larry, if you mean about Nora's adoption, well, Kit has her own reasons for keeping that part of her family a secret. As for me, well, I only just found out myself and I'm as shocked as you. Plus, we've been busy here—"

"Yeah, dead bodies keeping you busy; I get it. But obviously not too busy for Kit and Nora to go shopping."

"It wasn't so much shopping; they just needed to have some sister time, now that . . . well, now that it's all out on the table."

"Never mind that—for now. Sister Magdalene told me recent events have caused them to reopen some records, including and especially Nora's, since they've received some inquiries about her birth. *Police* inquiries. Or maybe it was the Mounties." Larry chuckled, and then, sounding guilty, he continued. "She told me everything was complicated because of the American/Canadian thing."

"Larry, was this nun from . . . from a place . . . where young pregnant girls went to—"

"Sort of. Before she joined the order she's currently in, before she was even a nun, she was involved with an organization where young girls used to be sent—from both

Canada and the United States—to wait out their illegitimate pregnancies. But how did you know that, Val?"

And so I briefly filled him in. Well, maybe not so briefly, because Culotta walked by me, pointing to his watch in an apparent attempt to let me know he had places to go and people to see.

"Yes, the babies were to be put up for adoption," Larry said, obviously continuing to put two and two together as he spoke. "And in a way, they were, but now authorities know that many of them were sold. To people, apparently, who Nora's new *husband* and other scum like him had lined up." He sounded outraged.

I felt a little light-headed, realizing Larry was talking about the place where Arthur had sent Nora's birth mother and Louetta and who-knew-how-many others. If only all the babies had been placed with parents like Nora's, as imperfect as Beverly was, I could happily accept it—right, wrong, or otherwise. But Roger's human-trafficking charge made me fear the worst for many of the babies, not to mention their young mothers.

As predicted, I'd squelched the retail buzz Kit and Nora had sat down with. They both looked as sick as I felt.

"Is that all, Val?" Kit asked at last. "Is that all Larry had to say?"

"*All?* Isn't that enough?"

"Yes," Nora said a little too loudly. She'd been so quiet, I almost forgot she was there. And she was the star of our not-so-little drama. "It's more than enough—"

"Did this Sister person shed any light on who Nora's mother is?"

"Beverly is my mother, Katherine."

"You know what I mean. Did Sister Maggie tell Larry anything about Nora's birth mother?"

"She told Larry she would speak further on that subject only to Nora and instructed him not to share with anyone what she'd said." I'd been surprised Larry hadn't kept secret all Sister Magdalene had told him. I've always known him to be a superhuman secret keeper, in stark contrast to his wife. He obviously knew the stakes were just too high not to share what she'd told him. "But yes," I answered Kit, "Larry said she did know the name of Nora's birth mother."

***

"We obviously need to call Mother Superior." Kit drained her wineglass.

"I don't think this nun is the Mother Superior," I said. "And shouldn't we call Beverly first—"

"I was talking about Beverly. We'll get to the nun later. Nora, finish your wine and let's go back to the hotel." Kit swiftly picked up her sister's glass and drained the remains.

As we made our way across the hotel lobby, headed back to our room, I saw Tom standing at the bank of elevators. I'd almost forgotten he was in California and felt guilty that I hadn't at least called to check up on him. His suit jacket was hanging over his shoulder, suspended from his index finger. His crisp white shirt was unbuttoned at the collar. This was Tom's idea of casual; at least he wasn't wearing a tie. But I noticed his cheeks were unusually red. A suntan already? Rather, a sun*burn*.

"Where have you been?" I asked, alarmed.

He spoke around the unlit cigar in his mouth. "I've been having drinks at the poolside bar with your boyfriend."

"Kevin Costner is *here*?"

Kit looked annoyed. "We don't have time for your childish games, Tom." She reached past him and punched the elevator button several times, even though it was already illuminated.

"Ah, so that's how it works? You have to *punch* the button." Tom took on a look of exaggerated wonder.

The elevator doors opened at last, and Tom ushered us all in. "I need a ride to the airport in about fifteen, Val," he said. "If you can tear yourself away."

"Already? You just got here." I pushed the button for our floor, since no one else had.

"I can see you're okay," he said, looking only at Nora. "And I have a game in Reno lined up."

"Poker?" Kit asked.

"It ain't Go Fish."

When we reached our floor, we headed down the hall and Tom stopped at his room. "See you in the lobby in fifteen, Pankowski," he said, unlocking his door.

"What an ass," Kit said, a half second before it closed.

"Why, I think Tom is actually—"

"Shut up, Nora." As always, Kit was in no mood to hear favorable closing arguments about Tom. "Call Culotta, will ya, Val? Let's see what he thinks he knows. And Nora, you call Mother."

CHAPTER TWENTY-THREE

I was back down in the lobby to meet Tom five minutes later. I left Kit and Nora having a heated debate on who should call Beverly. Neither one wanted to confront her, even by phone. I wanted to be a witness to the call even less.

The lobby was quiet, except for one man sitting by the waterfall in an overstuffed leather armchair. I'd seen this man before. He was the guy I'd stood behind at the reception desk. One and the same.

Mr. Tippon.

I spied a newspaper on the glass coffee table in front of him, and I headed in his direction to grab it. As I got closer, I saw him put a cell phone up to his ear. He glanced at me and then began nodding amiably as he listened to his caller. I took the newspaper and sat down in the matching chair across from his.

I removed my reading glasses from my purse and stuck them on my face. I recalled that this man had turned and briefly smiled at me while checking in, so perhaps the glasses would offer some disguise to keep him from recognizing me. I wasn't sure what harm it would do if he *did*. But just in case he thought I was a stalker, I pretended to study the headlines in the newspaper. KIM KARDASHIAN GOES PLATINUM IN PARIS. GWYNETH PALTROW DONS TUBE TOP. MAN CONFRONTS FEMALE STALKER. *(Huh? Was I really making the news already?)*

As I turned the pages to the business section, he looked in my direction and smiled. He was nice-looking, probably early fifties, dressed in the California casual that Tom had yet to master. He had salt-and-pepper hair, cut short, and a pair of expensive-looking sunglasses on top of his head. I watched him remove the glasses and chew lightly on the end of one of the earpieces.

I smiled back and then turned my attention to the Dow, not sure if it had gone up or down.

" . . . yes, it's all gone down," I heard him say, and then realized he wasn't channeling my thoughts on the stock market but was talking into his phone.

I desperately wished Kit were with me. She would know how to get him off the phone and start a conversation. I debated texting her, but I didn't want to interrupt the phone call I hoped she and Nora were making back in our room.

" . . . yeah, you worry too much, Roger. I'm telling you it's all taken care of. You just stick to the plan. I'll see you soon; I'm leaving shortly." He laughed at something Roger said.

Roger? Roger of Roger Carpenter? Of fake British Arthur/Roger? Or was it simply Roger Rabbit? We were, after all, in the state where even cartoon rabbits might receive phone calls.

"Are you a guest here at The Palms Hotel?" I asked, as soon as he hung up. It was the only thing I could think of to say, but it seemed important that I set up some kind of rapport with this guy.

He looked up from his phone, where he appeared to be scrolling for messages. "Sorry. Did you say something?" he asked.

"Yes," I said in a normal person's voice (apparently I'd been whispering). "I just wondered if you were staying here. I'm wondering if the spa is any good."

He laughed a little. "Sorry, I don't really do spas. I'm not even sure what happens there."

"Me neither," I said, half truthfully, as he shut down his phone and put his glasses back on top of his head. "What about the restaurant?" I was determined to keep him from leaving, but I wasn't exactly sure why, and I certainly didn't know how. "Have you eaten here?" I asked.

His easygoing smile disappeared. So he clearly had me pegged as a real stalker, or a moderately priced hooker wearing a shirt that was held in esteem by a Chicago-area cop.

"Sorry," I said. "I don't mean to be so nosy. I'm just a little—"

"Nervous?"

"Oh, do I appear nervous? Yes, I guess I am."

"Nothing I said, I hope."

"No, it's not you. Of course it's not you. I ... er ... have a job interview with a real tough guy. I'm meeting him here—"

"Whatever it is, I'm sure you'll get it." He crossed his legs in a leisurely manner and leaned back in the armchair. "Good luck. I'm sure he'd be very fortunate to get you."

"Oh, I don't know about—"

"Pankowski!" I heard the boom of Tom's voice from across the lobby, and I turned to see him standing at the front desk. "You ready?" he yelled.

"He *does* seem tough." My new buddy glanced over at Tom and then leaned toward me to whisper, "Do what I always do. Pretend you don't need the job."

***

"In case you're hurrying out of town so you don't have to tell her she's adopted," I started to explain to Tom as we drove toward the airport, "Nora—"

"I'll tell her. In my time."

"Yeah, right." I laughed and then told him she already knew, so he was off the hook.

He grunted before changing the subject. "Who was that guy you were talking to in the lobby?"

"I'm not sure. But his name is Tippon. So he could be—"

"Related to Arthur aka Keith aka dead guy found in the mountains?"

"What a way with words you have."

"I'm not done. Nora's stepson?"

That thought alone made me not want to discuss my discovery with Tom any further. And I couldn't wait to dump him at the airport and return to Kit. She would have some ideas.

***

When I was finally alone and driving back to the hotel, I made a quick stop at a Starbucks for a grande mocha. Then I set my phone on speaker and called Culotta. We had a lot to talk about.

Mainly young Mr. Tippon.

"Dennis," I said brightly, after he answered on the first ring. "It's me."

"How good of you to call, Valerie. Last time I saw you, we were having breakfast, until you got up and left the table—"

"No. I took an important call, and you disappeared on me. I thought you and the waitress were going to take in a movie or something."

"Oh yeah, her. Did you know her mother is a vegetarian?"

"Ugh."

"You don't like vegetarians?"

"I don't like waitresses who inject themselves into their customers' conversations."

"Hmm. Well, I don't like customers who take calls during—"

"Oh, Dennis, get over it. It's the twenty-first century, in case you haven't heard. Look, I have something I need you to do."

"Wow. I didn't see *that* coming. *You* have something for *me* to do? A strange turn of events, Valerie, and rest assured I'll drop whatever it is I happen—"

"There's a guy staying at the hotel named Tippon—"

"Um, in case *you* haven't heard, this is the twenty-first century, and I believe that guy, Tippon, is no longer living in it."

"Not him. Another Tippon. I heard his name when he checked in the other day. And I heard him talking on the phone today to someone called Roger."

"Roger Moore? The best Bond?"

"Sean Connery was the best Bond; everyone knows that. And no, I don't think he was chitchatting with a former movie-star spy."

"Who, then? Roger Carpenter?"

"Could be. Arthur/Keith's old partner. This guy in the lobby could be the son that Arthur lost contact with. Maybe he took back his father's real name. We need to know what he's doing here and where the hell Roger Carpenter is. Can you check him—"

"Call Tag Mason. He's got to know this stuff."

"Yes, I will; and yes, he certainly should know, but couldn't you just—"

"Call the police, Valerie. And do it now. Before this goes any further." Then he hung up.

Instead, I called Kit, but her phone went straight to voice mail. I wasn't too far from the hotel, and I couldn't wait to talk to her. But I'd have to.

***

I rushed through the lobby to the elevator, and when the doors finally opened on our floor, I hurried down the corridor that extended to our room.

Then I stopped.

At the end of the long hallway, I could see our door was wide open. Standing guard outside was a man in blue, Palm Desert–style. (His Hawaiian shirt was fuchsia laced with large white tropical flowers, but his shoulder holster and gold badge proved he was a cop and not a hotel guest.) I walked slowly toward him, but he kept his gaze just a few inches above my head. When I finally reached him, he put out a hand to stop me.

"I'm Valerie Pankowski. I'm staying in this room." I peered around him and saw Kit and Nora both seated on the end of one of the beds. In front of them stood Detective Tag Mason, and leaning against the wall was Dennis Culotta.

"Oh, *Valerie*," Nora shrieked as soon as she saw me. She hopped up and came over to wrap her arms around me. "Thank goodness you're here. You just won't believe what's happened now."

"Sit." I urged her back onto the bed. "And you?" I addressed Culotta. "What are you doing here? And how did you get here so quickly?"

"Sorry, Valerie. I thought I'd call Detective Mason for you. You know . . . in case you had trouble *reaching* him." He moved out of his nonchalant position and came toward me. "Val, tell Detective Mason what you told me earlier on the phone. Do it now."

"Well," I said, joining the sisters on the end of the bed, forcing Kit, who had remained silent, to move over a little. "What I told you on the phone . . . well, remember, it was just what I overheard. I'm not sure—"

"Oh, this is all bullshit," Kit suddenly found her voice. "It seems another body has been uncovered—"

"Er, not really uncovered," Nora said. "As Detective Mason explained, a body was found with a fatal gunshot wound, fully visible—"

"And so naturally," Kit said, "the police rushed over here, and once again Nora is suspected—"

"Who was it?" I asked, alarmed. "Who was shot?"

"Looks like Roger Carpenter," Culotta said.

"Oh no, that's not possible. I just heard . . . I mean, not even two hours ago . . . he was . . ."

"Ms. Pankowski," Detective Mason spoke through his chewing gum for the first time, "I think you need to accompany us down to the station."

"Her?" Kit sounded almost jealous that I was the only one being hauled in for questioning.

Ignoring my friend, he continued, "Detective Culotta seems to think you may have some information pertinent to this homicide, and I'd like a formal statement from you." He cracked his gum when he finished his long-winded sentence, and I wondered if he was reciting from a police manual.

"Okay; I'll be happy to help you, but—"

Kit suddenly jumped to her feet and put her hands firmly on my shoulders. "Don't say anything, Val. I mean it. Not a word. Think of *The Good Wife*; that's the first thing Julianna Margulies tells murder suspects—"

"Good grief, Kit. I'm not a murder suspect. But Detective Mason is right; I might know something. In fact, I think I know who did—"

"STOP," Kit yelled. "Are you not hearing me? Is Tom Haskins involved in this? Because it sounds just like him. Let me call a lawyer."

"Ms. Pankowski is not under arrest," Tag Mason said.

I was a little unnerved that it had taken him so long to speak up.

"Shall we?" He extended his arm toward the door.

"Don't worry, Valley Girl," I heard Kit call, as Hawaiian Shirt moved slightly from his position to let us pass. "We'll be here when you get out—*if* you get out."

***

Culotta drove me home from the station, home being the hotel room. He had sat with me while I wrote out my statement confirming I had overheard a man, who the police identified as Alex Tippon, talking on the phone to someone he called Roger.

I'd thought I had it all worked out. I even called Kit from the station and told her everything was solved.

There was just one tiny problem.

Roger Carpenter had been found in a nearby hotel room with a gunshot through his temple at nine o'clock that morning. Hours before my chat with Alex Tippon in the lobby of the hotel.

"I feel like a fool," I said, as Culotta put his arm around my shoulders and steered me into the elevator.

"Don't. You're the smartest woman I know. Most of the time."

"But I was so sure I heard this Alex Tippon say the name Roger."

"The police spoke to Alex at the hotel," Culotta said. "No connection that they can find between him and Arthur Bainbridge *or* Roger Carpenter."

"Huh! None except the same last name as Arthur's, er, Keith's. Tippon."

Culotta did not respond as we stepped out of the elevator on my floor and made the long walk down the corridor to the room, stopping at the closed door. Although I could hear no sounds coming from inside, I knew Kit was waiting up.

"Thanks for staying with me and driving me back," I said.

"No problem."

"Dennis, are the police just idiots?" I took my key card from my purse.

He looked at me in amazement. "Are you kidding me? Why would you even say a thing like that?"

"Well, they seem to always be a step behind us. How in the world can there be no connection between the two Tippon guys—"

"Whoa. First of all, you don't know what their thinking is. They're working on a lot of stuff you know nothing about—"

"Yeah, stuff that we provided. And why do you police guys act like—"

Suddenly, I felt his arm wrap around my waist in a swift motion as he cupped my chin in his other hand and raised my face just enough to kiss me. I felt a surge of excitement course through my body, and I had to reach out to the door behind me to stop from sliding to the carpet.

When our lips parted, Culotta's forehead rested gently on mine for a few seconds. His eyes were closed, and I thought he might speak. But instead, he silently straightened up, and I watched as he walked down the hallway to the elevator.

If I hadn't been able to still feel his lips on mine, I might have been convinced it never happened.

The elevator doors closed, with him inside, yet I was still unable to move. I'm not sure how long I stood there, but after a while the door behind me was abruptly opened, and Kit yanked me inside.

"Get in here," she hissed. "While you and your dreamboat were making out, Nora and I figured out how he did it."

CHAPTER TWENTY-FOUR

ow who did what?" I asked, as I heard Kit shut and lock the door behind me.

"How Arthur managed to lure everyone out here," she said.

"It's not *how* he did it that's important," Nora said. "And Katherine, *lure* is a poor choice of words. It has a misleading connotation. It's *why* Arthur *invited* so many of the principals out here that's important."

"Whatever," I said, thinking this was no time for semantics. "Whatever you call it, how does it help us? Why do we care what Arthur did? Or how he did it? He's dead. It's his *murderer* we're looking for."

Neither of them seemed to be listening to me. Both of them looked pensive, as if still figuring out whatever it was they were so proud of having figured out.

"Val, shut up and listen," Kit said.

"Today was the day Arthur was supposed to give his presentation at the conference," Nora began. "It made me sad when I realized that. Arthur had so much to give the world, so much wisdom—"

"Nora. Stay on point. We might not have much time," Kit said. And then she just told me herself. "Arthur's topic, you see, was the black market that was formed when young girls were sent from the United States to Canada to give birth and then supposedly decide whether they wanted to put their babies up for adoption. That whole thing—the fact that the girls were told the babies had died, and then the babies were sold—has been greatly exposed, and Arthur was to speak on the legal rights of those mothers and the babies who were removed. A euphemism for *stolen*," Kit added, as if her air quotes accompanying the word *removed* hadn't already made the same point.

"Arthur felt terribly guilty, you see," Nora reclaimed the narrative from her sister. "He wanted to do what he could to help those mothers and babies find one another. Many of the babies are already looking for their birth mothers, but some of the mothers, of course, don't even think the babies—er, their offspring—exist. They think they were stillborn. Although more and more mothers are finding out, thanks to the publicity."

"Wait a minute." I opened the door of the as-yet-unused minibar. It was cleverly disguised as a chic mahogany storage unit, so I wasn't surprised it was the first time I was noticing it. I took out a can of Diet Coke and a Snickers. The discreet price list taped to the inside of the door told me the two items cost more than the shoes I was wearing. "Okay, I'm confused," I said, tearing the paper off the candy bar.

"Oh, Val, don't go into a number. That's standard pricing for snacks in this type of hotel, so chomp away on your nine-dollar treat. It's on Larry, not you."

"It's not the cost of these things, although it's outrageous, but why are we only just now learning what this seminar is about? Why didn't we know this before? You should have told us, Nora."

She took a piece of paper out of her briefcase and handed it to me. "It wasn't a secret, Valerie. Look at this. It's even posted on the events calendar in the lobby."

The glossy flyer showed a picture of Arthur, and the text beside his picture read: *Arthur Bainbridge, JD, noted authority and expert on the North American underground economy as related to infants, offers a symposium on his nonpartisan study in the main ballroom at 4:00 p.m.*

"Give me that." Kit snatched it out of my hand and glanced over it. "I suppose you wrote this, Nora?"

"I had no hand in it," she said stiffly.

"Why couldn't it just say come and hear some old guy talk about lost babies?"

"That's exactly how it reads."

"Yeah, if you were looking to hook up with Oliver Twist—okay, let's forget about this for now and finish telling Val what we know. In English this time." Kit tossed the flyer onto the bed.

"Arthur has been volunteering to help the cause," Nora continued, "with this order of nuns who have been trying to piece everything together. And they had no way of knowing where a lot of the birth mothers are, let alone the—"

"Nursing homes would be my guess," Kit said.

"Could we just move on to the present?" I asked. "You said we didn't have much time—"

"Right," Kit said.

Nora continued. "Arthur apparently contacted as many people whose names he had—mothers and babies alike—asking them to come here this week; he wanted them to hear his talk today, and he wanted to meet with them afterward. He was prepared to completely confess and take his lumps."

"What a magnificent humanitarian your husband was," Kit couldn't resist saying.

"Why would he do that?" I asked. "Why would he risk—"

"Because of his advancing age," Nora said. "He knew he wasn't going to be around forever. And it was important to him to make amends as best he could. But not everyone was supportive—"

"No, I imagine not," I said, crumpling the empty Snickers wrapper. I hadn't meant to interrupt her. I was just thinking out loud as I realized how Roger, especially, might not share the need to come clean and relieve his conscience. No wonder he'd been chasing Nora and probably Arthur around Palm Desert—and in the mountains.

But if Roger had killed Arthur, who had killed Roger? And how many more were going to die before someone solved this friggin' killing spree?

"The natural assumption would be that Roger killed Arthur/Keith," I continued thinking, aloud now. "Just because his partner in crime wanted to clear his conscience wouldn't mean Roger was equally willing to spend his last years on earth behind bars. And of course Celia had to go too. But Roger himself?"

"Yes, that would seem to narrow the field of suspects, of course," Nora said.

"And about that field? The suspects are . . . ?" I asked.

"Unfortunately, we can't know them *all*," Nora said. "I found a mailing list in one of Arthur's files, presumably all the people he invited to hear him speak either at the conference or, informally, afterward. Louetta Powell was on the list, and Alex Tippon." She paused and took a deep breath. "And Katherine, our *mother's* name was on there." She paused again to let that sink in, before adding, "But none of the other names meant anything to me."

"Of course," I said, relief for Nora flooding over me. "Everyone on that list could be a suspect, if they'd been duped by Arthur. And Roger." I thought of how suspicious Alex Tippon had acted and how protective Dale Powell had been of his wife. To name just two.

"I would think so," Kit said. "Along with Nora. And our mother is definitely—"

"Katherine, I think we're safe to rule me out. If the police had any real evidence against me, they would have arrested me by now. And you know Mother would never *murder* anyone. I think *you* should stay focused."

I shuddered. "Well, the police will eventually figure it all out. Obviously, we aren't going to. I say it's time for a little vacay and then a flight home." I wanted to see more—much more—of Emily, and then it sounded like a little piece of heaven to crawl into my own bed at home and watch some *Law & Order*—with a bowl of Ben and Jerry's Chunky Monkey, of course.

And then there was *the kiss*. Thinking of it, I gently put my fingers to my lips.

"Val, do ya think you could rejoin us here on earth for a moment?" It was Kit, bringing me back to the present.

I put the cherished memory into storage. "Yes . . . sorry."

"I don't think Nora's going anywhere until this is solved," she continued. "The police may not have any evidence against her, but she's definitely under their microscope. And I'm not leaving if she can't."

"Even if they put me in prison out here? Why, Katherine, you'd have to—"

"Silence, Nora. You're not going to prison. *Is* she, Val."

It wasn't a question, but I answered, anyway. "No, of course she isn't." I sighed, realizing I probably wasn't going home any time soon. *Or* visiting Emily. "So you figured out Arthur invited certain people to come here. And what he planned to do. Is that all?"

"It's a start," Kit said defensively.

"Actually, there's something else I know," Nora said. "Something else now makes perfect sense."

***

"Why are you being so stubborn?" My ex-husband's name had appeared on my phone screen, and I'd stepped out into the hallway to take the call. I let him rant for a few minutes.

"How can you encourage her to give up her career at this point and move to Europe?" I heard David yell.

I could have reminded him that even though we both considered Emily a great actress, she hadn't yet won an Academy Award. Her last paying job, in fact, was for a television commercial where she displayed unnaturally white teeth, and some other actress's voice was dubbed over hers to announce the new and improved whitening product. But I said nothing.

Instead, I thought of the last time I'd stood in this hallway, and how Culotta's hand had gently cupped my chin and pulled my face toward his. I closed my eyes for a second and relived the kiss. With Culotta still on my mind, I hung up on David without saying a word.

As I shoved the phone into my pocket and looked down the long corridor, I saw Dale Powell heading toward me. And he looked as furious as if someone had just told him Texas was going to annex Oklahoma.

"Mr. Powell. Dale," I said, thoughts of Culotta and his kiss gone, replaced by fear. I started to insert my key card into the door, but was surprised to find my hand trembling. I was reminded of a game my brother, Buddy, and I used to play when we were kids, pretending a monster was after us as we frantically used our shaky fingers to get our front door open. Usually, my mother was behind us in the driveway yelling at *me* to quit acting like a fool.

"Stop right there, little lady." My childhood monster had materialized.

This was not the congenial Dale Powell.

"I beg your pardon," I said, masking my fear with bravado since I couldn't get the key card in and thus escape the imminent threat.

He was close, looming large, a white cowboy hat on his head making him appear even taller than his six feet plus. "Cut the bullcrap. I need some answers. Now. I have one upset little woman back at my hotel, and *she* needs some answers."

When I looked up, I saw his lips had formed a grim line. Thinking of what Nora had just told us, I wondered if I should share it with him. Would it put him out of his misery? Or add to it? Or was it already too late? *Was he the killer?*

Just in case, I decided we needed to be in a more public place. *Immediately.*

"Let's talk down here." I walked quickly past him toward the hospitality area, praying there would be others relaxing there.

But no such luck. "Let's go down to the bar," I said, when we reached the tables of drinks and snacks that apparently no one wanted right now. I kept walking toward the elevator, but Dale Powell grabbed my arm.

"No. We'll sit here. Or go to my hotel."

"Here's fine." I sat down in the closest chair, knowing I wouldn't budge until help came. And surely he wouldn't harm me right here in the open. I relaxed a bit and thought about what Nora had said.

"I found out from Arthur's papers," she had told Kit and me shortly before I'd stepped out into the hallway, "that the son he raised was Louetta Powell's by birth. Arthur insisted she was a rather unhinged young lady, and he truly felt he was doing the baby a favor—"

"Not to mention his wife, Elizabeth," Kit said.

"Go on, Nora." I gave Kit my *shut up* stare.

"Of course. Her too. Anyway, when Alex turned eighteen and Arthur shared this information with his son, Alex became . . . a bit unhinged himself. And from that time on, Arthur's greatest energy was spent trying to win Alex back. But after his son graduated from college and cut all ties, Arthur finally lost track of where he was. He was aware, however, that Alex always knew how to reach *him*, and that's what really hurt. That Alex could have contacted him at any time, but didn't."

I brought myself back to the present, unnervingly aware that I was still alone with Dale Powell.

" . . . is beside herself," he was saying. "She deserves justice—she deserves some answers."

I glanced at the elevator doors, willing them to open and a squadron of army guys to spill out. But the doors remained closed. I again debated sharing what Nora had told Kit and me, but I found myself chiding Dale instead. "Well, your answers might have died in the mountains with Arthur Bainbridge," I said, thinking *you shouldn't have killed your source.*

CHAPTER TWENTY-FIVE

D ale. You and Louetta came here to attend the conference." I was really thinking aloud, but he nodded in agreement.

"That was our plan. But there was also another reason we came out to this damn state. Louetta's doctor is here."

"Is she sick?"

I was expecting him to say her doctor was a plastic surgeon, but his eyes began to water and he swallowed hard before answering. "Breast cancer," he said. Then, after a second, he continued. "Final stages. So, when we were contacted by this Arthur Bainbridge fella, and he told us about this meeting he had going here, it was like . . . it was killing two birds with one stone, if you catch my drift."

I caught his drift, all right. "Dale, I'm so sorry."

"Yeah, we've had our troubles. What with the illness, and looking for her child, she's just about wore out. But let me tell you, since the first day I clapped eyes on my wife, she's been looking for her missing child. It ain't been easy watching her suffer all these years. I won't tell you how much money I've spent on detectives and whatnot, trying to figure out who stole her kid."

"You believe the circumstances of the adoption were fraudulent?"

He stared at me long enough for me to grow even more uneasy.

Relieved to hear the elevator doors open, I turned from Dale's gaze to the welcome sight of a young couple exiting on our floor. They had their arms around each other, and the man was holding an open bottle of champagne. The girl had the man's suit jacket over her shoulders, and they looked like models in a glossy-magazine ad. I was aware of them nodding to us when they passed by, and heard the sounds of laughter as they walked down the corridor to their room.

"Fraudulent?" Dale said at last, his voice rising. "I'd say it was that and much worse. And as far as I can tell, there weren't no adoption. More like stealing a baby from a young girl that didn't know what the hell she was doing. Much less have the smarts *not* to give her flesh and blood away."

"And you thought Arthur Bainbridge could help you?"

"Help us? Damn it, are you listening? He didn't help us in any way. He's the son of a bitch that stole the baby."

I still debated how much I should share with Dale Powell. Although his words were harsh, his demeanor had softened to the point where I felt a rush of sympathy for him. "Dale, do you know Alex Tippon?" I asked.

"Alex Tippon? Never heard of him. Who is he?"

"I'm pretty sure he is Louetta's son."

"And where is he now?"

"He's staying in this hotel."

"Then we gotta find him. And quick-like. This might be just the shot in the arm Louetta needs. I don't think she's got a lot of time left."

As he stood, I reached out a hand to stop him. "Please be careful, Dale. I have a feeling about that guy. Where is Louetta now?" I thought about Alex Tippon in the armchair in the hotel lobby, how casually he mentioned Roger on his call when I was in earshot.

Was it deliberate? Was he establishing some kind of an upside-down alibi?

"She's back at our hotel resting."

I stood too. "Why don't you go back there and be with her. And call the police from your hotel. Ask for Detective Tag Mason and tell him what you've told me. The police have already spoken to Alex Tippon once, but they might need to keep an eye on him."

"You got it," he said. "Y'all keep in touch. Do you still have my number?"

"Yes, I have your card."

Dale gave me a little salute and took off to protect his wife.

***

When I got back to the room, both girls were already sound asleep. I ripped off my clothes and slid my arms through my T-shirt. I was in bed two seconds later. And asleep a few seconds after that. I dreamed I was married to Culotta. I looked rather like Nicole Kidman—tall, slim, and very blond—and we had three little boys, all with pure-white hair.

When I awoke the next morning, my luscious dream ended, Kit's side of the bed was empty and Nora was sitting at the table by the balcony window, staring out at the glorious view.

"Oh, I hope I didn't wake you, Val." She turned to face me.

"No, not at all. Where's Kit?"

"She said something about coffee. I expect she went to Starbucks. She does love her coffee . . ." She stood and moved tentatively to the end of my bed. "You know Kit so well."

"Yeah, I guess I do." I stretched my arms up and then patted the side of my bed. "Come sit here, Nora. Are you okay?"

She walked over and then crawled in beside me, pulling the covers up. It was a tender side of her I'd never seen before. "You are so lucky to have each other," she said. "You two are closer than she and I ever were."

"No," I quickly assured her, although I knew she was right. "We were just closer in age than the two of you, and . . ." *And what? What was I going to say next?*

"I'm so sorry I dragged you both into all this mess. You know, my only intention was to just learn who my real . . . my birth mother was. I don't expect you to understand; you are so lucky to have been raised by Jean. She's a magnificent woman, Val."

I nodded in agreement, but luckily I wasn't forced into arguing about my mom. She certainly has her good points; but if she were here right now, she'd want to know why I hadn't taken my makeup off before going to bed and why I hadn't had a manicure since my nails resembled those of a coal miner.

Nora pulled the covers up a little higher. "You know, when I was a little girl, I used to daydream that Jean was really my mother. Is that awful? Oh, maybe not *her*, since she already had you and Buddy, but someone like her. Someone who hugged me every chance she got and was worried if I stayed out late—"

"Oh, believe me. You wouldn't have wanted my mother—"

"But I would. May I tell you a secret?" she asked. Then, not waiting for an answer, she continued. "Sometimes I'd get home late on purpose, just to see if Mother noticed, and then I'd get there and discover she hadn't even known I wasn't home. Although I didn't find out until recently that I was adopted, I think I always really knew it. I think I have spent my whole life searching for my real . . . my birth mother. It's a strange term, isn't it, Val? *Birth* mother. An unknown woman who carries you for nine months and then disappears from your life."

I put an arm around her shoulders, and she snuggled against me—the way Emily used to when she was an infant. "Beverly and your dad love you very much. Of that I'm sure."

"Oh yes, I believe they do. In their way. I did my best to make them proud of me, but I always felt I didn't belong to them. When I was a teenager, I began having dreams about my birth mother, even though I had no idea at the time that she even existed."

"Oh, we all do that, honey." I remembered a time when I was about nine or ten and my brother told me I was adopted and that my "real" mother had left me in a basket outside the 7-Eleven. I remembered rather liking the idea for a few months, believing my birth mother was some kind of heiress or movie star who would eventually come find me. But Mother Jean had immediately dispelled that notion when I'd blurted it out in one of our arguments, her reason being she would never be caught dead at a 7-Eleven. You were just asking to get your purse snatched at that sort of place, and worse.

That was why she always made sure my father filled the car with gas.

I squeezed Nora's shoulder. "You were lucky to have been adopted by Beverly. She may not show it very much, but she loves you."

"Yes." Nora nodded glumly. "I guess it could have been worse."

"A lot worse. Look at the tremendous life you've had. We're all so proud of you."

"You are a good friend, Valerie. I'm so fortunate to have you . . . and Katherine. Do you mind if I consider *you* a sister as well?"

This time I grabbed her hand and then planted a kiss on her cheek. "Mind? I'd be honored, for heaven's sake. You two girls—"

And then the door opened and Kit appeared, carrying a cardboard holder with three Starbucks cups.

"See? We're both lucky." I sat up and took the cup Kit handed me.

She gave Nora her coffee and then sat down on the edge of the bed. "I woke early and couldn't resist a Starbucks run. By the way, have I mentioned how much I appreciate your coming out here with me—"

"Shut up and let me enjoy this in peace," I said. "And yes, you've told me a million times."

Nora sipped her own coffee and smiled.

"Good morning, beautiful," Kit addressed her.

But poor Nora, not accustomed to such tender words from her sister, simply stared at her in alarm. "What's happened?" she whispered.

"Nothing has happened. But here's what's going to happen. I have reservations at The Palms Cafe for breakfast. Then we're all going to the spa and getting the works done. How does that sound?"

We all three raised our coffee cups in a toast.

***

Nora and I took our time showering and getting dressed while Kit sat immobilized on the bed, held rapt at something on her iPad. I'd filled them in on my talk with Dale Powell the night before, so no doubt she was googling for more information.

"I'd like to call the Powells, just to make sure he and Louetta are okay," I called to her from the bathroom.

"All right. Do you have their number?"

"It's in my purse," I shouted above the noise from the blow-dryer.

When I finally emerged from the bathroom, feeling fresher than I had since I'd arrived in California, both sisters were sitting at the table. They stood up as I emerged.

"Okay, let's go," I said. I opened the door, and they walked toward me. "Did you speak to the Powells?" I looked at Kit.

"No answer. We'll try again later."

I nodded, stepping into the long, empty corridor. As we headed toward the elevator, we passed the room I had seen the gorgeous young couple go into. There were no sounds from behind their door, and the Do Not Disturb sign hung from the door handle. As we reached the elevator, and before we could press the button, the doors opened, revealing a cleaning cart. The same maid we had seen when we first arrived, the one Kit had tricked into letting us into Nora's room, was behind it.

I noticed her name badge. "Good morning, Rosa," I said as she exited the elevator and then stopped.

She gave me a smile that displayed brilliant-white teeth.

"Good morning, *señoras*," she replied, nodding her head at each of us.

"*Buenos días, señora. ¿Cómo estás hoy?*" This of course was from Nora, who apparently spoke perfect Spanish.

"*Muy bien, gracias,*" Rosa said. Then her dark eyes flipped from Kit to me. "This lady," she said, indicating Nora, "she is the bride, *sí?*"

"Yes," Kit said.

"Ah," Rosa crossed herself. "I am so sorry for trouble that happened. Very bad." She shook her head.

"Yes," Kit said again. "Very bad."

"But you are safe?" Rosa asked, giving us the once-over. "You and the other lady that was in the room?"

"Er, no," I replied. "Unfortunately, the other lady died. Remember, you saw her body?"

"*Sí, sí.*" Rosa nodded again.

After she and her cart departed, we entered the elevator. I pushed the button for the lobby, and we watched in silence as the lights indicated we were headed down. But when we reached our destination and Nora and I began to leave, Kit remained pressed up against the back elevator wall.

"What is it?" I asked.

"She said the *other* lady." Kit's face showed she was deep in thought.

"Yes, she meant Celia—"

"Maybe. Get back in. We need to speak to Rosa."

***

We found the cart outside one of the rooms halfway down the corridor. The door was slightly open, and Kit led the way, pushing it enough for us all to enter. Rosa was pulling sheets off one of the king-size beds and looked up at us in shock. I figured she was sick at the sight of us.

"You need help, *señoras*?" she asked.

"Rosa," I began, "you said the *other* lady. And you didn't mean the lady on the bed that was mur . . . the one . . . that we found . . ."

"The dead one," Kit succinctly finished my unfinishable sentence.

If anything, Rosa looked a little relieved. "*Sí*," she said, letting go of the sheet she was holding and putting one hand in her pocket, the other to the crucifix at her neck. "I mean the older lady with the pretty silvery hair."

"Do you know her name?" Kit asked.

"*Sí*, of course; she was staying in hotel too, but I think she and her husband moved out. Missus Powell." She stretched Powell into *Pow-well*.

Nora looked at Kit and me, then spoke. "And you witnessed her in the vicinity—"

"Was she in the Bainbridge room?" Kit asked.

"*Sí*. I saw her come out earlier. Just before you got here. She waved at me, a very nice lady. But she was . . ." The maid looked distressed.

"How was she, Rosa?" I asked.

"This Missus Powell, she was looking a little . . . a little not very good. I think she is sick, perhaps."

"Rosa, did you have to open the door to the Bainbridge room for her?" I asked.

"Oh no." Rosa fingered her crucifix again. "No, she was already let in; no need for her to get key from me." She frowned, worried perhaps that allowing Kit and me access that day would come back to bite her. "I didn't do anything wrong."

"No, of course you didn't." I tried to sound calming. "Rosa, did you tell the police this?"

Poor Rosa looked positively frightened. "No . . . policeman did not ask me. I tol' him only that I let you and your friend in, but good reason, *sí?* To get surprise ready for bride, *sí?*"

"Yes," I said. "Good reason; nothing to worry about. But I think we need to contact Detective Mason."

After my call to the police, we retreated to the comfy chairs of the lobby area to await their arrival—all except Rosa, who stood by her cart, guarding it as if it were a Rolls Royce.

"I not in trouble?" she asked me, her dark eyes watching the elevator buttons as if they were the hands of a clock.

"No, you are not in trouble," I said. "I promise. You just have to tell the detectives what you saw."

"Yeah," Kit agreed, reaching across to Nora's chair and grabbing her hand. "And it could go a long way in clearing this up." She smiled at her sister, a sweet, loving smile. An *it's gonna be okay* smile.

And I believed it really would be.

CHAPTER TWENTY-SIX

What's this?" I watched Tom slowly slide an envelope across his desk toward me.

"Open it," he said.

"It's not a pink slip, is it?"

"Open it and see." As he spoke, he held a flame from his Dunhill lighter over the end of the cigar that sat precariously in one side of his mouth. It was probably illegal—the lighting part, not the lighter—but Tom does it anyway. His office, his rules, as he's told me a thousand times.

I picked up the envelope and opened the flap. Inside was a company check written in Tom's bold hand. The amount was ten thousand dollars. I gasped and looked at him, and after he had blown a smoke ring into the air, a broad smile spread across his face.

"Well, it's not a pink slip," I said. "What in the world is this for?"

"For the outstanding job you did the past twelve months. Just a little token of my appreciation. Same for Billie. You guys have gone without a bonus for too long."

"And Perry?"

"Yeah, and him too. Although he should be paying me."

"Well, thank you. But I didn't expect—"

"The company is recovering, Kiddo. Listings are up; sales are up. And I won the bad beat in Reno."

"Well, that's good," I said. "No, that's great." Tom has explained to me many times how the bad beat poker jackpot works. But just like the rules of football and what my son-in-law does for a living, it isn't something I fully understand. "Thank you, Tom."

"You earned it." He smiled again, leaning back in his leather chair. "So, tell me everything."

"Everything? As in—"

"As in how the hell things ended in Palm Desert."

I'd been back home for a week, but this was the first time I'd seen my boss. After his obviously successful Reno trip, he'd moved on to Las Vegas, his favorite town. "Well," I began, "I guess you know who the murderer was, right?"

"I don't know anything, other than what you tell me, Valerie. Start from the beginning, and give me all the details. But don't take too long; I've got a lunch date."

I started with Louetta Powell. She had hired a hit man, unbeknownst to her husband but using his money, and had Keith Tippon, aka Arthur Bainbridge, killed while he was taking an innocent hike in the mountains. Roger Carpenter had been shot and killed in his hotel room by the same man. Her motive for eliminating the two men was a kind of motherly revenge for her missing son and their part in stealing him from her. I suspected she was more than a little out of her mind with the need for some retribution for the hell she'd carried with her for over fifty years.

The biggest tragedy for Louetta might have been that she was not more than a few miles from her son while she was in California. If she had known, perhaps it would have been different. When they were finally reunited, it was bittersweet.

"As for Celia Decissio," I told Tom, "Louetta took care of her personally, although it probably wasn't planned. On the day she murdered Celia, she'd seen her enter Nora's hotel room using a key card Nora had left for her at the reception desk. Celia had arranged to meet Nora in the room to further discuss her findings, and even though Nora wasn't there, she'd let herself in to wait."

"Big mistake," Tom said.

I gave him a *no kidding* nod and continued. I told him how, when questioned by the police, Louetta had confirmed that she'd followed Celia to Nora's room, where the unsuspecting private investigator had opened the door, thus admitting her killer.

"Big mistake number two," Tom said. At least he was paying attention.

"Louetta has admitted that while she was in the room, she saw evidence of Celia's investigation, including a report that mentioned Elizabeth Tippon's hit-and-run. Which, it turns out, was Louetta's *first* murder—"

"Holy crap." Tom slapped his forehead with the palm of his left hand.

"Yes. Come to find out, though, there was no actual *proof* mentioned in the report. But Louetta didn't take time to find that out. In her panic, she decided she couldn't let Celia live with any knowledge she might have uncovered about who committed the hit-and-run."

"That broad really got around," Tom interrupted me again. "So you're saying she ran over Elizabeth, the ... er ... first wife?"

"Yes. And I'm thinking it added to Arthur's— Keith's—motivation to hightail it out of California and build a whole new identity and life for his son and himself in New York. He probably figured someone was trying to get revenge."

Smart move on his part, I thought, as I recalled our first conversation with Louetta, when she had chatted so aimlessly and asked what we knew of the dead girl found in Nora's room. And the subsequent conversation about how she and Dale were searching for Arthur—when she knew full well he was already dead. I marveled at her cunning, not to mention her composure (which, as Kit pointed out to me, was no doubt one of the benefits of a face-lift).

"A very smart move," I said aloud.

"So, this Alex guy, he was . . . who was he? Remind me."

"Alex Tippon was Louetta's son. He was stolen by Keith Tippon—"

"Keith Tippon?"

"Yeah. *Arthur*. And he was presented to his wife, Elizabeth, probably as a legal—or at least ethical—adoptee when he was a baby. It's not clear how much Elizabeth knew. But we do know that the grown-up Alex came to California to attend the seminar in the hopes of meeting his biological mother."

Alex Tippon had been on a mission. He figured out who I was and that I had a connection to Arthur's new wife, Nora. His bogus talk on the phone with a person called Roger—which he made sure I overheard—was a ruse to get me talking to him, so he could find out what I knew about his adoptive father and Roger Carpenter. "And I might have shared stuff with him," I told Tom, "if I hadn't had you yelling at me across the lobby for your ride to the airport."

"Hmm," Tom said, "so basically this guy is Nora's stepson."

"Basically, yes."

"And what *about* Nora? Where is she now?"

"She's back in New York. Actually, as she would say, she's considering giving up practicing law and is thinking about teaching. She did stop on her way home to spend some time with Beverly Rudolph. She wants her mother to come clean."

"Yeah, she better plan on hitting a few bars for that to happen. By the way, did she find out who her birth mother was? Don't tell me *she* was at the damn conference, or seminar, or whatever the hell it was."

"No. Nora's biological mother died many years ago. Sister Theresa Magdalene—"

"Who?"

"Oh, she was the nun who was helping the authorities in Canada contact the mothers and now-grown children who were victims of the scam. Nora's mother was an eighteen-year-old girl from Clark Fork, Idaho. She moved to Los Angeles when she discovered she was pregnant. She was penniless and homeless and just about perfect for Keith's and Roger's purposes. She was transported to Canada, gave birth to Nora, and then moved on. She ended up going to Dartmouth on a scholarship. She never married and worked for the government at Quantico in a high-powered job. She didn't ever try to contact Nora, and unfortunately, she died when Nora was about fifteen—"

"Wait. So Nora is Canadian?"

"I guess technically she might enjoy dual citizenship, although I never thought of that. Beverly and her husband adopted her when she was just weeks old. Although, if you really want to get technical—"

"I don't; I really don't—"

"Since the adoption wasn't even legal, I wonder if—"

"Don't wonder, Val; just finish the story."

"Well, that's about it. I think you know everything."

"Except why Nora and Arthur tied the knot in the first place. I can see what was in it for him, but her?"

"I think she really loved him. And although we never met, I like to think he felt the same about her. I guess he sought her out, to hire her. And I do wonder if he just wanted to . . . I don't know, maybe keep tabs on her. She would no doubt seem like someone who could unravel and expose his past. But then he came clean with her, and I have every reason to believe he really fell in love. And she did too."

"Yeah, and since he was close to kicking it, anyway—"

"Closer than he thought, thanks to Mrs. Powell—"

"What will happen to Louella?"

"Loue*tta*. With two t's. She gave up the name of her hired killer, and he's in custody. And she'll be tried, of course, although there's some doubt whether she'll even live long enough for the trial."

I suddenly thought of her husband, Dale, and a wave of sadness washed over me. I clung to the hope that he and Alex Tippon could form some kind of bond. Alex had two kids, and maybe there was a grandfather role that Dale could fill.

"I guess you gotta hand it to the old gal. She took care of the two assholes, Keith—Arthur . . . whoever he was— and his sidekick Roger."

"Yeah, you could look at it that way. But what about the two innocent women she killed, Elizabeth and Celia?"

"Yeah, true. Celia was Culotta's pal, right?"

"Right. He's pretty upset about her."

At the mention of Culotta's name, a familiar feeling came over me.

We had never repeated our kiss, and the day that Louetta was taken into custody, he left California. He claimed he was going to take a slow drive across the country to Chicago, and that he'd call me when he was back in town.

"You know," I said to Tom, "I never really understood what Culotta was doing in Palm Desert. He said he was on vacation, but—"

"He was doing me a favor. Keeping an eye on you."

I wasn't sure how I felt about that. I preferred to think he wasn't just doing Tom's bidding. And I knew Tom had been just as concerned, if not more so, about Nora. But I held on to the hope that Dennis would get in touch at some point.

Tom changed the subject, no doubt feeling it was getting too mushy. "And Emily? Did you see much of her?" he asked.

"Never enough. And now she's moving . . ."

"Yeah, but how great for her. I take it Asshole, I mean David, has a problem with it? What's that all about?"

I gave a humorless chuckle. "It's about *him*, of course. Turns out he has plans to be in England for much of the time Emily and Luke will be living there. Some part-business-part-pleasure thing he's been planning for a long time, without having shared those plans with Emily, by the way. And now I'm guessing he's afraid she'll cramp his style. Because I'm guessing he's not going alone, or at least not wanting to be available for fatherly duties while he's there."

"So he really is a total jerk." Tom shook his head.

I tried to hide my pleasure at his assessment of my ex as I slipped the generous check back into its envelope. "Say, I have a question for *you*."

"Shoot." He looked at his watch.

"About Nora? What happened with you two?"

"What do you mean?"

"You had a . . . what? A thing? A love affair? What?"

"I think I already answered this question."

"Well, tell me again."

He tipped the end of his cigar into the Waterford ashtray on his desk, and we both watched half an inch of ash fall into the glass. He waited a few seconds before answering, as if choosing his words carefully. "You know, when we were kids growing up, Nora was really something—"

"She still is—"

"Yeah. You're right. But back then, I guess I was a little in awe of her. She was so damn smart and so damn gorgeous, and yet she was never really part of anything. She moved outside any circle, always different enough from the rest of us so as not to be included. I don't know; I just had a . . ."

"Crush on her?" I could see that. My own mother had a crush on her, so why not Tom?

"Yeah, I guess so. But later, when she and I hooked up in New York—which was quite accidental, by the way—I began to see she wasn't anything like I had remembered her from high school. I always thought she was so confident and a little aloof, but it turns out, beneath all those ten-dollar words, she's just a schmuck like the rest of us. I felt like she needed looking after. All those brains, and she couldn't cross the street without getting run over by a bus."

"So, it wasn't really an affair?"

"I'm not saying that. But she's not really my type; you know that, Pankowski. I don't like my women to be . . ."

"Smarter than you?"

"As if." He started to laugh and then changed the subject. "So, what're you gonna do with all your money?" He nodded toward the envelope still clutched in my hand. "Why don't you move out of your rabbit hutch and find a decent place?"

"Tom, I love my rabbit hutch, as you so rudely call it." That was very true, and even more so upon my return from Palm Desert and a hotel room shared with two other women. My hutch felt like a mansion.

"Just do me one favor. Don't go blowing it at Walmart or wherever you shop. Treat yourself to something good."

"Oh, I will; don't worry. I will. When Emily is settled in England, Kit and I are going over there. And it will be *my* treat."

Foreign Relations

*W*hen *a man is tired of London, he is tired of life.* Samuel Johnson, a British essayist and poet, wrote this in 1777. Imagine how he might have upped his opinion if he'd been able to walk across the

River Thames on the Millennium Bridge; take a ride on the London Eye, with its spectacular view of the capital; or visit the dazzling Tate Modern art museum.

Kit James and I were in London, and I was giddy with excitement. In my nontransatlantic life, I am a Realtor working for a small outfit in Downers Grove, Illinois. My boss, Tom Haskins, owner of the company that boasts four full-time employees, including himself and me, claims to have been to the city several times. He assured me we could see the whole place in about forty minutes.

"In 1777, maybe," I'd countered.

"Nah, it would have taken even less time back then, Kiddo."

"How could it, seriously?" I had laughed. "Tom, are you sure you've actually been to London, because—oh, forget it."

"I've been, and just remember, Val, they're not big on ice over there, so don't go nuts. And they drive on the wrong side of the road, so make sure you look both ways when you cross the street."

"Hmm, wouldn't that apply to any city?"

"Just do it."

Forty minutes, indeed! We spent twice that amount of time in the Tower of London gawking in awe at the Crown Jewels.

***

I had booked us a room at Queen Anne's Chambers, a hotel located within walking distance of a lot of famous stuff, not the least of which was Buckingham Palace.

"So, which is it?" Kit asked when I first told her about our travel plans. "Are they chambers or a hotel? And what do they mean by chambers, anyway? Why don't we just stay at a Hilton?"

"No. We can do that anywhere. Queen Anne's place sounds so . . . English."

"Okay, but your Queen better have decent Wi-Fi, that's all I'm saying."

On our first day in London, ignoring any jet lag, we took a boat ride on the River Thames. Together with a million or so other tourists, we embarked at the majestic Tower Bridge and set sail down the river toward Greenwich, where, if nothing else, we could set our watches to mean time, whatever that actually means.

As our vessel glided lazily on the water, our tour guide explained points of interest on either side of the river. To our right was the site of the original Globe Theatre, where Shakespeare himself had ruled the roost, and the pub next door, where his actors ran to change costumes, among other things. To our left were shimmering towers of glass where Cher and Robert De Niro supposedly owned apartments. During our brief sojourn in London I'd already become accustomed to the amazing architecture that spanned hundreds of years in the blink of an eye, from the timber used in Tudor England in the 1500s to the innovative glass and steel of the twenty-first century.

Our jam-packed four-day extravaganza included afternoon cucumber sandwiches and tea at The Savoy Hotel, champagne cocktails at The Ritz, and a couple of shows in the famed theaters of the West End.

"Do you think King James ever thought about refurbishing?" Kit asked, as we settled into our snug seats in the Dress Circle of the theater named for him.

"Funny you should ask that." I consulted the playbill I had purchased with a ten-pound note. "They did refurbish several times after the original structure was built in 1688. Last update was . . . let's see . . . oh, 1790."

"I thought I recognized this green velvet."

On our last evening in London, we joined the throng of people strolling along the Thames embankment, heading toward Westminster Bridge. Across the river we took in the splendor of the Houses of Parliament, bathed in gold as the sun began its descent. We stopped to take phone pictures, wedging between two Canadian twentysomethings with Maple Leaf appliqués on their backpacks and an Asian couple who had some serious cameras dangling from straps around their necks.

"It's really a beautiful city," Kit said, surprising me a little. She is not a big fan of old-timey stuff.

"Yes," I agreed. "It's bloody magnificent."

***

For the remainder of our time in England, our plan was to rent a car and drive a couple of hours out of London to enjoy a stay in the County of Sussex. There my daughter, Emily, had found a cottage for us to lease. Her husband, Luke, had been transferred for a year to Chichester, a nearby city where he did, well, whatever it is he does . . . something in computers (I'm never exactly clear what).

"Are you sure we're on the right road to the village?" Kit asked. "I think we've passed those sheep at least three times."

The sky was clear and very blue, the weather was warm, and we appeared to be the only car on the two-lane road. Even with the wind blowing through the rolled-down windows, Kit's chin-length auburn hair cascaded perfectly, outlining her face and making her appear like a model doing a shoot for fabulous fiftysomethings.

Mine, not so much. Wind tunnel came to mind when I pulled down the visor to grab a look at my blond bob in the mirror. I snapped it back quickly and turned to watch as we sped past the seemingly endless green pastures. The dozen or so sheep, all staring at us transfixed, did indeed look familiar. "The guy in the pub told us this was the way to go," I said.

"The one with the lazy eye?"

"No. Not him. The one in the other pub. He was sitting on his own in the corner and looked a bit like Charles Manson."

"Oh great. You took directions from a death row inmate? Where was I?"

"Well, he's no longer—oh, never mind. You were in the restroom. He told me he had great respect for Americans, in particular our marching bands, and he admired our ability to throw a parade."

Seeming not to care about the Charles Manson look-alike or his opinion of Americans, she asked, "Don't you mean I was in the *loo*?"

She took her eyes off the road for a few seconds, turned toward me, and we both burst into a peal of laughter. I was consumed with joy to be with my best friend of more than forty years and driving on the wrong, or at least the other, side of the road in a car that was not much bigger than my microwave oven.

And it was true that we'd taken ourselves on a little pub crawl on the way to our destination. The King's Head, The Queen's Arms, The Prince's Big Toe (okay, I made that last one up). After another five miles or so, a sign appeared in the hedgerow along the road.

Village Centre Ahead.

"That's it!" I yelled. "We just passed the sign. Look! There's another one."

LITTLE DIPPING. Population 576.

Kit slowed the car down as we entered a street lined with shops and small restaurants on one side and a church behind a large expanse of green on the other.

"Look for Magpie Lane," I said, as she slowed the car even more and the street became transformed by houses on either side, some with thatched roofs. "Oh, here it is. Turn here. Number 6. Oh my, it's adorable."

We had arrived.

***

"I'm Brown Owl," the woman announced, as soon as I opened the front door of our cottage. She said it with such authority, she might have been informing me she was the prime minister.

"Okaaaay." I extended my hand to shake hers. "It's very nice to meet you, Miss . . . Ms. . . . Mrs. Owl? Did you say Owl?"

She was tall and thin, with overly permed short gray hair. She wore an expensive-looking tailored suit and sensible lace-up shoes. I noted her pallor and thought she could have benefited from a little makeup.

"Kit," I yelled over my shoulder, my voice easily reaching down the short hallway to the kitchen at the back.

"What the hell kind of oven is this?" she yelled back. "Am I supposed to cook in this thing—"

"Kit, dear, we have a visitor, Ms. Brown Owl—"

"Brown *what?*" Kit appeared behind me, a kitchen towel draped over the shoulder of her cashmere sweater. She looked surprised to find a woman rather than an actual owl. "Kit James," she softened her tone and extended her hand in greeting.

"Brown *Owl.*" The woman laughed a little. "Sorry; that might sound strange to you, but it's how we sometimes address the leader of the Brownies. Some packs don't stick to the tradition, of course, although here in Little Dipping we do. But please call me Vera. Vera Wingate. I run the pack over at St. Matilda's. I thought I'd just stop by and welcome you to our village . . ."

She hesitated so long I decided she would probably rather be doing more important Brown Owl stuff. I noticed beads of perspiration on her top lip, which was surprising, given the mild day. Finally, with a shake of her head, as if to clear it, she spoke again. "The oven, by the way, is an AGA. And yes, you'll probably be using it—if you plan on cooking, that is."

Just then a little girl stepped from behind her. She was wearing a blue-and-white-checked dress, belted at the waist, that appeared several sizes too big for her tiny frame. On her head was a navy beret from which several unruly red curls had escaped. "Are you from America?" she asked in a voice too loud for her slender body.

"Yes," I said. "We are. Please, come in, ladies." I leaned back, giving them space to pass through. Charming as our cottage was, and although larger in square feet than my own tiny apartment back home, the walls separating the individual rooms made it appear much smaller.

Vera Wingate put her hands on the little girl's thin shoulders and steered her past me and into the living room. "This is Ivy," she announced. "She insisted on coming with me."

"Well, hello, Ivy," I said. "That's a very pretty name."

"No, it's not. It's poison. And I didn't insist on anything, Brown Owl; I just happened to be going in the same direction." Freeing herself from her elder's grip, her eyes darted around the small room before she plunked down on the end of the old brown chesterfield (which we Americans call a couch). "So, are you two from Florida or what?"

"No." Kit sat down next to her. "Not Florida. You're thinking of Disney World, I bet."

"No, I'm not," Ivy said. She had picked up a small silver bell from the end table beside her. "Are you from California, then?" She studied the bell.

"No, sorry; nowhere that exciting."

"Texas?" She shook the tiny bell and then returned it to the table.

"Wrong again."

"New York?"

"We're from Illinois," I cut in, saving Ivy the arduous chore of naming all fifty states.

"Never heard of it." She sniffed, her ginger eyebrows raised in disbelief that there was such a place. "What's there?"

"Chicago, for one thing," Kit said. "You seem to know so much about America, Ivy, I'm sure you have heard of that."

"No, but my dad probably has. He's been all over the world."

"Good for him," Kit said, trying to sound impressed. "So . . . Brown Owl . . ." She turned her attention away from the child and toward the older woman.

"Vera, please."

"Vera. Can we offer you coffee or something? Tea, perhaps?"

"Got any cake?" Ivy asked. She had crossed her thin legs in a mature fashion that looked all wrong on someone so young. I noticed one of her white knee-length socks was twisted around her ankle.

"Ivy, that's very rude," Vera/Brown Owl admonished. "And pull your sock up."

"I like your dress," I said to Ivy, although it reminded me more of a candy striper's uniform than something a little girl would wear. "It's very pretty."

"No, it isn't. My dad was in the navy once, and he had a very nice suit."

"Ivy, your sock," Vera repeated. "Fix it." And then, turning back to Kit, she said, "Thank you, but no, we won't stay for tea. Another time, perhaps. Just wanted to pop in and say hello."

Reluctantly, Ivy stood, muttering as she did so. "Yanks don't know how to make tea, anyway; my dad told me that." She began pulling up the errant sock, but it immediately fell back down around her ankle. "Have you ever met Taylor Swift?" She looked up at Kit.

"Yes. Many times," Kit lied. "Have you?"

"No, but I don't reckon she's all that."

"I'll be sure to tell her what you think of her—"

"Nooooo," Ivy began to wail, "don't you dare go and tell her—"

"For goodness' sake, Ivy," Vera said, "don't you know when someone's pulling your leg?"

"Oh." Ivy stopped wailing. "She shouldn't tease children. It's not very nice."

"How old are you, Ivy?" Kit asked sweetly.

"How old do I look?"

"Hmmm." Kit rested her chin in her hand, as if deep in thought. "Let's see . . . twenty-six?"

"Don't be daft. I'm nine."

"She's eight and very naughty." Vera looked annoyed.

"You're just confused again," Ivy said, but the look in her eyes convinced me she was taunting this Brown Owl. I had no doubt Ivy was eight.

"I can assure you the other Brownies are much better behaved," the Brownie leader said.

"Is Emily here?" Ivy changed the subject quickly, which seemed to come naturally to her.

"Emily? You know Emily? She's my daughter."

"Yes. I was here when she came to rent this place for you. She doesn't look like you; she's very beautiful, and she's an actress, you know. She lives in Los Angeles; that's in California. But her husband, Luke, is working in Chichester for a little while. He's the IT person; that means information and technology, and he specializes in programming nautical code. He likes the Chicago Bears. Emily does too, of course, but I think I can get her interested in Manchester United. They play football, but my dad told me you call it soccer in America, which is so dead wrong."

"Well, I expect you'll bring Emily around to your way of thinking, Ivy," I said.

She dug her hands into the pockets of her dress. "Yeah. Emily's really nice. I hope she gets that part in the play they're doing at The Beamlight Theatre. She's a brilliant actress."

"Really?" I hadn't spoken to my daughter since we'd arrived in Little Dipping, so I wasn't really up on the latest Emily news, but it seemed she had a fan already. And I was also grateful to learn what it is my son-in-law does for a living. "I thought Emily had already been cast in the play."

"Nah." Ivy took a seat again and leaned over to carefully roll both her socks around her ankles. "She's only the understudy. That means if Doreen gets herself killed, then Emily can go on—"

"Ivy!" Brown Owl said. "What nonsense you talk. No one is getting killed."

"Probably not. But Doreen—she's my sister—isn't half as good as Emily. Did you fly here on a plane? 'Cuz you know, you could have come by boat. My dad was on loads of boats. Of course you wouldn't want to be on the *Titanic*. That hit a big iceberg, and everyone died."

"Not everyone." Kit said it kindly, but I still couldn't believe she was actually correcting this little girl.

Ivy just shook her head and adjusted her navy beret, roughly shoving some ginger curls back in place. "Most of the Irish did, like Leonardo."

"He wasn't Irish, ya know." Now Kit's kind tone held an edge of smugness, and I *was* impressed with her sudden cinematic knowledge. Generally, she either talks or sleeps through a movie.

"Yes, he was," Ivy insisted.

"No, dear. Actually, he was from Wisconsin." Now Kit looked triumphant.

"Wiswhat?" Ivy scrunched up her little face. "Where's that, then? It must be somewhere in Ireland, right?"

"Wisconsin is the state that borders Illinois to the north, in America, where we come from, remember?"

"If he was American, why was he staying down in the bottom of the ship with the poor people?"

This would have been a great opportunity for Kit to teach Ivy that not all Americans are rich. But no. "Good question," she said instead. "He should have been in first class, and then he might have made it."

"Oh, for goodness' sake," Vera Wingate interrupted them, and I was grateful. "Enough with you, child. Let's leave these two ladies in peace." She yawned. "Forgive me. I didn't get a very good night's sleep." Then she reached for Ivy's thin arm with her own thin arm and gently pulled her off the couch. "I live three doors down, at Number 9, so if you need any help, please give me a knock. And welcome again. Hope you enjoy your stay in Little Dipping."

"Phew," I said, as I closed the door after our visitors left. "She's really a little pistol, isn't she?"

"Yeah, but I kinda liked her."

"Yeah, you would. And by the way, how did you think we were going to make them tea? Or coffee, for that matter. I hope we *can* get a decent cup of coffee in Little Dipping."

Later, when I was upstairs unpacking in one of the two bedrooms that were separated by a rather large and obviously remodeled bathroom, I heard Kit call me from the floor below.

"Hey, Valley Girl, did you move that silver bell thingy?"

"What?" I called back down, leaning over the banister.

"It's gone. Remember? It was on the table by the end of the couch."

"Why would I move it?" I went down the steep stairs. "Really? It's gone?"

"Yeah." Kit was sitting in the same spot the disgruntled Ivy had occupied an hour earlier. "I think the little stinker pocketed it."

And once again we both burst out laughing.

Patty and Roz
www.roz-patty.com

About the authors ...

Now a proud and patriotic US citizen and Texan, Rosalind Burgess grew up in London and currently calls Houston home. She has also lived in Germany, Iowa, and Minnesota. Roz retired from the airline industry to devote all her working hours to writing (although it seems more like fun than work).

Patricia Obermeier Neuman spent her childhood and early adulthood moving around the Midwest (Minnesota, South Dakota, Nebraska, Iowa, Wisconsin, Illinois, and Indiana), as a trailing child and then as a trailing spouse (inspiring her first book, *Moving: The What, When, Where & How of It*). A former reporter and editor, Patty lives with her husband in Door County, Wisconsin. They have three children and twelve grandchildren.

No. 1 in
The Val & Kit Mystery Series

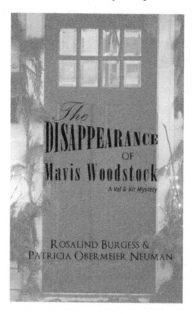

The Disappearance of Mavis Woodstock

Mavis Woodstock (a vaguely familiar name) calls Val and insists she has to sell her house as quickly as possible. Then she fails to keep her scheduled appointment. Kit remembers Mavis from their school days, an unattractive girl who was ignored when she was lucky, ridiculed when she was not. She also remembers Mavis being the only daughter in a large family that was as frugal as it was wealthy. When Val and Kit cannot locate Mavis, they begin an investigation, encountering along the way a little romance, a lot of deception, and more than one unsavory character.

FIVE STARS! "I highly recommend this novel and I'm looking forward to the next book in this series. I was kept guessing throughout the entire novel. The analogies throughout are priceless and often made me laugh. . . . I found myself on the edge of my seat. . . . The ending to this very well-written novel is brilliant!"

FIVE STARS! "I recommend this book if you like characters such as Kinsey Millhone or Stone Barrington . . . or those types. Excellent story with fun characters. Can't wait to read more of these."

FIVE STARS! "A cliff-hanger with an I-did-not-see-that-coming ending."

FIVE STARS! " . . . well written, humorous . . . a good plot and a bit of a surprise ending. An easy read that is paced well, with enough twists and turns to keep you reading to the end."

FIVE STARS! "Very enjoyable book and hard to put down. Well-written mystery with a great surprise ending. A must-read."

FIVE STARS! "This is a well-written mystery that reads along at a bright and cheerful pace with a surprisingly dark twist at the end."

FIVE STARS! "I really enjoyed this book: the characters, the story line, everything. It is well written, humorous, engaging."

FIVE STARS! "The perfect combo of sophisticated humor, fun and intriguing twists and turns!"

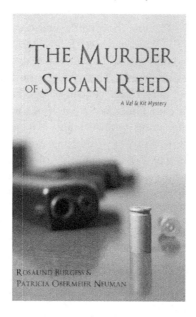

The Murder of Susan Reed

When Kit suspects Larry of having an affair with one of his
employees, Susan Reed, she enlists Val's help in uncovering
the truth. The morning after a little stalking expedition by
the lifelong friends, Val reads in the newspaper that Susan
Reed was found shot to death in her apartment the night
before, right around the time Kit was so certain Larry and
Susan were together. *Were* they having an affair? And did
Larry murder her? The police, in the form of dishy Detective
Dennis Culotta, conduct the investigation into Susan's
murder, hampered at times by Val and Kit's insistent
attempts to discover whether Larry is guilty of infidelity
and/or murder. As the investigation heats up, so does Val's
relationship with Detective Culotta.

FIVE STARS! "I couldn't wait to get this Val & Kit adventure after reading the authors' first book, and I was not disappointed. As a fan of this genre . . . I just have to write a few words praising the incredible talent of Roz and Patty. One thing I specifically want to point out is the character development. You can completely visualize the supporting actors (suspects?) so precisely that you do not waste time trying to recall details about the character. . . . Roz and Patty practically create an imprint in your mind of each character's looks/voice/mannerisms, etc."

FIVE STARS! "Even better than the first! Another page-turner! Take it to the beach or pool. You will love it!!! I did!!!"

FIVE STARS! "Great writing. Great plot."

FIVE STARS! "Once again Val & Kit star in a page-turner mystery!"

FIVE STARS! "I loved this book and these two best friends who tend to get in trouble together. Reminds me of my best friend and myself."

FIVE STARS! "Ms. Burgess and Ms. Neuman are fantastic writers and did a great job with their sophomore effort! I enjoy their writing style and they really capture the genre of cozy mystery well! I highly recommend their books!"

FIVE STARS! "Val and Kit's interactions and Val's thoughts about life in general were probably the best part of the book. I was given enough info to 'suspect' just about every character mentioned."

Death in Door County

Val embarks on a Mother's Day visit to her mom in Door County, Wisconsin, a peninsula filled with artists, lighthouses, and natural beauty. Her daughter, Emily, has arrived from LA to accompany her, and at the last minute her best friend, Kit, invites herself along. Val and Kit have barely unpacked their suitcases when trouble and tension greet them, in the form of death and a disturbing secret they unwittingly brought with them. As they get to know the locals, things take a sinister turn. And when they suspect someone close to them might be involved in blackmail—or worse—Val and Kit do what they do best: they take matters into their own hands in their obsessive, often zany, quest to uncover the truth.

What readers are saying about . . .
Death in Door County

FIVE STARS! "I really enjoyed this book. Not only was I in Door County at the time that I was reading it and Door County has always been one of my favorite places, I am also a homeowner in Downers Grove, IL, which is where Val and Kit also live. I did read the first two books in The Val & Kit Mystery Series which I also thoroughly enjoyed. Being from Downers Grove, I got quite a kick out of the real names of most of the streets being used in the stories because I could just picture where the events were taking place. Even though all three books were mysteries, they were lighthearted enough to hold my interest. I would love to see more stories in this series."

FIVE STARS! "Whether you are a mother, daughter, grandmother, great-grandmother or best friend . . . This is a heartwarming and hilarious read that would be a perfect part of your Mother's Day celebration!!! I loved getting to know Val and Kit better. Their relationships with their loved ones had me laughing and weeping all at the same time!!! I loved ending my day with Val and Kit; it just made it hard to start my day as I could not stop reading *Death in Door County*!"

FIVE STARS! "Another page-turner in the Val & Kit Series! What a great story! I loved learning about Val's family."

FIVE STARS! "Really enjoy the Val and Kit characters. They are a yin and yang of personalities that actually fit like a hand and glove. This is the third in the series and is just as much a fun read as the first two. The right amount of intrigue coupled with laughter. I am looking forward to the next in the series."

FIVE STARS! "*Death in Door County* is the third installment in the series, and each book just gets better than the last."

FIVE STARS! "The girls have done it again . . . and by girls, do I mean Val and Kit, or Roz and Patty? The amazingly talented authors, Roz and Patty, of course. Although Val and Kit have landed themselves right smack dab in the middle of yet another mystery. This is their third adventure, but don't feel as though you have to (albeit you SHOULD if you haven't done so already) read *The Disappearance of Mavis Woodstock* and *The Murder of Susan Reed* in order. This book and the other(s) . . . are wonderful stand-alones, but read all . . . to enjoy all of the main and supporting characters' quirks. . . . I can't seem to express how much I love these books. . . . Speaking of characters . . . This is what sets the Val & Kit series apart from the others in this genre."

FIVE STARS! "This third book in the series is my favorite, but I felt the same about the first two as well!"

FIVE STARS! "Just the right mix of a page-turner mystery and humor with a modern edge. I have read all three books and am waiting impatiently for more."

FIVE STARS! "Love, love these two writers! I'm these authors' best fan, and I can't wait for these lovely ladies to write more!"

Lethal Property

In this fourth book of The Val & Kit Mystery Series (a stand-alone, like the others), our ladies are back home in Downers Grove. Val is busy selling real estate, eager to take a potential buyer to visit the home of a widow living alone. He turns out not to be all that he claimed, and a string of grisly events follows, culminating in a perilous situation for Val. Her lifelong BFF Kit is ready to do whatever necessary to ensure Val's safety and clear her name of any wrongdoing. The dishy Detective Dennis Culotta also returns to help, and with the added assistance of Val's boss, Tom Haskins, and a *Downton Abbey*–loving Rottweiler named Roscoe, the ladies become embroiled in a murder investigation extraordinaire. As always, we are introduced to a new cast of shady characters as we welcome back the old circle of friends.

FIVE STARS! "OK . . . so I thought I knew whodunit early in the book, then after changing my mind at least 8-10 times, I was still wrong. (I want to say so much more, but I really don't want to give anything away.) Just one of the many, many things I love about the Val & Kit books. I love the characters/suspects, I love the believable dialogue between characters and also Valley Girl's inner dialogue (when thinking about Tina . . . hehe). I'd like to also add that (these books) are just good, clean fun. A series of books that you would/could/should recommend to anyone. (My boss is a nun, so that's a little something I worry about . . . lol) Thanks again, ladies. I agree with another reviewer . . . it IS like catching up with old friends, and I can't wait for the next one."

FIVE STARS! "Reading *Lethal Property* was like catching up with old friends, and a few new characters, but another fun ride! I love these characters and I adore these writers. Would recommend to anyone who appreciates a good story and a sharp wit. Well done, ladies; you did it again!"

FIVE STARS! "As with the other books in this series, this can be read as a stand-alone. However, I've read all of them to date in order and that's probably the best way to do it. I'm to the point where I don't even read the cover blurb for these books . . . because I know that I'll enjoy them. This book certainly didn't disappoint. Plenty of Val and Kit and their crazy antics, a cast of new colorful characters and a mystery that wasn't predictable."

No. 6 in
The Val & Kit Mystery Series

Foreign Relations

After sightseeing in London, Val and Kit move on to a rented cottage in the bucolic village of Little Dipping, where Val's actress daughter, Emily, and son-in-law are temporarily living and where Emily has become involved in community theater. Val and Kit revel in the English countryside, despite Val's ex-husband showing up and some troubling news from home. The harmony of the village is soon broken, however, by the vicious murder of one of their new friends. The shocking events that follow are only slightly more horrific than one from the past that continues to confound authorities. The crimes threaten to involve Emily, so Val and Kit return to their roles as amateur sleuths, employing their own inimitable ways.

And if you want to read about the mystery of marriage, here's a NON–Val & Kit book for you . . .

Dressing Myself

Meet Jessie Harleman in this contemporary women's novel about love, lust, friends, and family. Jessie and Kevin have been happily married for twenty-eight years. With their two grown kids now out of the house and living their own lives, Jessie and Kevin have reached the point they thought they longed for, yet slightly dreaded. But the house that used to burst at the seams now has too many empty rooms. Still, Jessie is a *glass-half-full* kind of woman, eager for this next period of her life to take hold. The problem is, nothing goes the way she planned. This novel explores growth and change and new beginnings.

What readers are saying about . . .
Dressing Myself

FIVE STARS! "Loved this book!!! Another page-turner by talented Burgess and Neuman, my new favorite authors!!! I loved reading this book. It was very heartwarming in so many ways!!! Ready to read the next book from this writing duo!!!"

FIVE STARS! "I love these authors. I love the real feelings, thoughts, words, actions, etc., that they give to their characters. I love that it feels like a memoir instead of fiction. I love that it depressed me. I want to say so much more about what I loved, but I don't want to give too much away. A classic story that draws your emotions out of you to make you root for it to go one way, then in the next chapter, make a U-turn; just like the main character. It makes you reflect on your own life and happiness. It makes you check your husband's e-mails and credit card statements. I simply love your writing, ladies. Can't wait for the next one."

FIVE STARS! "I couldn't put it down! Great book! Maybe I could relate with the main character too much, but I felt as though she was my friend. When I wasn't reading the book, the main character was constantly on my mind! The ending was unpredictable in a great way! I think the authors need to keep on writing! I'm a huge fan!"

FIVE STARS! "Wonderful book! A fast read because once you start, you just cannot put it down; the characters become like your family! Definitely a worthwhile read!"

FIVE STARS! "Delightful! I so enjoyed my time with Jessie. I laughed with her, and ached for her. I knew her so well so quickly. I'll remember her story with a smile. I hope these authors keep it coming. What a fun read!"

FIVE STARS! "Love these writers!! So refreshing to have writers who really create such characters you truly understand and relate to. Looking forward to the next one. Definitely my favorites!"

FIVE STARS! "This book is about a woman's life torn apart. . . . A lot of detail as to how she would feel . . . very well-written. I have to agree with the other readers, 5 stars."

FIVE STARS! "What a fun read *Dressing Myself* was! . . . I have to admit I didn't expect the ending. . . . It was hard to put this book down."

FIVE STARS! "Great, easy, captivating read!! The characters seem so real! I don't read a lot, but I was really into this one! Read it for sure!"

FIVE STARS! "Loved it! Read this in one day. Enjoyed every page and had a real feeling for all of the characters. I was rooting for Jessie all the way. . . . Hope there's another story like this down the road."

FIVE STARS! "*Dressing Myself* deals with an all-too-common problem of today in a realistic manner that is sometimes sad, sometimes hopeful, as befits the subject. My expectation of the ending seesawed back and forth as the book progressed. I found it an interesting, engaging read with fully developed characters."

FIVE STARS! "Great book! It has been a long time since I have read a book cover to cover in one day . . . fantastic read . . . real page-turner that was hard to put down . . . Thanks, Ladies!"

Made in the USA
Monee, IL
03 January 2022

87912071R00154